PAL A
CAFE

PALPASA CAFE

Narayan Wagle

RANDOM HOUSE INDIA

Published by Random House India in 2010
1

First published in English by nepa~laya, 2008

Random House Publishers India Private Limited
MindMill Corporate Tower, 2nd Floor, Plot No 24A
Sector 16A, Noida 201301, UP

Random House Group Limited
20 Vauxhall Bridge Road
London SW1V 2SA
United Kingdom

978 81 8400 142 6

Typeset by SwaRadha Typesetting, New Delhi

Printed and bound in India by Replika Press

To my dear Nitika

PROLOGUE

A paper bird came flying down from the balcony and landed by my seat in the Birendra International Convention Centre. On it was written, 'When's your novel going to be published, Mr Coffee Guff?'

The curtains would soon be raised and singer Deep Shrestha would begin his performance. Seconds before the lights went down, I passed the note to my friends. They read it and chuckled.

Over the next two hours Deep sang many songs, old and new, his voice flowing with the rhythm of the orchestra. 'I came from afar,' Deep sang while I read the note again and wondered who'd written it. I looked up at the balcony, straining in the darkness, but could make out only a black mass of people. When Deep began to sing 'Sainlibari in the tea garden', I thought I saw someone in the balcony wave to me, but I couldn't be sure.

I'd stopped writing my weekly column 'Coffee Guff' in the *Kantipur* daily newspaper to make time to finish a novel. One of my colleagues quipped, 'You're a newspaper editor. What makes you think you can write?' Another chided me, 'A journalist shouldn't write fiction.' Even events in my country seemed to be conspiring against my novel. A series of shocking incidents had occurred at breathtaking speed in the lives of my countrymen and in the life of my protagonist. The line between fact and fiction was blurring.

***

Kathmandu had been washed clean by the winter rains. I headed for Thamel, taking in the cold air mixed with the scent of wet earth. I passed some young people on motorbikes heading for Nagarkot. 'It must be snowing up there,' they shouted to one another. There was a long line of cars going to Bhaktapur. I thought that if the sky cleared I might even get a glimpse of snow-capped mountains from a rooftop restaurant.

Just as I was about to climb the stairs, a waiter called from the top, 'I saw a photograph of you recently.' I stopped at the bottom. He said, 'You were writing and exhaling smoke.'

So what's the big deal? I thought. At least it wasn't smoke from the barrel or a gun.

The waiter went on, 'Were you writing in one of the restaurants around here?' I didn't bother to answer.

'Is a table free up there?' I asked.

I went upstairs, sat down, ordered a pot of coffee, and called Drishya from my mobile. 'I'm on my way,' he said, sounding harassed. I hung up.

I wanted one last interview with him before finishing my book. It was based on his story, after all, and I needed a few more details to make it as true to life as possible. The novel was a portrait of his world. It was the music of his experience and his imagination. A painter, he was my novel's only rightful critic. He was the one who'd inspired me to write it in the first place. Drishya was like a painting to me and I, his enraptured viewer. I'd written my novel in such a way that readers could take his story for my own.

Drishya had a dream project: he dreamed of blending art and coffee on the canvas of the western hills. He wanted to establish a resort built in the local architectural style and surrounded by sprawling coffee plantations where connoisseurs of art and coffee could experience something unique. The resort would have a library, an art gallery, and internet facilities. He'd told me about his dream. He'd named it Palpasa Café.

Drishya was going to the hills soon to begin his project. I wanted to read my novel out to him before he left. Palpasa Café was his future. He'd told me a ladder spiralling up from the left of the art gallery would take visitors past the library to the café. From there, they'd see a wonderful view of hills and, in clear weather, the mountains in the distance, covered with snow. Palpasa Café would have gardens with flowers that perfumed the air all year round, where migrating birds could rest on their seasonal flights. Visitors would be able to reach the base camp of the mountains after a four-day trek.

I wasn't sure the situation in the country was conducive to the realization of his dream. How, I wondered, could Drishya find the strength to face all the uncertainties? His determination impressed me, especially because I thought that the country had already raised its hands in surrender, defeating his dream. He alone was standing, defiant.

A cat miaowed, approaching my table. An article about my novel published in *Nepal* magazine had mentioned another cat in another restaurant I frequented, my favourite restaurant. This cat looked like that one and, like the other cat, jumped onto and curled up on my lap. Beside my table, the flowers of the potted poinsettia thrust themselves forcibly out of the budding stage. After I finished my coffee, I phoned Drishya again.

'Five friends have arrived,' he said, still sounding harassed. 'I'll come after they leave.'

Which friends? I wondered.

'Order something for me in the meantime,' he said before hanging up.

I'd soon find out these weren't his friends at all. The cat on my lap looked at me serenely as I sipped my coffee. Unaware of all the events taking place in the lives of the people around it, it lived in a blissful world of its own. Not many cats were so lucky. Tourists from all over the world came to this restaurant. Even now, a tourist at a nearby table was turning her camera towards me to take a photo of the cat. I wasn't sure if I was included in the frame but nonetheless grew wary. In times like these, even small things make us paranoid.

My mobile rang. A reporter was calling. The Maoists had looted and bombed a bus. 'No casualties,' he said, 'but my report might get there a bit late. The district headquarters is still very tense. There was the sound of gunfire this morning and now students are throwing stones from inside the campus.'

'Why don't you buy a bloody computer and e-mail your reports like everyone else, instead of relying on the PCO fax machine?' I said, unable to hide my irritation.

I would've if you'd approved an advance,' he shot back. I hung up.

Drishya still hadn't arrived. I began to wonder whether he'd come at all. I was fascinated by his dream project and wanted to know more about it. What did the villages around Palpasa Café look like? I imagined small houses with slanted roofs, dark wooden doors, and clay-washed walls, their verandas dotted with tiny pits made by raindrops. I hoped Drishya would take me there one day.

I phoned him again but someone else picked up the phone.

'They took him! They took him!' she cried. I recognized the voice of Phoolan Chowdhary, Drishya's secretary.

Now it was my turn to panic. 'What? Where?' I asked.

'Five strangers came,' she said breathlessly. 'They said they needed to ask him some questions. They said they were security personnel but they weren't wearing uniforms. He didn't even take his mobile!'

Had Drishya's 'friends' abducted him? 'Are you sure?' I asked.

'Absolutely!' she shouted. 'Can't something be done?'

Phoolan's panic infected me. How could Drishya have been abducted in broad daylight? Since the men had been wearing ordinary clothes, no one on the street would suspect anything. I learned later that they had made him walk a short distance, then put him in an unmarked van parked nearby.

And all the while I'd been sitting in this restaurant, waiting for him, thinking about his dream project. I'd been waiting to read him his story while he, the protagonist of my novel, my first reader, was being abducted.

I phoned an army general I knew. He said nothing could be done 'at this time'. I knew only too well that it was now common practice to arrest people without a warrant. And I also knew how difficult it was to discover the whereabouts of such people once they'd been arrested.

But I called around nonetheless, trying to talk to the chief of the army. He was apparently in a meeting. 'Talk to the spokesperson,' a major advised me.

When I hung up, the waiter, always very eager to serve, asked, 'Have you placed your order, Sir?'

'What order?' I snapped.

My mobile rang again. It was another district correspondent. 'I'm sorry but I have to dictate a story to you,' he said. 'No one's answering the phone at the district bureau.'

What timing! I picked up a napkin to jot down the story: '*A patrol of the unified command lost contact with district headquarters after being ambushed by Maoists this morning about eight kilometres to the east...*'

This was nothing new. We published stories like it every day. Today's newspaper carried an almost identical story; tomorrow's would as well. It was the same thing every day: security personnel losing contact with headquarters, land mines, bomb blasts, the killing of suspected spies, deaths of victims being rushed to health posts... Did newspapers here exist only to publish body counts?

'Is that it?' I asked the reporter.

'There's one more report,' he said.

I picked up another napkin. '*Seven children died after temperatures dropped to a record low due to heavy snow in the western part of the district...*'

Afterwards, I re-read what I'd written. The ink on the napkins seemed to have changed from blue to red, as though my writing had somehow changed languages. I folded the napkins and put them in my pocket. My coffee was cold.

From the street outside the restaurant, I could hear some students chanting: 'Democracy forever!' I asked the waiter what was happening and he said security personnel had fired at the students after failing to control them with batons. I ordered tomato soup and French fries. It was growing windy and cold. I could hear Tibetan music playing somewhere. From where I was sitting, I could see on the main road a sign written in large letters: 'Democracy Forever! Long Live Nepal!'

What had happened on the campus was this: a loudspeaker had just announced the results of a mock referendum held by the students. Democracy had won by a landslide. Shortly after this announcement, police officers had entered the campus, trampling on 'Democracy Forever! Long Live Nepal'. The students were demonstrating in protest.

My thoughts returned to Drishya. Who'd abducted him? And where had they taken him? Would he come back safely? What if his abductors were to claim later that he'd been killed in an 'encounter'? Then I'd have to search for the right words to cover the news of his death. How many columns would that take?

And what did it matter anyway? It was all nonsense.

But who were these men? And why had they abducted him? Did they want to question him about the trek he'd done? Had they found out about his friendship with Siddhartha? Was there something about his dream project that made them suspicious?

Evening set in. Thamel came alive with coloured lights. The car jumped off my lap onto the table and examined the notebook in which I'd made my notes on Drishya's life. I started leafing through the pages, thinking about the constitution of our country. Every paragraph made me think about the fundamental rights our constitution was supposed to guarantee. But now it was possible for the protagonist of my novel to disappear because those responsible for upholding these rights had become their most flagrant violators.

First they hijacked the constitution, then they kidnapped Drishya.

Should I publish the news of his abduction today? Phoolan was sure to issue a public statement appealing for his release. Colleagues in my newsroom would say, 'There are a few similar appeals. Put them all into one report.' And Drishya would become just another name in the long list of the 'disappeared'.

Phoolan phoned again. 'You should be careful,' she said. 'Those men also took away some documents and photos.'

'So?' I asked.

'You're in some of the photos,' she said.

CHAPTER ONE

A mysterious shadow was moving outside the window of my room.

I could tell it was the shadow of a woman. Was the hotel owner's daughter trying to tease me? I rubbed my sleepy eyes. The shadow disappeared, then abruptly reappeared, moving along the verandah. Was she taking a morning walk? Couldn't she find a better place to do it? She seemed to be carrying something. It looked like a pineapple.

I got up and went out onto the verandah, then realized I was naked. I went back in, wrapped a towel around my waist, and went out again, heading for the sea. The waves had fallen silent. The sea here had a peculiar way of raging through the night, then falling asleep in the morning.

Where was the hotel owner's daughter? I looked around and saw her underneath a coconut tree, trying to knock down a coconut with a pole. I wanted to call out to her, 'Come. Let's drink coconut milk from the same straw', but she wouldn't have heard me. I let it go.

By the time I got back to my room, the newspapers had arrived. I picked them up and went to the bathroom. Reading cartoons while sitting on the john makes the whole thing more enjoyable. If the cartoons aren't any good, a laptop will do. There'll always be a few jokes from someone.

This has become one of my habits.

Later, as I dressed, I again noticed the shadow outside my curtains. This teasing was unbearable. I opened my door, saw the hotel owner's daughter disappearing into another room, and realized the guest next door must've ordered a coconut. The pungent smell of cigar smoke wafted up from the verandah of the floor below.

I went to pay my bill and say goodbye to the hotel owner. Her daughter was now halfway up the coconut tree, trying to knock down another coconut. I wondered if there was any point in going to stand underneath her, but no, she was wearing trousers. 'Bye,' she called as a coconut fell with a thud. I didn't deem it necessary to respond. Nearby, a tourist was folding a sheet of paper into a bird to peck his girlfriend.

I went to check out Goa's historic church. There was a long queue outside it. As I joined it, I realized I was standing behind Palpasa. On impulse, I covered her eyes with my hands.

'Who is it?' she asked, startled.

Her friends turned and, seeing me, smiled like accomplices.

'Who is it?' she said again. I didn't say anything. Her eyelashes were soft against my palms. One of her friends joined in the fun. 'Take a guess,' she said.

But Palpasa slipped out of my grasp, turned around, and saw me. 'Oh, you!' she said, playfully punching me in the chest. 'Haven't you gone to Kerala yet?'

'Does it look like I've gone?'

'You aren't going then?'

'I'm still thinking about it.'

''When does your train leave?' she asked.

'It's already left,' I said.

'You missed it? But why?'

'Because of you.'

She looked surprised. 'Me? What did I do?'

'Nothing.'

'So?'

'I just missed it. That's all.'

'But what actually happened?' she asked.

'I lay awake all night, thinking of you,' I said. Her friends began to giggle and whisper among themselves.

'So you woke up too late?' Palpasa said.

'I just got out of bed.'

'Well, what a free spirit you are!' she said.

'The spirit should always be free,' I said

Then she introduced me to her friends. One of them said, 'It seems she's finally met someone who can stand up to her.'

'So none of you can?' I joked.

'She's too much for us,' the friend said. 'But we wish you all the luck in the world. You're going to need it.' The others burst into laughter.

'You...!' Palpasa said. Still laughing, they moved forward in the queue.

Palpasa and I stepped out of the line. She turned to me. 'It seems everyone's against me,' she said. 'What am I going to do?'

'Make a documentary,' I said.

'About you?'

'Why not? And I'll make a painting of you.'

She laughed. 'I'd be honoured if you did that.'

'The honour would be all mine,' I said.

'Well, it seems I'm blessed by the stars,' she quipped.

'No. It'd be a good opportunity for me.'

'Fate smiles on me!' she said.

'Do you think I'm an opportunist?' I asked.

'And do you think I'm a fatalist?' she replied.

I laughed. 'We don't need to tie ourselves to any "isms". Our meeting's a pleasant coincidence, that's all'

'Maybe we could call ourselves coincidentalists?'

'But it does seem fate has brought us together,' I said. 'I was meant to leave for Kerala, after all.'

'Do you mean we'd never have met again if you'd left?'

'It would've been difficult.'

'Why?'

'I forgot to get your phone number yesterday.'

'I'm a fool. I forgot to give it to you. I'm sorry.'

'No need to be sorry. I didn't ask for it.'

She said, 'So you're telling me that's why you missed your train?'

'Partly,' I said.

'What do you mean?'

'Well, last night I wandered around everywhere, looking for your hotel.'

'Oh, didn't I tell you where I was staying?'

'No, and I didn't ask.'

'Then you're a fool as well!'

'I wasn't before I met you.'

'What do you mean?'

'I lost my senses when I met you.'

'You idiot!'

'You mean I haven't worked my magic on you?'

'You have, but now you're messing it up.'

We were standing by a bench in the churchyard. We saw Palpasa's friends coming out of the church, which had stood stable and rock solid for more than three centuries. The only unstable thing in the churchyard was me.

'Let's meet again in Kathmandu,' Palpasa said as her friends approached.

'So you want to say goodbye?' I asked.

'Did I say that?'

One of her friends interrupted us, 'Excuse me. Have you two finished your conversation?'

'We're only just beginning,' I said and her friends laughed. I watched them leave, wondering what to make of Palpasa.

That evening I sat on the verandah outside my room, drinking wine and watching the sunset paint the ocean as if it were a vast canvas. Seagulls were swooping down to scoop fish from the waves. To my surprise, Palpasa left her friends and came to join me. She also ordered a glass of wine, while I considered moving on to something stronger. She made me nervous and I wanted to get plastered.

In the courtyard across from my room, the hotel's loudspeakers were blaring, Bob Marley urging his listeners, 'Get up; stand up; don't give up the fight.' I didn't know what to say or do with Palpasa. I was afraid of my feelings for her. Why lure this girl into love? And why surrender myself to her? Was I a fool? I pinched myself, then rested my hand on my knee. I held myself back, trying to look cool.

Marley was soon singing another song, asking his listeners, 'If you don't know your history, how can you know where you're coming from?' After that, the first song came back on: 'Get up; stand up..."

All I could do was to drink and, tongue-tied, listen to the music. Eventually Palpasa left, retreating beyond the shadow of a coconut tree and disappearing into the night. Long after she'd gone, I could still smell the perfume of her hair. I regretted I hadn't said goodbye to her properly and couldn't remember if she'd bid me goodbye or not; my forgetfulness was probably a combination of the relaxed atmosphere, my own mood, and the fact that I'd drunk too much wine. These things happen in a place where you lose your identity and become just another anonymous tourist. I wondered if I'd meet Palpasa in Goa again.

I paced backwards and forwards on my verandah. Cigar smoke was again wafting up from downstairs. I felt like going down and giving the smoker a slap. And where was the hotel owner's daughter? The sight of her might've cheered me up. I looked at the trees to see if anyone was there, still trying to knock down coconuts. On the trees, the leaves danced madly; the wind was picking up. The sea was loud. Music was still blaring from the loudspeakers.

I switched on my laptop. There were three new e-mails, but I wasn't in the mood to reply. Some idiot had sent dirty jokes.

CHAPTER TWO

I'd met her the day before at the Coconut Bar and Pineapple Restaurant in a traditional Portuguese-style building. A local band was playing Beatles songs. Goa was teeming with Christmas visitors and all the tables were occupied. I was sitting on one chair with my feet up on another. I'd just sent Tshering an e-mail, telling him I was on the lookout for a girl.

'I feel sorry for them, whoever they might be,' Tshering replied. I told him to come to the chat room later that evening.

The band was playing 'Norwegian Wood' at my request. I was enjoying its fusion of eastern and western styles. I thought about Ravi Shankar and the fact that George Harrison had learned sitar from him. A waiter stood nearby, with his eye on my laptop. He looked at it every time he passed, probably hoping I'd connect to some porn sites. I ignored him. He poured more of the local drink, feni, into my glass. As I raised it, out of the corner of my eye I caught sight of a shadow moving among the shadows of the coconut trees cast by the moon on the white walls of the restaurant. Someone was coming towards me.

'Excuse me,' a young woman said, waving her hand to catch my attention. 'Can I take this chair?' She pointed to the chair on which I was resting my feet.

It was my last night in Goa. I was going to Kerala for the New Year.

The girl was wearing blue jeans and a v-neck shirt printed with a scene of a Goan sunset. That day, as I'd walked barefoot over the dry sand of Anjuna Beach, the cool waves had lapped around my ankles, refreshing me. It was as if a wave had brought her to me. I could see the girl's dangling earrings shining. Her long hair was like the waves of the ocean. This girl will be my girl, I thought.

'What if I don't want to give you the chair?' I asked, testing her.

She raised her dark, beautiful eyebrows. Her eyes were large and clear, the eyes of a dreamer.

'Sorry?' she said, pretending not to have understood.

I took another sip of feni. Just then, the waiter brought me my rice and fish. We Nepalis can't do without rice, no matter where we are. Should I eat with my hands? I decided not to. The girl still stood there, waiting for my reply.

'I'm sorry to keep you waiting,' I said as I raised my fork.

'So I can take it?' she said. I looked at her cleavage as she bent forward to lift the chair. I made my move.

'I'd rather you joined me,' I said.

'I wasn't asking to share your table,' she said. Her voice was deep and dripping with honey. Her eyes seemed to beckon me. Who'd pass up this opportunity?

'You can see the band better from here,' I said.

'But you can hear them better from there,' she replied. I realized this girl would be a challenge.

'Can I join your table then?' I asked.

'Our table's already crowded.'

I made myself clear. 'I'd like to talk to you.'

'I'm busy,' she said.

'I've got a good reason to talk to you,' I said.

'What reason would that be? I don't know you.'

'But I know you.'

'Oh, come on. We've just met.'

I looked into her enticing eyes. 'In fact, we met a few hours ago.'

'What are you talking about?' she said.

I asked, 'What were you reading today on Anjuna Beach?'

'An art book.'

'Aha,' I said.

'So?'

'So, I wrote that book,' I said. 'It's about my paintings.'

Her eyes widened. 'That can't be true.'

'You don't believe me?'

'I don't know how I could prove or disprove it,' she said. 'The book doesn't have the author's photo on the cover.'

'Check the name.'

'But the author's Nepali.'

'Do I look like a westerner to you?' I asked in Nepali.

Startled, she took a step back. I looked into her eyes again to better gauge her reaction. I was drawn to her like a bee to nectar.

'Wow!' she said, finally interested. She looked at my face closely, examining every feature.

'I hope you'll join me now,' I said. 'I'd like to hear your thoughts on my book.'

Like an obedient student, she sat on the chair she'd earlier wanted to take. 'Namaste,' she said, pressing her palms together. I reached over and shook her soft hand. She was biting her lip; I could tell she was nervous. The shadow her body cast against the wall moved rhythmically with the music, tempting and erotic. It reminded me of a charcoal sketch come to life.

All the time I was looking at her shadow, the girl was examining me closely. Did she think I was good-looking? I wondered.

'My name's Palpasa,' she said.

'Hi,' I said and offered my hand again.

'I've just graduated from college in the States. I'm hoping to be a documentary filmmaker.'

'Nice to meet a fellow artist,' I said.

'I'd like to introduce you to my friends,' she said, starting to get up.

'No,' I said, 'please don't introduce me to anyone.'

She sat down again. 'But you just introduced yourself to me,' she said.

'You're different.'

'I really like your paintings,' she said. 'They're simple but your style's totally original.'

'I'm flattered,' I said. 'Can you imagine how an artist might feel seeing a girl obviously from overseas lying on a beach in a swimsuit engrossed in his book?'

'How did it feel?'

Why reveal my true feelings? I thought. 'I'm still trying to decide.'

'This is the first time I've had an experience like this,' she said.

'Like what?'

'It's the first time I ever met a writer whose book I've read.'

I asked, 'When you read a book, do you imagine the author?'

'Of course. And with art books I picture the artist. But the way I picture him or her changes with each page, with each work I look at. With each painting, I get more curious about what the artist might be like.'

'So how did you picture me?'

'Middle-aged,' she confessed, 'wearing a hat, smoking a pipe, carrying a guitar, and humming with the wind.'

'A romantic figure, in other words?'

'And I haven't changed my opinion,' she went on, 'though you do look a bit younger than I'd imagined.'

'But still old?' I said, trying to prolong our conversation. The waiter came back, intent on invading our privacy. I would've liked to pull a few hairs out of his goatee.

'Did I say that? I just meant you look too young to have created such mature work,' Palpasa said.

'Thank you,' I said. 'No one's ever said that to me before.'

'You're just saying that to flatter me.'

'No. It's you who's flattering me.'

'You don't look like someone who'd care what other people think,' she said.

'That's where you're wrong,' I said 'Artists care very much, especially when they find someone who appreciates their work, as you do.'

'I'm just an ordinary person who happens to love art,' she said, 'though my friends might disagree. They say that when I find something that interests me, I get so impassioned about it I almost become obsessive. But I think of myself as an uncomplicated person with simple tastes.'

'This is the first time I've ever wanted to introduce myself to anyone who's read my book,' I said, trying to impress on her the uniqueness of the occasion.

'In fact,' she said, 'I lead such a simple life, I sometimes wonder why I didn't become a nun. Maybe I'll end up in a nunnery some day.'

Unhappy with the turn the conversation was taking, I said, 'It's better to lead an active life, out in the world.'

'I want to understand things,' she said, 'to seek knowledge. I want to know myself. If documentary filmmaking doesn't satisfy me, I'll become a nun and seek inner knowledge. Wouldn't a search like that constitute an active life?'

Wishing she'd stop this nonsense, I said, 'This is the first time I've ever met anyone who wants to be a nun.'

'I really like your paintings,' she said.

'What do you see in them?' I asked.

'The dreams and desires of the people you paint. How do you choose your subjects?'

'Just the way I met you.'

'Oh, I could never be a subject for one of your paintings!'

'Who said I wanted you to be?'

'Nobody,' she said.

'But the impressions you've given me, even in this short meeting, could be the basis for some future work.'

'This is impossible,' she said, exasperated.

'What's impossible?'

'Talking to artists.'

'So you've talked to many?'

She laughed. 'I mean talking to an artist.'

She stretched then and seemed to open up for the first time. Her arms looked soft and her fingers playful. By then the band had performed several Beatles numbers. I'd sent a request for two songs written on a napkin and 'Strawberry Fields Forever' was yet to be played. The night was passing with the sound of the waves. I wanted to be in bed by midnight. I had to be at the train station by noon. I ate my dinner while she sat there. Just as I finished, I heard the first notes of 'Strawberry Fields Forever'.

'Isn't it late for you?' I asked

'My friends keep looking over here,' she said. 'They obviously want to leave.'

'How long are you staying in Goa?' I asked.

'A few more days,' she said. 'And you?'

'I leave for Kerala tomorrow'

'Oh.' She raised her eyebrows. 'Artists must lead such free lives.'

'You have to be free to express yourself freely,' I said.

'Are you preparing another series of paintings? Will you include them in a new book?'

'I don't believe in preparing too much. I wander, read, meet people. And when I find inspiration, I pick up my brush.'

'That's why your works seem so romantic.'

'How many pages of my book have you read?' I asked.

'The whole thing. More than once, in fact.'

'Really?'

"Yes. I don't get tired of it. Every time I look at it, I find something new. I've got ten other books with me, but none of them interests me as much as your book.'

'That's wonderful.'

'Make sure your next book's just as good,' she said seriously. 'Your paintings in this book are really evocative. Can I tell you something? I identify with the female figure in the painting *Rain*. I feel that figure is me. It might sound strange but the more I look at that painting, the more I see myself. It seems to capture my deepest feelings.'

I looked at her inquisitively.

'Maybe everyone feels the same,' she went on, 'but your paintings have made a big impression on me. Photography has limitations. Paintings are more complex and more interesting because the viewer's imagination is an essential and integral part of the whole. The true depths of a painting lie in the mind of the viewer.'

'You're right,' I said. 'I feel encouraged when I meet someone who understands things the way you do.'

'Well, you're an inspiration to me,' she said.

'With your understanding of art, I'm sure you'll be a good filmmaker; I said.

She lit up. 'Finally, I've found someone who believes in me. No one, and that includes my friends and family, understands me. They just want me to marry and settle down in the States.'

'You have to make your own decisions,' I said.

'I'm still thinking about it.'

'If you do intend to do creative work,' I said, 'I feel it's better to be in the east than the west. The west's more advanced, of course, but it's running out of stories. Here in the east, there's a much wider gap between problems—social, cultural, and natural—and their solutions. That gap fuels creativity; we have more space to work.'

'You know, we really think alike,' she said. 'Could we meet again in Kathmandu?'

'I don't know when I'll be back,' I said.

'But you must have a contact address?'

'I'm a traveller. I never stay in one place long,' I lied.

She laughed. 'Your permanent address is in the heart of your readers.'

A man came up to Palpasa. I could tell from his appearance he was also Nepali. He looked angry or maybe I just thought he was. He said something to Palpasa, then abruptly took her arm and led her back to the table where her friends were waiting.

I didn't want to give her up. I got up and started to go over to their table, but before I could reach them, they stood up and left the restaurant. The band was still playing 'Strawberry Fields Forever' as I left as well.

It was past midnight. I walked behind Palpasa and her friends for a while. Finally, near a coconut tree, she turned and said, 'Have a good trip to Kerala.' I shook hands with her and said, 'Having met you, I feel encouraged as an artist.' I didn't look at her friends, especially not at the man who'd ended our conversation so abruptly. As we shook hands, I brushed against her gently. She didn't seem to mind.

Then I walked away. The perfume of her hair sailed with me. All the way back to my hotel, I thought about her hair, her eyes, her voice, and the curves of her body. I cursed my bad luck for having had to let her go. Only the two of us knew about the gentle touch we'd shared.

In my hotel room, I didn't want to switch on the computer. Tshering was sure to ask if I'd found a girl. I stood by the window for a while. The ocean looked like a giant lump of coal and the lights from ships like flickering embers. A western couple was walking along the beach, locked in an embrace. The sea was still noisy, its waves crashing against the shore. Someone downstairs was still smoking a cigar. I wanted to forget the disappointments of the day and start a new one afresh.

CHAPTER THREE

Dear Writer,

I'm addressing you as a writer because I've read your book, just as I'll address you as an artist after I visit your gallery. I presume you do have a gallery. I'm sure I can find its address in your book somewhere. But for now, I want to keep your studio in the realm of my imagination. Your paintings suggest to me that your gallery must be high up in the hills, above the clouds, because how could you create such beautiful work in Kathmandu?

Your paintings capture the beauty of the hills. They're the heart of your work, but their presence in your work isn't always obvious Instead, it's implicit in your brushstrokes and the way you use symbols. Your brushstrokes hide the hills, making the viewer hungry to see them. Maybe the divine's at work in your art. Logically, I know divinity's just an illusion, but sometimes it seems the divine does manifest itself through art. Maybe there's a spark of the divine in all artists?

I need to apologize for not meeting you today and just leaving this letter instead. I can imagine what you must be thinking, finding this letter instead of me. But I have my reasons. Or maybe I don't. I'm confused.

I'm an admirer of your work and always will be. As I write, your book's lying on my pillow beside me. Your work's left its mark on me. All my friends are tired of my always having my nose in your book, but I don't care.

As I told you, I'm a simple girl. You said I'm a mirror of you; maybe I am. Sometimes I do feel I'm not a sentient being. But the thing is, though I understand what you said and I don't mean to disagree with it, I don't know what I am. Don't misinterpret me. Don't think I'm saying I'm an object for others. I'm not. But how can a person who's not sure about herself mean something to others? I might sound like a pessimist saying that, but I'm not. I'm an optimist, in fact. Remember we joked about being 'coincidentalists'? I've never lost hope about anything and never will.

Meeting you was one of the most amazing experiences in my life. I met the writer of a book I've read and re-read. And I wouldn't have got to know you if I hadn't asked for that chair, and, before that, if you hadn't coloured me with your brushes through your book. If we'd met under other circumstances, we might not have even talked to each other and I'd never have known who you were.

Why did I decide not to meet you today? Why did I do it? When we met, I felt exactly as you did—that we reflect each other—but I didn't have the words to express it. That's the difference between an artist and a viewer, between a writer and a reader. Writers touch the hearts of readers, giving them pleasure and expanding their visions. Words can be a mirror of the self. Can you see my reflection in these words? They are a mirror in which you can see me instead of yourself. We could even call these words my photograph.

But maybe you see me as a painting. If that's the case, it makes me nervous because I know you're not seeing me as I really am. You're not seeing me as a real person but as someone created by your imagination.

I guess writers must receive many letters from their readers, but they rarely appear in their readers' lives. I don't imagine I'll ever meet another writer the way I met you. And, even if I did, I wouldn't be as open with him as I've been with you. You're special because you're exactly how you appear to be. There's no difference between what you say and what you write. You live according to your beliefs and expect others to respond with the same sincerity. Maybe that's where I failed. I wasn't as honest with you as you were with me. I wanted to be more than just an admirer of your work. I wanted to be your friend. Perhaps that's why I can't meet you today.

We've known each other for just two days, but I feel as if I've known you for ages. I first opened your book a long time ago. It isn't set in any particular time. It describes no particular events. It raises no questions about when, who, why, and where. People who look at your book are allowed to lose themselves in their imaginations. I feel the paintings and words in your book are a reflection of your personality, so I don't need to ask any questions. There's already an intimacy between us created by your images and words. I'm surprised that, intellectually, you're exactly as I imagined. Even if I hadn't read your book, I still would've been impressed by you. To me, there's no difference between reading what you write, looking at your paintings, or listening to the words you speak.

As I told you, I feel the girl in the painting 'Rain' is me. I can't tell you why I feel that way. Maybe your art's cast a spell on me. You told me that I made you lose your senses, that because of me you missed your train to Kerala, that because of me you found something different in yourself. I don't doubt you. These words came from your heart, so how could I not be moved? I don't imagine you said these things just for effect, but I've been affected nonetheless.

Both of us going to Goa for Christmas, your seeing me reading your book on Anjuna Beach, both of us going to the same restaurant that evening, our table needing a chair and my being the one to ask you for it—this was a wonderful series of coincidences. And I feel such coincidences will continue. To think I mightn't have gone to Goa at all. Or you might've celebrated Christmas in Kerala and the New Year in Goa. Or you mightn't have walked on Anjuna Beach when I was there. Or I might've been reading another book when you saw me. Or, even if I had been reading your book, you mightn't have noticed.

I wonder why you didn't approach me when you saw me reading your book. If we hadn't been in the same restaurant that evening, we'd still be strangers. I won't say our meeting was fated but I'm compelled to reflect on what made it happen because meeting you has somehow changed me. It's boosted my self-confidence, my self-esteem. I feel charged with energy. My desire to be creative has doubled. You've inspired me to follow through on the things I've wanted to do. Maybe it's not that you've changed me exactly but that you've energized me and helped me find an inner strength I hadn't known was there. But now I know it always was. I'd just never made the effort to tap into it. The mist has cleared, I've become my own mirror; I understand my own heart. And the credit goes to you.

Still, I'm letting you down by not meeting you. On the one hand, I'm giving you credit for all you've done for me while, on the other, I'm failing you. You see, there's a contradiction inside me. You've given me strength, but you've also created a conflict inside me. The mist has cleared, but a new set of clouds has appeared on my horizon. I'm confused and you're the architect of my confusion. I'm grateful to you but I'm also beginning to blame you. Am I a perceptive art lover? I don't know the answer to that question any more. By giving you both credit and blame, I fear I'm dragging my favourite writer into a whirlpool. But I think you can understand the contradictions inside me. And perhaps contradiction-filled feedback from admirers of your work is nothing new to you.

When I came back from meeting you at your hotel, I stayed up very late thinking. Was I getting too close to you? Was it natural to feel so close to someone so quickly? Would getting to know you better affect my admiration for your work? Would being close to a writer change my feelings for his words? Would I love your book less?

After tormenting myself with these questions, I decided not to meet you again, at least for the moment. I want to maintain a healthy distance from someone whose work I admire so much. I want to limit myself to knowing you through the pages of your book. Have I made the right decision? I can't say. All I know is that it was a difficult and painful decision to make. For the first time in my life I'm truly suffering.

You're different from anyone I've ever known. That's why I'm trying to be open with you. I hope my frankness doesn't offend you.

Only moments ago, I was looking at one of your paintings, the one in which a long yellow leaf is falling. The leaf falls and falls but never touches the ground. I feel like that leaf. You've made me that yellow leaf, which falls continuously, never finding a place to rest. I want to stop falling. I want to stand up and fight my inner battles on solid ground. That's all I want to say.

Yours truly,
Reader

CHAPTER FOUR

Palpasa was standing under the coconut tree by the gate. She was wearing a maroon shirt tucked into her trousers. She was carrying a book. It was clear she was watching the gate, waiting for me. She stood immobile, like a statue, an object devoid of life. Only her eyes were moving.

I came down the stairs and went over to her. It seemed she'd been in that place for a long time, like a leaf falling and falling.

Noticing me, she came to life. 'Forgive me,' she said.

'No. It's my fault,' I said.

She fixed her gaze on me. 'Why?'

'I offered you an illusion.'

'So everything you said was a lie?' she asked.

'No. But I gave you the wrong idea.'

'Which is?'

'You know. That's why you had to write the letter.'

'I wrote it in a moment of weakness.'

'I've never received such a beautiful letter,' I said. 'I read it over and over last night.'

A smile appeared on her lips. 'The way I read and re-read your book?'

'You write beautifully,' I said.

'I'm sorry I didn't come to meet you,' she said.

'No. Don't be sorry. It's good you made yourself clear.'

'Did I make myself clear?'

'You made your inner conflict clear,' I said.

'So I'm clear in my confusion?'

'There's energy in inner conflict,' I said. 'It drives human beings to search for clarity and resolution, and that gives their lives meaning.'

'Did I hurt you?' she asked.

'Your words took away the pain,' I said. 'You've touched my heart. You've given it a fresh beat.'

'I don't understand what you're saying,' she said.

'Does a bee ever wonder if a flower gets hurt by its sting?'

'Bees don't think about things like that!'

We both laughed. She tried to hold her laughter back initially but couldn't. The tension in her face disappeared.

The shadow of the coconut tree kept pace with the movement of the sun. The hotel was bustling with tourists coming and going. We talked.

'This trip's become a special one,' I said. 'I received the most beautiful letter in my life.'

'You see beauty in everything,' she said.

'I picked that up from you.'

'Nonsense.' She pretended to be annoyed.

'It would definitely have been incomplete if I hadn't met you.'

'The trip, you mean?'

'No. My life,' I said, and stole a glance at her.

'Don't be silly!' She blushed. 'Stop playing with me.'

'I'm still confused about one thing though,' I ventured.

'Yes?'

'I don't know which is more beautiful, you or your letter.'

'Was my letter really that beautiful?' she said, looking pleased.

I said, 'Reading your words and being with you are equally lovely.'

'Then I must be good at fooling people.'

'No. I'm not wrong about this.'

'Were you wrong earlier?'

'Yes. Before I met you, I had some misconceptions,' I said.

'What misconceptions?' she asked.

'I didn't believe I could ever talk to a girl as beautiful as you.'

She laughed. 'You fool!'

'And now I've done it.'

'But you didn't just talk to me. You stole from me.'

'Oh? What did I steal?'

'My heart,' she said.

I smiled. 'So, you're calling me a thief?'

'You're a thief of hearts.'

'Is it only your heart I've stolen?' I asked. 'I wanted to steal all of you.'

She smiled. 'You're doing that as well.'

'Am I stealing you away from someone else?'

'No. I take care of myself.'

'I hope you don't feel insecure with me,' I said.

'Oh? You could even do that?'

'Do what?'

'Save me from my desires,' she said. 'It's only my desires that make me insecure, the desire to meet you, for example.'

I asked, 'Did you really think meeting me was the wrong thing to do?'

'Reading my letter, you must've understood I felt that way,' she replied.

'Then why have you come to meet me now?'

She threw my question back at me. 'Was it wrong of me to come?'

'You could've stopped yourself but you didn't.'

'I wouldn't have come if I could've stopped myself.'

We both laughed gently.

After a while, we went to look for a restaurant. The sun was at its hottest, though there's no such thing as summer or winter on a tropical beach. The scene's the same, only the characters change. The beach was at its most crowded, and in that crowd was an admirer of my work who made me feel special.

I looked at her surreptitiously and was taken aback. She seemed to be wilting before my eyes. Earlier she'd been guarded. Then I'd said something that made her blossom like a flower. Now she was aloof again, separating herself from me. The flower was fading and who knew when it might bloom again.

At the restaurant she ordered only orange juice.

'I thought we'd never meet again,' I said.

'It's a small world,'

'And round,' I joked. 'Our paths might've crossed some day.'

'Why do you put it so abstractly?' she asked. 'I came to your hotel, remember?'

'Maybe you just took the wrong path?'

'No, it was the way I chose to go,' she said.

'I'm surprised.'

'Why?'

'Well, what brought you here today?'

'The book.'

'What do you mean?'

'I wasn't sure if we'd meet again and I wanted you to sign it.' She put the book on the table in front of her.

I stared at her incredulously. 'You mean you came to see me just for an autograph?'

'What did you think?'

'Why didn't you tell me earlier?' I snapped. 'In that case, you must be eager to be on your way.'

'You're the one who seems to be in a hurry,' she shot back.

'Time has meant nothing to me,' I said, 'since the evening I met you.'

'The way you use time is entirely under your control,'

'In that case, would I have missed my train to Kerala?'

'Well, make sure you don't miss the train to Kathmandu.'

'There are no trains to Kathmandu,' I said.

'Then to wherever it is you're going.'

I said, 'Actually, I thought I might've reached my destination.'

She stared at me for a few moments. 'I thought so too. But it turns out that there are tracks leading away.'

'Why?' I asked, 'Have the tracks been reserved for someone else?'

'No,' she said. 'I just think the train's crying to run before the tracks have been laid.'

She slid the book towards me. I wrote, '*To my dear reader*,' and signed it.

Without further ceremony, she stood up. As she turned to go, she spoke quickly in English, 'You'll always be in my heart. All the best and bon voyage to wherever your travels take you.'

She walked away. The air shimmered with her body heat as she moved.

A few words kept echoing in my ears: 'One last thing. Never miss a train.'

'But I've already missed the one I wanted,' I said under my breath as I watched her go.

The leaf was falling again and couldn't stop even though it wanted to. I wondered where it would go, cut loose from its stem.

CHAPTER FIVE

Kathmandu was basking in glorious sunshine. A gentle breeze was showering blue jacaranda flowers onto a parked Volkswagen Beetle. A girl wearing faded jeans was taking in this sight, oblivious to the flowers landing in her hair. Nearby, a group of Tibetan children were picking the flowers off the ground and stuffing them into each other's vests as though the flowers were snowballs. They laughed as they played. The blue flowers kept drifting down, making me think of the shepherds in the mountains and the way snow fell on them in winter.

A man on an Eliminator motorbike screeched to a halt near the girl. She pulled a purple shawl out of her bag and shook her hair, making the blue flowers fall. Then, wrapped in the shawl, she got on the motorbike.

I called Tshering on my mobile. I knew he was working on a feature called 'Jacarandas and Love' and wanted him to come and photograph this sight.

'I can't come now,' he said crossly.

There were very few vehicles on the road that day. Another young couple drove up in a car and parked behind a jacaranda tree. They stepped out of their car, their arms raised to receive a shower of blue blossoms. This girl was also wearing jeans. They fitted her like a second skin. I couldn't take my eyes off her legs. On the other side of the street was a wall painted with an advertisement for 'Fair & Lovely' cream. The couple lay down on the ground, between the car and the wall. No one could see them except me and the jacaranda tree.

The young man leaned over and kissed the girl on the lips, then on the cheek. His lips were a paintbrush with which he coloured her. She blushed in pleasure and passion, her body moving tenderly with each stroke of his brush. Soon, a painting was in the making, its final result impossible to predict.

My mobile shouldn't have rung at that moment. Everything should've been banned there except the flowers, the lovers' lips, and my eyes. I should've been transformed into a branch of the tree on which I was leaning. My clothes should've turned into camouflage. Nothing in the world should've interfered. But my mobile rang.

If I answered it, I'd ruin the lovers' rendezvous. They'd fly away, cursing me, like a pair of frightened doves. Most likely they'd never enjoyed any privacy or a chance to kiss like this. They'd have to wait another year for another afternoon like this, when the streets were empty and the blue flowers showering down. And who knew what might happen to their relationship by then? They mightn't even be on speaking terms. A bomb might explode in the city, claiming one of their lives. Or the man might get caught in crossfire while travelling outside the capital. His car might be ambushed. Anything, anything could happen to deprive the couple of another afternoon like this.

The young woman's eyes were still closed. The man was gently picking flowers from her hair, the jacaranda tree replacing each blossom he removed. The woman was a jacaranda tree in full bloom; the man, her spring.

The Tibetan children shouldn't have been spying on the couple. Suddenly, the young woman heard a giggle, opened her eyes and, seeing the children watching, melted with embarrassment.

Still hiding, I answered my phone. It was Tshering. I hissed, 'Come quickly. This might be your last chance to see the jacarandas in full bloom.'

'Sorry, Drishya,' he said. 'I'm here waiting for the right light to take some shots of migrating birds. I want to capture the afternoon sun. It's for a travel magazine. Please don't disturb me.'

I pictured Tshering perched on a tree, his camera focused on a nest below in which a mother bird was tending to her newly hatched chicks, their eyes not yet open. What more peaceful image could there be for a travel magazine than a migrating bird raising its chicks in Kathmandu?

I got in my car and drove down the alley under the rows of jacarandas, heading towards the highway. I drove aimlessly. At a police checkpoint, I stopped behind a truck packed with chickens. There were some boys in school uniform on the truck. One sneezed violently. The boys looked at the armed police guarding the checkpoint and the police stared back.

'Look! We've reached Kathmandu,' another boy said, pointing excitedly towards the city.

'Yes, Kathmandu,' the first boy said. He sneezed again.

A rooster jumped about in a bamboo cage, flapping its wings in alarm.

The sun shone brightly. The sky was blue and the hills that stood like dutiful guards around the Kathmandu Valley were clearly visible. A mass of clouds was rolling towards the Langtang range to the north.

'Look at the frog!' one of the boys on the truck shouted, pointing at me. The rest joined in the fun, shouting, 'Frog! Frog!' I realized they were referring to my Volkswagen Beetle.

'Where are you boys from?' I shouted above the noise of the chickens.

'School,' one replied.

'The village,' said another.

'Which village?' I asked.

'Below Dhanchuli Himal.'

I started. My eyes welled with tears. Fifteen years ago I'd come from the same region. When I entered the 'Nepal valley' for the first time, I'd been like these boys, excited and uncertain. That was the first time I'd ever seen a road full of vehicles. I'd arrived during a SAARC summit and we'd had to go through countless checkpoints. The truck I'd come on had been carrying sacks of rice but, fortunately, I'd been able to sit up front with the driver. I'd arrived late and my boarding school was locked up for the night. I'd had to sleep in the guardroom.

I looked at the boys on the truck, pitying them. One of them was about to say something to me, but the truck started up with a rumble. The other boy sneezed loudly and the rooster flapped its wings.

I watched them go, filled with nostalgia. One of the boys waved at me and then the others waved too. I remembered the day I left my village. I'd run all the way through the paddy fields till I found my way blocked by a herd of cows coming back from the pastures. A startled calf attacked me, tossing me over a shrub. I'd overheard someone at a nearby tea shop say, 'Look. Our teacher's son is leaving for boarding school.' It seemed like yesterday.

My best friend, Resham, had been waiting for me below the paddy fields. 'Don't forget us,' he'd said, offering me a poinsettia flower as a parting gift. He and I had scampered down together till we reached the suspension bridge. He had been crying. I'd wanted to comfort him. From my bag, I'd taken out two bananas and given them to him. 'I'll come for the Dashain holidays,' I'd said. 'We'll play on the swings, I promise.' 'You can teach me English when you come back,' Resham had replied.

***

Further along the highway I looked for the truck with the chickens and the boys but couldn't distinguish it from the other trucks. I started to cross the highway, but a car whizzed past. Then a boy darted across the highway, chasing after a wheel that had rolled off a speeding van.

It was dark by the time I got home. I was hungry. I heated some bread and sausages, cut a few slices of cheese, poached an egg, and made some tomato chutney. Then I sat down, eating at my computer.

A sixteen-year-old girl had entered the chat room.

'Sweet sixteen,' I wrote. 'I'm twice your age!'

'No problem,' came the reply. 'I like mature men.'

She said her name was Lara, but I suspected she was a Nepali. No matter. She sounded saucy. I'll catch her, I thought. She, too, might be a falling yellow leaf. Who knew, maybe she'd also go on about needing a firm place to land. And what better place could she find than my lap! Right, Tshering? The idiot was probably already asleep, and not just asleep but snoring his head off. His wife had left for a pilgrimage to Mansarovar and the bastard was enjoying a few days' peace and quiet.

'I'm a Sherpa,' I wrote to Lara. 'I just got back from an expedition to Mt Everest.'

She wrote back, 'Did you see a yeti?'

'Yes. But it ran away.'

'Why?'

'Because I was riding a yak.'

'So you didn't climb Mt Everest. You climbed a yak.'

'I climbed Mt Everest on a yak.'

'It's the yak that reached the peak. You just sat on its back like a bottle of oxygen.'

My mobile beeped then. Tshering had sent a message, asking what I was up to. 'Busy in chat room,' I texted back. I hoped he wouldn't call to invite me to his place for dinner so late. He didn't. He just sent another message: 'Who with?'

'Teenager,' I replied.

'Congrats,' he wrote. 'Feel young again?'

I didn't reply. If he wants to talk, let him come online, I thought. He'd probably had a hard day, photographing his migrating birds. He was probably tired.

I asked the teenager, 'Have you ever read of a yak climbing Everest with a man on its back?'

'It's the first time I've heard of such a thing,' she wrote back. 'Shouldn't it go in *The Guinness Book of Records?*'

'I'm thinking about it.'

'And what did you see from the top of the world?'

'Contrary to what you might expect, I didn't see any mountains or the Tibetan Plateau or any Lhasa-bound aircraft. Instead, I saw fairies, smiling and waving at me. Among them was a girl named Lara.'

'How romantic! We should go on a date,' she wrote back.

I didn't hesitate. 'Sure.'

'When?'

I wrote, 'Whenever you're free.'

'How about now?'

Was she kidding? 'It's a bit late, isn't it?' I wrote back.

'Do you only date in the afternoon?' she wrote.

I laughed and wrote, 'I'm flexible.'

'So what's the problem with now?' she insisted.

'OK. But let me ask you one thing.'

'What?'

'Are you a virgin?' I wrote, a bit crudely.

'What difference does that make?'

'Just asking,' I pressed on.

'Stupid ooloo,' came the reply. And then, 'Ha ha ha...'

'Who is this?' I asked, 'Tell me who you are, if you have the guts.'

My God, it was Tshering.

Outraged, I switched off the computer but immediately wondered why I'd done it. Angrily, I switched it back on and put on a CD. I wanted to fall asleep to the sound of music but the song I'd chosen wasn't right. Still irritated, I went to the cupboard and took out a Narayan Gopal CD. I put it on: 'I don't know where I'll be going after I get up in the morning...'

Tshering rang just then. 'Want to get together for a drink?' he asked.

I heaped abuse on him, using every swear word I could think of, then hung up with a bang.

I was still cursing him as I got ready for bed. Then I started laughing at myself for trying to pass myself off as a Sherpa to the son of a Sherpa, for claiming to have climbed Mt Everest, for asking the 'girl' if she were a virgin. I was sure Tshering must be laughing at home as well.

I was right. He called back. 'So how was your chat?'

'Not bad.'

'I did a wonderful thing today.'

'What was that?'

'I punctured a balloon that was flying high in the air.'

'You're totally useless!' I shouted, and hung up again.

CHAPTER SIX

I didn't go to my gallery yesterday. I wasted my time reading a bad Nepali novel, a recent release. It took real effort to finish it. It had nothing new in substance or in style. I would've been better off watching a movie, going to a restaurant, or visiting Nagarkot or Kakani. I prefer Kakani to Nagarkot because it's closer to the mountains and windier; my imagination runs free in the breeze. Standing on a windy hillside, I feel far away from Kathmandu. But the shoddiness of the novel truly upset me. Why had I wasted my money on it? I couldn't sleep and spent the whole night painting. It was morning before I finally went to bed.

I woke up in the afternoon. The first thing I did was to put the novel on top of a pile of newspapers bound for recycling. I felt better after that. I resolved not to read another Nepali novel for at least a few months.

To refresh myself, I drank a lot of cold water, then put the kettle on for coffee. I made some toast. Where was the jar of strawberry jam? I peeled and chopped some potatoes, then fried them with cumin. Then I fried some salami. After breakfast, I cleaned up.

I wasn't satisfied with the painting that hung on my dining room wall. I hadn't been myself when I painted it. I still wasn't able to think of a title for it. I wasn't even sure what to do with it.

I went to get the newspapers. The newspaper boy had left them wedged in the fork of a tree. I took them with me to the bathroom. The headlines were depressing but the cartoons were funny. I'd just gotten out of the shower when the phone rang, but I couldn't get to it in time. I thought, if it's important they'll call me on my mobile. And then there was e-mail. There was no reason to hurry in this country. Time was standing still.

Later, Phoolan called. A French diplomat wanted to see my paintings and had asked when I'd be at the gallery. I told her to make an appointment at any time convenient for him. Back in the kitchen, I spread some jam on a piece of bread. It was about time I bought some fresh bread. Perhaps in the evening I'd stroll through Thapathali and Durbar Marg to the bakery in Thamel. The weather outside looked pleasant. And the streets might still be carpeted with blue jacaranda flowers.

I'd started a series of paintings on jacarandas. But I'd stopped halfway through the first painting, dissatisfied with one of the figures, a college girl on her way to campus, walking along a street strewn with blue flowers. I still couldn't find the inspiration to finish it. If I saw that street again, perhaps I'd be able to capture its light. Light's always been my greatest challenge.

I had an easy time with watercolours but preferred oils. They were more labour-intensive but allowed me to explore the depths of my subjects and tested my ability as an artist. My subjects were usually drawn from local life. I wanted to depict the times I was living in and the places around me.

I missed my college days and longed to enrol in a good art school. I'd always dreamed of studying in Paris. If I could sell a few paintings at high prices, perhaps I could afford to go. But it'd probably be too expensive. I could always go to the J.J. School of Art in Mumbai or to Shantiniketan in West Bengal, but, if I could afford it, my first choice would definitely be Europe. The galleries and museums there are institutions of learning in their own right. I could spend months just exploring them. The only things I'd need in Europe would be devotion to art and the ability to deal with stress. But where would I find inspiration? I'd been feeling a bit empty for some time.

I wasn't close to any other artists in Kathmandu. I didn't find any of them inspiring. I rarely went to their exhibitions, finding the atmosphere sterile, with viewers moving tight-lipped from one painting to another. People never discussed art at these exhibitions. And I truly disliked the custom of having 'important' people do the openings. Why? For the media coverage they attracted, or for their thick wallets and the hope they might buy a painting or two?

I feel artists should try to attract the younger generation, Palpasa's generation, to their exhibitions. If that generation developed a taste for art, it'd be its future market. And they'd look at paintings with critical eyes and offer valuable feedback.

A few months ago, a young Dutch woman spent a whole day in my gallery. Before she left, she said, 'You make beautiful paintings but they're cold. In most of them, the colours don't seem to suit the subject matter.'

I was stunned. It was the first time anyone had said anything so critical about my work. I felt like I'd been slapped in the face. Till then, most of the people who'd said they didn't understand my art were visually illiterate and I'd never taken their comments seriously. But I could tell this woman understood art. I couldn't dismiss her criticism lightly. I couldn't think of a response even as she gathered up her bag and walked towards the door. She was already going down the stairs when I finally spoke.

'Excuse me. Could you tell me why my paintings look cold?'

Her face brightened in the darkness of the stairwell. She smiled and said, 'You'll have to find the answer to that yourself. You're the artist.'

Then she left, leaving me speechless again.

I turned to my paintings and spent a long time examining them. I was dismayed. It felt as though she'd switched off the music which had been playing in the gallery. But I was glad she'd made me question the quality of my work.

I drank wine late into the night, brooding. I found a box of Cuban cigars a tourist had given me ages earlier. I lit one and took a strong drag.

Phoolan told me later that the Dutch woman had come to the gallery the following day as well. She'd spent three hours there, studying two of the paintings in particular. She'd also come the day after that. Phoolan had had to keep the gallery open for two extra hours, just for her. After studying the paintings in silence, the woman had told Phoolan she was leaving Nepal the next day. She'd taken my visiting card and some digital photos of my paintings before leaving. I was thrilled when Phoolan told me that.

I'd never been able to have even a single solo exhibition. For artists, exhibitions are like books for writers, stage shows for singers, or by-line stories for journalists. I dreamt of having solo exhibitions not only in Kathmandu but also in Delhi and even, one day, in Paris. I wanted my paintings to be shown at the National Gallery of Art in London and the Metropolitan Museum of Art in New York. To be hung in the Louvre would be the pinnacle of success.

But my paintings were cold, the Dutch woman had said. They'd never attract the attention of international critics. I realized I still had a lot of work to do. The Dutch woman had left me with the most difficult homework of my life.

The days passed as I painted the Chandragiri Hills orange. My inability to find ways to get rid of the coldness in my works brought me down. I became increasingly depressed and reclusive, and eventually didn't even dare to pick up a paintbrush. When I looked out my window in the evenings, all I saw were birds of prey—eagles and vultures—circling in the sky.

Phoolan phoned several times during this period. She was worried about me. She kept asking how I was and I'd hang up after giving her one curt reply or another. I spurned dozens of invitations to exhibitions I read about later in the newspapers. Journalists mentioned that so-and-so's exhibition had been opened by so-and-so but never ventured an opinion on the art itself.

I didn't even meet my friends during that time, and they, assuming I was busy, didn't contact me either. They stopped sending e-mails. I hadn't heard from Tshering for a long time, but I didn't disturb him. I figured he was busy, finalizing his book of photographs.

One day, I noticed my kitchen stank of sulphur and realized some eggs had spoilt. I cleaned the whole house and felt better afterwards. The phone rang just as I was finishing. It was Phoolan.

She said, 'There's a personal letter for you, Sir.'

'I've told you not to call me "sir",' I said.

'Sorry, Sir,' she said. 'I mean, sorry, Dai. I didn't open it since it's personal.'

'I'll read it later.'

'Aren't you ever coming to the gallery?' she asked. 'A few customers are asking for appointments, Sir. Oh, sorry! I said "sir" again.'

She sounded flustered. She was probably getting anxious. I hadn't paid her for the past few months and was feeling guilty about it. I wondered if she was still going to college in the mornings.

I'd brought Phoolan to Kathmandu from Dang District, assuring her parents I'd send her back after she got a university degree. She was a Tharu. She'd attended an English-medium school and gotten a first division in the School Leaving Certificate. I wanted her to make her community proud. She now lived in a women's hostel, attending classes in the morning and looking after my gallery in the afternoon. I wondered what she thought of my bohemian ways.

'The letter must be from that Dutch woman,' Phoolan said.

'What makes you think so?'

'It comes from the Netherlands. Who else could it be?' she replied.

I was intrigued but also worried about what the letter might say. Later that day I walked to the gallery with a heavy heart. A Japanese aid project had set up new traffic lights at one intersection. They eased the flow of traffic slightly, but the majority of people simply ignored them. Which politician was it who'd promised to make Nepal as developed as Japan? Only after Nepal was as developed as Japan would these traffic lights serve any purpose. The old traffic lights in front of Singha Durbar were out of order. As I neared the gallery, a jeep passed, narrowly missing me, its horn blaring. I followed it and found Phoolan waiting for me at the gallery door.

'You've lost weight,' she remarked.

'Where's the letter?' I asked.

She had it in her hand, as though she'd been waiting to me.

It was from the Dutch woman. I read:

Dear Nepali Artist,

I felt lost for several days after returning to Amsterdam. I thought about your paintings a lot. There are many art galleries here. I visited several of them and concluded that the medium you used and the colours and brushstrokes in your work are actually brilliant. There's motion and melody in your art. Still, I told you your paintings were cold and you asked me why. Let me tell you. I now realize the problem doesn't lie in your work. It's actually the colour of your gallery walls. The green walls are all wrong for your work. That green doesn't do justice to your paintings. It lessens their impact. Please forgive my thoughtless comment. I hope you'll paint your gallery walls a different colour. The next time I'm in Nepal, I'll visit your gallery first thing.

Written at the bottom, in slanted letters, was her name—Christina.

She'd also sent a picture of a gallery in Amsterdam and a book on painting.

I thanked her silently.

CHAPTER SEVEN

The house looked like it could've been built in the Malla period. In front was a small garden with a statue of Lord Buddha. The garden was so peaceful I felt like chanting 'Om mani padme hum'. I stopped by the statue and looked into Buddha's eyes. They were beautiful enough to cast spells; the statue must've been the work of a master sculptor. Artists live on a higher plane. They create a separate world, another reality. They conjure characters from their minds. I wondered what the real Buddha had looked like. This one looked into my eyes with great compassion.

If I ever made a Buddha, I'd make its eyes quite different. The eyes of my Buddha would be crowded with illusions.

But I can't make a Buddha, and I won't.

I opened a small, dilapidated door and went into the house. Everything was a silent. I moved with quiet, cat-like steps, climbing the stairs in semi-darkness. On the first floor I found my Shangri-La—a capacious sitting room lined with books. There were so many books you'd need a catalogue to find the one you wanted.

In one corner of the room sat an old, bespectacled woman. 'Namaste, Hajur Aama,' I said. She looked up and smiled sweetly. Her hair was white and her cheeks were wrinkled. 'I was told I could find old books here,' I said.

'I don't know,' she said. 'Feel free to look around.'

She was rolling cotton *batti* for worship. An antique radio sat on the table in front of her. It looked like one of the radios that had been brought to Kathmandu during the Second World War. There was an equally antique telephone beside it. I felt like I'd come to a museum.

Books on history, geography, culture, philosophy, politics, and literature were preserved lovingly on the shelves. As I browsed through them, the old women switched on the lights and came up to me.

'I'm an artist,' I said. 'I'm looking for a book on ancient Nepal.' In fact, I was looking for a book about the balance of colour and light in traditional Nepali art. I wanted to examine the relationship between the colour of my gallery walls and the paintings hanging on them. I wanted to understand how the quality and intensity of light could change a painting. I didn't know if anyone had actually written about the dynamics of colour in Nepali art, but someone had given me the address of this private library and it was worth a try.

'Most of these books look old,' the old woman said.

I said, 'The libraries in this city seem to have every book except the one you want.'

'I suppose that's why people come here.'

'Your collection's excellent,' I said.

She smiled. 'I wouldn't know but everyone says so.'

I picked up a book that didn't have a cover and leafed through it. The old woman went and turned on a cassette player. A song drifted through the room:

It rained heavily on a monsoon night,

The maize leaves played music in the fields...

The book I'd picked up was the diary of an Englishman. The page dated July 17, 1957, said:

I took a Dakota plane from Patna to Kathmandu. As it came into the Kathmandu Valley, I saw a mountain peak. It was a clear day and visibility was perfect. It was my first time in Kathmandu and its beauty overwhelmed me. I saw the green valley surrounded by hills. In the middle of the valley was a dense settlement. The rest of the valley was covered with greenery. It was like a peaceful dream.

After I checked in at the Royal Hotel, I discovered that there was no other hotel in the valley. Not even another restaurant! At the Yeti Bar, I had a long conversation with the hotel owner, Boris Lissanevich, a Russian citizen. He described the lifestyle, culture, and customs of the place. I learned that the elite of Kathmandu occasionally came to the hotel for dinner. There weren't many. Boris surprised me by counting them on his fingers. He also told me that everyone could name the people who had telephones in their homes.

Boris introduced me to some Sherpas. I asked them about the mountain I'd seen from the plane but they couldn't identify it. Maybe I didn't describe it well enough. They told me foreigners had started coming only five years ago. Naturally, no one knows the names and heights of all the peaks. They told me to come back next year and they'd take me to the mountain I'd seen.

The airport existed even before roads were built. People got on planes before they boarded buses. I'm beginning to believe there are more temples here than houses and more gods than people. At night, hymns being sung far away can be heard from the hotel window, while the rest of Kathmandu is completely silent. I feel as if I'm in a peaceful temple where worshippers sing hymns through the night, lighting oil lamps. Gazing at mountain peaks is an encounter with God. Above stand the snow-capped peaks and below live these God-fearing people, singing hymns though the night.

The old woman came back, offering me a cup of tea.

'You shouldn't have gone to the trouble,' I said.

She smiled. 'It's no trouble, ooloo.'

'Isn't anyone else at home?' I asked.

'I've got a maid. My granddaughter's out now.'

'Granddaughter?'

'Yes. When she's at home, she's always reading,' she said, 'And when she goes out, you never know when she's coming back.'

'And your son?'

'He lives with his wife in Amrika.'

'Have you been there?'

'Who'd go to a country where they eat beef?'

'So you're alone here?'

'Well, the gods are here and so are their temples.'

'Don't you feel bored?'

'People like you come here to read,' she said. 'Some are like my sons; some, like my grandsons.'

'I understand.'

'If you feel close to people, you don't feel lonely.'

'Oh.'

'How's the tea?'

'It's good.'

'You're just saying that to please me.'

'No. I really mean it.'

'You like it because it's sweet.'

'It's perfect.'

'How many children do you have?'

'I'm not married.'

'Oh?'

'And you?' I asked.

'I've got a son, a daughter-in-law, and a granddaughter.'

'An ideal family.'

'But what's the point when I hardly see them?'

'Oh.'

'I hope you don't intend to go to Amrika?' she asked.

'You just said the gods and temples are here, didn't you?'

'So you also go to temples?' she asked.

'You see, Hajur Aama,' I said, avoiding the subject, 'I'm an artist. For a Nepali artist like me, the inspiration, subjects, and colours of my work all come from this place.'

'You sound like my granddaughter,' she said, beaming.

'Oh,' I asked, 'is she an artist too?'

'I don't know. She's always carrying a camera.'

'Yes?'

'Once she filmed me and I saw myself on television.'

'You were on television?'

'No, no. It's something you put into something and a picture appears.'

'I understand.'

'Carry on reading,' she said. 'I'm just prattling on.'

'On the contrary,' I said, 'what you say is interesting. I'm enjoying our conversation.'

She smiled. 'You're just being polite.'

'No. I mean it,' I said.

'Thank you. You've brightened my day.'

'And you're beautiful as well,' I said. 'I can only imagine how you looked when you were young.'

'Oh, I don't know that I was beautiful and, even if I was, I don't have any photographs to prove it. There were no cameras in my day.'

'I understand.'

'Have you ever seen my granddaughter?'

'No,' I said. 'Why do you ask?'

'I think she's like me when I was young.'

'Well, she is your granddaughter.'

'It's more than just her physical appearance. She even behaves the way I did.'

'That must make you happy?'

'Of course,' she said. 'Her parents keep pressuring her to go back to Amrika but she's determined to stay here.'

'How could she leave a grandmother like you?'

'No, it's not because of me. She says this is her country. She wants to work here. This is where she belongs.'

With that, the old woman started rolling *batti* again. I wandered through the house, moving from room to room. The floors were wooden and the bricks of the walls seemed to belong to another age. There were things of beauty everywhere. Small statues of gods sat in niches in the walls, with paintings and photos hanging above them. The house's inner rooms were wonderfully peaceful. None of the doors was locked. I wandered into bedrooms with clean white sheets on the beds. Elegant lamps stood on mahogany tables. I felt as if I'd gone back in time.

The whole house felt as if it had come from another era. It felt as though some Englishman nostalgic for Victorian times had decorated it. But the amenities were modern. I could've wandered for hours just looking at the décor. The carved wooden doors and windows filled me with wonder at the skilled hands which had created them.

Then I looked out of the window. Outside was the chaotic clutter of an unplanned concrete city. It hurt my eyes.

I returned to the drawing room and found the old woman rewinding the cassette cape. She played the same song again:

It rained heavily on a monsoon night,

The maize leaves played music in the fields...

I said, 'You really love that song, don't you?'

'It reminds me of the old days,' she said.

'It takes you back?'

'Yes. I used to dance to that song when I was young.'

'How did you dance? I'd love to see.'

She laughed. 'Oh, I'm too old for that now.'

'Why don't you give it a try?'

'Old women like me don't dance!'

'Why not? Who says so? Is it written in religious texts?' I asked.

'The gods in the walls might laugh.'

'Well, I'd love to hear the gods laughing.'

'Do you really think gods laugh?' she said. 'I meant I'd look ridiculous.'

I insisted. 'But you yourself are like a goddess, so what are you afraid of?'

'Do you know something? My name is actually Devi.'

'A divine coincidence!'

'A priest gave me that name.'

'Well,' I said, 'he must've been a wise priest. That explains why I feel I'm in the presence of the divine.'

She said, 'I wonder when I'll enter the house of the real Devi.'

'To me, you are the real Devi,' I said, 'so I've come to the goddess's house first.'

'Smarty!' she laughed.

'And I'm stubborn as well,' I said. 'I won't leave till I see you dance.'

'You're just as stubborn as my granddaughter,' she said.

'And you just said she's like you.'

The grandmother stood up. She rewound the tape and played the same song again. Then, putting aside her walking stick, she danced, her body suddenly as light as an alpine flower. Her arms moved like leaves dancing to the music of the wind. Reaching out, she pulled me to her and tried to make me dance as well. I tried to copy her steps but couldn't keep up and felt embarrassed to be so clumsy. She was like a moth dancing around a light.

Loud laughter interrupted our dancing. It was Palpasa, standing in the doorway watching us. She was obviously surprised and delighted to see me there. I was amazed to see her too. After so many months, I'd come straight to her doorstep! Having been caught dancing, her grandmother became as shy and embarrassed as a child, hiding her eyes behind her hands like a little girl ashamed about revealing a tear in her dress.

CHAPTER EIGHT

On the wall by the table was a black and white photo of the Blues Brothers. They were lighting cigarettes. A blues song was floating from the bar. This particular restaurant was packed with tourists, though the number of visitors to the country had dwindled. Dried corncobs and red peppers were hanging from the ceiling, dancing in the evening breeze. By the time Palpasa arrived, I'd already got my order—a steaming chicken sizzler.

'That was the first time I ever saw my grandma dance,' she said.

'Well, I couldn't make *you* dance,' I said.

'She still talks about you.'

'But the person I want to talk about me doesn't.'

'Why do you think I'm here?'

Laughter erupted from a nearby table. Some tourists had just come back from trekking and were looking at photos they'd taken in the Annapurnas. They seemed to have brought the cool breeze of the Thorang Pass back with them. Looking at one photo, they burst into raucous laughter again. I thought I glimpsed a photo of someone who'd slipped on the snow but I couldn't be sure.

I realized Palpasa was still standing.

'Are you here just to borrow a chair?' I asked.

'I haven't done that since Goa,' she replied, taking a seat.

'Any regrets about that?'

'No, but one chair was enough for me.'

I divided my food, putting half onto another plate. I ordered another glass of wine for Palpasa. I didn't look at her, pretending to be annoyed. She didn't look at me either. Eventually, I stole a glance at her. She was even more beautiful than I remembered. I felt close to her. I felt as if I were meeting a lost lover after a long separation and we had a lot to talk about. But Palpasa was like a fruit that had to be peeled slowly to get to the core.

'My grandma's one of your admirers,' she said.

'Why? Has she seen my paintings?'

'No. Because you made her dance.'

'But she danced on her own.'

'Then why haven't I seen her dance like that before?'

'Maybe you didn't want to.'

'She told me you insisted that she had to dance.'

'Yeah. Only old people take notice of what I have to say.'

'Excuse me. Do you listen to young people?'

I said, 'No. My problem's with the young.'

I began to eat. She kept looking at me. Her eyes looked lovely, inviting.

'Are you fasting today?' I asked.

'I'm watching you in order to learn how to eat.'

'The food's getting cold.'

'You made it cold.'

'But the steam's still rising!'

'My heart's getting cold.'

'Did I put ice on it?'

'You divided up that food like you were removing ice cubes from a tray.'

'But I did it because of my feelings for you.'

'I felt you did it with scorn.'

'Would you have preferred to eat from my plate?'

'Would you have dared to feed me with your fork?'

'It's a bit early for that, isn't it?'

'Early for what?'

To provoke her further, I took her plate, put the food back on my own plate, and began to eat it. She watched, speechless, her face getting flushed. Her lips were tight with indignation. Without a word, I ate it all.

'Should I go now?' she asked coolly.

'Did I ask you to go?'

'Well, there's nothing left for me to eat.'

'But you can order something else, can't you?'

'True. After all, I didn't come here to eat someone else's food,' she said, beckoning a waiter.

'That's what I thought,' I said and emptied my wine glass.

She ordered a plate of momos.

Behind our table was a young Nepali couple having a heated discussion. The woman was angry, the man trying to calm her down.

'Do you love me?' I heard the man say.

'I hate you,' the woman hissed.

'Then I'm happy,' he said.

'Why?'

'I only fear people who don't have any feelings for me,' he said. 'Love and hate are two sides of the same coin.'

I looked at Palpasa. She was preoccupied with her plate of momos. She feigned such pleasure in eating the dumplings, it was clear she wanted to demonstrate that they were far tastier than my sizzler could have been.

'I love momos,' I said.

'I don't normally like them,' she said, 'but these are—wow!' And she ate another dumpling as if it were the most delicious food in the world.

'I'd really like to have one,' I said.

'Then call the waiter.'

'To ask for a fork?'

'No, to order a plate.'

'So you can put some momos on it?' I asked.

Calling the waiter, I asked for a plate. He brought it over immediately and I put it near hers. I looked at Palpasa, but she continued eating her momos without paying any attention to me.

'There it is,' I said.

'What?'

I gestured with my eyes towards the plate.

'Well, I didn't ask for it,' she said.

'But I did.'

'But why do I need it?' she said, putting another dumpling in her mouth.

'Some people are really selfish,' I said.

'Oh, yeah?' she asked, her mouth full of dumpling.

'For once I thought there was someone in this world who really cared about me.'

'Really? Why did you think that?'

'Not just because she'd give me some food.'

'Then what did you think?'

'I thought she'd feed me with her own hands.'

'Oh.'

'But today I saw...'

'What did you see?'

'I saw someone eating,' I said.

'And you've never seen that before?'

'Oh, I've seen people eating before,' I said.

'Then what?'

'I'd never seen before what I saw today.'

'And that was?'

'I'd never seen a person eating like she was afraid someone else was going to steal her food.'

'Oh!' she said. 'Oh, I see. You wanted to share my momos? I'm sorry! I just ate the last one. I was thinking about something else.'

'What were you thinking about?'

'I was wondering if you'd like a momo.'

'Well, I didn't come here to eat someone else's food,' I said.

'That's what I thought.'

'Should I go now?'

'Did I ask you to go?'

'I assume you want me to go?' I said.

'Some people seem to enjoy getting the wrong idea,' she said.

'Not me,' I said.

Beside us, the trekkers laughed uproariously again. They burst out laughing at the slightest opportunity, as if they seldom found occasion to laugh. They were still looking at their photos. I glanced over and saw a photo of a person who'd slipped on the snow while taking a photo of person who'd slipped on the snow. It appeared to be somewhere near Muktinath.

After a while Palpasa said, 'Hajur Aama wants you to come to our house again.'

'Why? Does she want to dance?'

'No. She wants you to come for lunch.'

'And who'll do the cooking?'

'She said she would.'

'But I'm worried you'll eat my food.'

'I'm not such a pig.'

'Yes, I saw that just now.'

Well, did I eat your food?'

'No.'

'So?'

'I ate your share of my food and now I'm afraid you'll take revenge.'

'Hajur Aama said you have the gift of the gab.'

'I'm not as talented as her granddaughter.'

'She knows me very well,' Palpasa said.

'She told me you're like her.'

'Yes. We're both equally straight.'

'But I saw your grandmother bend when she was dancing.'

'And she told me you were as straight as a rod.'

'That's because I am.'

'Yes, I've seen that'

'Your grandmother told me you're a great dancer.'

'Oh, rubbish!'

'No, really. That's what she told me.'

'I don't believe you.'

'She told me that once you take the floor, your family can switch off the television.'

'Nonsense!'

'She told me you dance like a goddess.'

'That's ridiculous' she said, looking annoyed.

'She even asked me to look for a suitable husband for you.'

'Oh, really?'

'She said she wanted to see you married to a good-looking guy like me.'

'You're impossible!' Palpasa laughed.

'And she was saying...'

She interrupted me. 'Enough, enough! So, when are you coming over?'

'The day her granddaughter's ready to dance.'

'That's not possible,' she said.

'What's not possible, my coming to your house?'

'No. My dancing.'

'Then it's impossible for me too.'

'You won't accept her invitation?'

'No. I won't dance.'

'But who wants you to dance?'

'I want to dance with you,' I said.

'You can dance with Hajur Aama.'

'What would happen if I didn't come?' I asked playfully.

'That would be fine by me,' she replied. 'Then I wouldn't have to dance.'

CHAPTER NINE

After repainting the walls, I threw a party at my gallery. Palpasa was the first to arrive. She looked absolutely stunning in brown jeans and a silk shirt. She'd brought a bottle of French wine. 'Hi,' she said, glancing around. 'Wow!'

It was her first time at the gallery. Some of the paintings in my book were hanging on the walls. She was immediately drawn to them. 'How lucky for me to be the first guest,' she said.

I said, 'I think of you as one of the hosts.'

She noticed my new denim shirt and pinched me for good luck. I wished she'd pinched harder.

Phoolan had set up a bar in a corner of the gallery. I placed the bottle of wine there. 'What can I get you, Madam?' Phoolan asked Palpasa.

Without turning her attention from *Rain*, Palpasa replied, 'As you please, Madam.'

I'd been trying to persuade Phoolan to drop this 'sir' and 'madam' business. She'd probably picked it up at college; she certainly didn't learn it in her village. If she continued with such affectations, I'd go to her college and slap the friends who were influencing her.

Palpasa was simultaneously looking at my paintings and checking her mobile for messages. I even saw her send a message. Maybe she'd sent someone a joke. Then she turned to the painting of the falling leaf.

Tshering arrived with his wife Kripa. As always, he began to complain about the lack of parking spaces. When he finally turned his attention to the paintings, Palpasa was still looking closely at the leaf.

'When's your flight?' I asked Tshering.

'I haven't decided.'

'Why not?'

'Why should I pay for my own ticket?' he said. 'It's just a photo exhibition.'

'Typical Nepali thinking,' I said. 'Exhibitions are good business opportunities. You can sell your photographs and also establish contact with international agents and galleries.'

'Not necessarily,' he said, 'and if money was my priority why would I have closed my trekking company to concentrate on photography?'

Kishore seemed to materialize from nowhere. It was unusual to see him without a guitar in his hands. A few days ago he'd said, 'I'm releasing my first album soon. Come to the release.' Then the next day he'd said, 'I'm making a music video. Can I use your gallery?'

'Is it a song about paintings?' I'd asked.

'Can there be a song about paintings?' he replied. 'It's about love.'

'Love?'

'Yeah, love. The title of my album's *The First Love before the Second.*

I laughed but he didn't notice. Even before Kishore had set foot in my gallery, he'd told me he liked the place. He'd said, 'If I shoot my video in your gallery, people will think I live in a really fancy house.'

The next day he'd shown up at my gallery. 'Dai!'

I was painting. 'Yes?' I said brusquely. "What is it?'

'I want you to appear in my music video.'

'Me? In a music video?'

'I need a character actor.'

'Would I have to sing?'

'No. Just lip-sync.'

I laughed. 'Where would your girlfriend sit to sing?' I asked.

'She won't be in it. We're just going to use her photo. It's a solo, after all, not a duet.'

Kishore had also brought a bottle of wine. I was surprised. Phoolan took it to the bar. I introduced him to Palpasa. 'This is my friend. He's a singer.'

'You know, Didi,' Kishore said, 'I'm releasing my first album soon. It's called *The First Love before the Second.*'

Just as Palpasa laughed, her mobile rang. She had an old Nepali song as a ringtone—*'Tiriri Murali Bajyo Banaima'*. She pressed the green button and said 'Hello'.

Kishore asked, 'What's so funny?'

'The title,' she said, as she pressed the red button.

'But it's a serious album,' he said. 'It's about heartbreak. You've got to come to the release.'

I saw two more people coming in and went to the door to greet them. They'd brought a bouquet of flowers. Its fragrance was lovely. I put it on the table beside my laptop. 'Meet my friends.' I was busy introducing people.

Within a few minutes, four more guests arrived. The oldest was Rupak. He is ten years older than I, but we're friends. He immediately noticed the fresh paint on the walls and voiced his approval, 'Beautiful! Am I in the right gallery?' Palpasa looked surprised.

She seemed to be getting a lot of phone calls. 'Hello,' she said again.

Rupak went on. 'Perfect,' he said. 'The colour of the walls really makes your paintings stand out. Finally, perfect.'

'Well, the credit goes to a Dutch lady,' I said. Palpasa, who'd got off the phone by then, looked a bit puzzled.

Another friend asked, 'So is that the reason for this get-together?'

'What do you think of the walls?' I asked him.

'They look great,' he agreed.

Suddenly, everyone was looking at the walls instead of my paintings.

From the corner, the CD player was playing Nusrat Fateh Ali Khan. I helped Phoolan put snacks on a few trays, though she kept insisting, 'No, no. I can manage.'

'But you're a secretary,' I said.

'Today I'm a party secretary.'

Kishore called out to me, 'You belong to the older generation. You can tell which generation a person belongs to by his taste in music'

Everyone laughed except Palpasa, who'd gone back to examining the painting of the falling leaf.

'You should've brought your album,' I said to Kishore. 'I could've played your music and been part of the new generation.'

Rupak turned to Kishore, 'So you're a singer?'

'Yes, Uncle,' Kishore said, pleased. 'I'm about to release my first album. You have to come to the release.'

Kapil's wife asked, 'How about us? Is it an album of pop songs?'

'The title says it all,' I said.

'What is it?'

Kishore said, 'It's called *The First Love before the Second.* It's got pop, rap, reggae, even blues. There's a slow song which is a bit serious and the last track's an instrumental piece.'

'My God,' Rupak teased him. 'The only thing missing is classical music!'

'Who listens to Raga Bhairavi these days?' Kishore said. 'I only sing bhajan to clear my throat.'

'Shreeman Narayana, Narayana, Narayana.' Kapil's wife sang a popular bhajan.

'That's a fast *bhajan,*' Kishore said. 'Don't you know any slow classical pieces?'

Soon the gallery was ringing with laughter as I poured more wine.

I took a bottle over to Palpasa, saying, 'Would you like some more?' and tilted it towards her glass. Her eyes were glued to the painting *Langtang 1995*. She turned so I could pour the wine and our fingers touched. I wanted to keep pouring and wished the glass would never fill. Perhaps she was thinking the same thing because we were both startled when the wine overflowed from her glass, dropping onto our shoes. We looked at each other, embarrassed. Her cheeks were redder than the wine.

She had a similar thought. 'Your cheeks are so rosy they look like they're about to drip.'

'Then hold your glass under them,' I teased back.

'Actually,' she said, 'I prefer things I can bite into. Like apples. I eat a rosy apple every day.'

'Only one?' I said, 'You could have several every day.'

Kapil interrupted us. 'Tell me, Drishya,' he said. 'What's the meaning of this painting *Langtang 1995*?'

'The meaning?' I said.

'Isn't it the same Langtang, whether it's '95, '85 or '75?' he asked.

Palpasa looked at me as I tried to explain. 'To understand paintings, you have to go beyond what's represented and try to feel the mood,' I said. 'In my Lantang series, you won't see many different Langtangs, but you'll see Langtang in many different moods. I'm not sure it represents exactly how things were in Langtang at the time. I was trying to capture the mood of '95.'

Kapil's wife joined us. She had no interest in the arts. Rupak was looking at my new painting.

'I don't understand art,' Kapil's wife said. 'It's above my head.'

'You don't need to do anything special to understand it,' I said. 'Just open your heart as well as your eyes.'

'Lots of people say that they don't understand my songs,' Kishore said, joining us, 'even my family! If my family can't understand, what can I expect from other people?'

'Maybe people don't understand because you mix up all sorts of languages in your songs,' Tshering said, rather sarcastically.

Kishore retorted, 'I hope you don't mind my asking this, Dai, but do you use only perfect Nepali when you're speaking?'

'Probably not,' Tshering said. 'I sometimes mix Sherpa and Nepali.'

'Exactly! So why can't I put some English in my songs?' Kishore said. 'Isn't that the way people talk these days?'

'That's the problem with songs these days,' Rupak said from a distance. 'You can't tell if the singer's singing or talking.'

'Yeah,' Tshering added. 'Singers don't sing nowadays. They talk. And while they talk, they shout, cough, and sometimes cry.'

Kishore blushed as everyone burst out laughing. 'But this friend of mine sings well,' I said, patting him on the back.

'Have you heard him sing?' Kripa asked, standing arm in arm with her husband.

'I've heard him rehearse,' I said.

'Where did you hear me?' Kishore asked.

'On the stairs. You were humming,' I said.

Tshering cut in, sardonic as usual, 'Maybe he was just clearing his throat.'

I took a tray of snacks from Phoolan and started passing it around. Soon I got tired and sat down on a stool. The others also began to take seats. Rupak and Palpasa were talking in a corner. I caught Kishore looking at Phoolan. I raised my wine glass to get his attention. 'Cheers,' I said and he raised his glass back. I knew Kishore was very taken with Phoolan, but she was determined not to get involved with any man before graduating from college. Kishore used to pester her to go out with him, but these days he left her alone.

Turning to Rupak and Palpasa, I said, 'A Dutch woman I met here in the gallery changed the way I look at things. In the beginning, I couldn't understand what she was getting at. But later I realized that the colour of my walls was detracting from my paintings.'

'Haven't you invited her today?' Rupak asked.

'If she'd been here, I would have. But she's left Kathmandu.'

'Ah!' Kapil said. 'So that's why you're looking a bit lost.'

'What do you mean?'

'My friend, your mind's far away, very far away, in fact, somewhere in the Netherlands.'

Everyone laughed, except Palpasa. That bastard Kapil was going to get me into trouble and all for nothing. 'Listen,' I said, trying to stop the laughter, 'She's an art critic and I accepted a suggestion from her. That's all. There's nothing more to it.'

'She's been a good influence on you,' Rupak said. 'There's a new atmosphere in the gallery. The walls do justice to your paintings at last.'

'Can walls do justice to art?' Kishore asked.

Tshering sniffed. 'That's what our host appears to be claiming.'

Of all people, Tshering, a photographer, should have understood the relationship between a painting and the wall it's hung on! I glanced at Palpasa. She'd become a falling leaf again, looking for a place to rest.

At that point, Phoolan said, 'I'm grateful to that Dutch woman. After she first spoke to him, Sir didn't come to the gallery for months. But in the end, she rescued him.'

I glared at her, displeased.

But Phoolan continued, 'When she sent a letter suggesting he paint the walls a different colour, he was suddenly very happy.'

Trying to save the day, I said, 'Westerners understand the relationship between paintings and the colours that surround them. For example, if the walls were painted blue, that'd detract from the sky in these paintings. In the Langtang series that Kapil was just talking about, the sky is prominent, symbolizing the flight of the human imagination. But it wouldn't look quite so evocative if the walls were also painted blue.'

Rupak raised his glass. 'Cheers, Drishya. I've known you for a decade and you've never accepted anyone's suggestions before. It's good you're listening to advice at last.' With a laugh, he went on, 'I bet this Dutch woman's a real beauty. And intelligent, charming, passionate...'

'Hey, Drishya,' Tshering said. 'Is this the same girl you met in the chat room the other night?'

I didn't see Palpasa leave, but when I turned around, she was gone. Only Tshering noticed that her departure made me sad. As for my other guests, they were injected with new life when Kishore started humming his songs. Palpasa had left without saying a word and I felt like a stem without a leaf. Kishore started singing his title song, 'The First Love before the Second'. He didn't have his guitar but it didn't matter. He moved his fingers in the air playing an imaginary guitar, and, though I had had only three glasses of wine, it felt as if his fingers were playing the chords of my heart.

CHAPTER TEN

I could hear an injured bird flapping its wings, trying in vain to fly. At midnight, the flapping shattered my dreams. Apart from the sound of the flapping wings, the city was silent. I got up and looked out the window. There was something sinister in the darkness. The phone rang. A panicky voice said, 'Have you heard?'

I couldn't figure out who it was and began to feel scared.

'Stupid, you haven't heard?' the voice said angrily. 'The country's been plunged into darkness. Everything's finished and you're still sleeping!'

All sleep vanished from my eyes and a chill ran down my spine. As I hung up, I heard a helicopter take off. It was the first time I'd ever heard a helicopter in Kathmandu at midnight. I went and switched on the television.

The phone rang again. 'Disaster's struck,' someone said.

'What happened?' I said. 'I don't understand.'

It was Tshering. He'd had trouble getting through to me; the network was jammed.

'Put on BBC,' he said.

BBC and CNN were carrying breaking news. The Indian television channels had also picked it up. I felt engulfed by a cloud. I couldn't see anything. Suddenly, I heard noises outside in the neighbourhood. I ran outdoors, terrified.

The king and queen had been murdered. The helicopter I'd heard was carrying the prince, who'd survived, back to Kathmandu. This much I learned from the crowd. How did the murders take place? When? Who did it? Why? So many questions remained unanswered. I left the crowd and went back inside. Nepal was the top story in the international media. Nepal Telecommunications Corporation had probably never handled as many calls. The phone rang so often I stopped answering it.

That morning there was not an empty spot on the streets. Everyone had come out of his or her house. A thick fog of uncertainty hung over us all. The state-owned radio and television stations were broadcasting sorrowful dirges. There was no official confirmation of the murders, let alone answers to our questions. People were grabbing photocopies of newspapers, hoping desperately to find out what had happened. There was grief and fury in their eyes. Crowds were gathering on every street corner in the city. Groups of young people were starting to chant angry slogans.

A speeding Maruti van appeared on the street nearby. Someone shouted, 'Smash it! Smash it!' The van turned sharply and sped away, narrowly avoiding some pedestrians. Large groups of police were out on the streets but behaving as if they weren't on duty. There was nothing they could do to control the crowds. The security situation was already out of hand.

When the state media finally broke its silence, the voices of the people on the street erupted in a deafening cry. The valley roiled on the brink of anarchy. In a crowd near the statue of the late King Mahendra, someone threw a stone at me. I left with a bleeding ear. All I'd done was to ask a few raging youngsters, 'How can you be sure there was a conspiracy at the palace?'

It was a stupid time to ask that question.

Soon men with shaved heads were everywhere in the crowds. It was risky for men who had not shaved their heads as a symbol of mourning to walk about. Anyone could accuse them of not showing respect to the murdered king and queen. All over town, neighbourhood clubs put up notices offering free shaves. Men with shaved heads held motorcycle rallies to Durbar Marg. One could predict there would be trouble just by looking at their faces. The leaders of these rallies carried photographs of all five of the royal family members who had been murdered. Nearby, a tyre had been set alight; its pungent smoke painted the sky black.

Not a single shop was open. I leaned on a tree, trying to listen to a distant radio. A curfew had been imposed. Security personnel began ordering the crowds to clear the streets. Near Rama Park, riot police resorted to baton charges. The crowd dispersed, leaving sandals and shoes scattered on the street.

The curfew continued for several days. Even after a landslide's over, stones continue to fall. Nepal would never be the same again.

Within two days of the massacre, a funeral procession headed for the Arya Ghat at Pashupatinath with the dead body of yet another king, the only king in Nepal's history to be crowned on his deathbed. It seemed we'd regressed to the Middle Ages. During this funeral procession yet another curfew was imposed. From the Army Hospital in Chauni, the body was transported along Ring Road on a truck; only security personnel were present. As the procession reached Pashupatinath, a pre-monsoon rain washed the valley clean. The last rites were performed in a rush.

It was a cool evening for early June. Evading a police patrol, I entered a narrow alley. Here and there, people were pelting stones at the police. Riot troops were out in force. Some people were arrested. Some were beaten. The police fired over the heads of the crowd, but people still refused to disperse. I heard the sirens of police vans but couldn't make out which way they were heading. Ambulances roared through the streets. A brick thrown at one of the police officers hit me in the back. I crouched in the doorway of a shop with closed shutters. When a police van sped past, I pretended to be passed out, drunk.

Only a few hours had passed since the crowning of the new king at Basantapur Palace. The ceremony had been telecast live. Government officials and political leaders had paid their respects to the new king, placing a coin at his feet and bowing before him. Then a carriage procession carrying the king headed towards Narayanhiti Palace. The grim expression on the king's face was mute testimony to the tragedy of the preceding Friday night. Soldiers, many on horseback, guarded the streets.

I ran into a Sherpa mountaineer I knew. Ang Phurba had just returned from an abortive expedition to Ama Dablam. His face was terribly sunburned. Five foreign mountaineers were with him. They were trying to find a taxi, but there were none on the streets. 'I had a bad dream in the first camp,' Ang Phurba said. 'We abandoned the expedition after the weather got worse the next day.' The foreign mountaineers listened intently. One of them, who had a nasty gash on his nose, pointed to his wound and said, 'Couldn't climb the mountain, but I'm taking this souvenir back to show my friends.'

Further along, I ran into a Spanish man I knew, rushing madly from Thamel to Durbar Marg. He'd once come to my gallery and almost bought a painting called *Winter in the Hills*. But he'd left without buying it, saying he'd come back later. Now, he looked panic-stricken, as though desperate for some life-saving medicine.

'What's wrong?' I asked.

'My plane's about to take off,' he wailed. 'But there aren't any taxis! I want to leave! Any place with journalists pouring into it isn't safe for tourists.' He vanished down the street. His speed made me think of Spiderman.

CNN and BBC journalists had landed in droves. It was as if the country were at war. Nepal had never received so much attention in the international media. On Durbar Marg, I saw hordes of foreign correspondents erecting satellite sensors and positioning their cameras for live telecasts. Others were dispatching news and photos from their laptops right on the street. Deadlines! The Hotel Yak & Yeti was bursting at the seams with desperate journalists.

All the tourists were leaving. All the journalists were coming. Were there more journalists than tourists in Kathmandu? I wasn't sure.

A never-ending queue of people was offering flowers and garlands to the murdered king and queen. Near me, two elderly men broke down while talking about the massacre before a television camera, their tears flowing like melting glaciers. Women carrying flowers and incense looked around, grief painted on their faces.

I headed home, my mind filled with ideas for two paintings I'd call *June First*.

As I neared home, I saw a man leaning against the peach tree beside my front gate. He was wearing a cap and dark glasses. Seeing me, he straightened. He was unshaven, tall, and lean, with prominent cheekbones. He carried a heavy bag. His bony face looked familiar to me.

'Namaste,' he greeted me. Then, seeing I didn't recognize him, he said, 'Drishya, it's me, Siddhartha.'

I felt like I was sliding on snow. Rattled, I looked down at my shoes, unable to say a word. I just stood there while he looked at me till, finally, I said, 'Come in.'

Inside, he stopped by a sketch hanging on the living room wall. It was a sketch of the primary school I'd attended, where the doors never closed properly, the roof leaked throughout the monsoon, the windows never stopped the winds from rushing into the classrooms, and the benches were always in disarray. The school's playground was always as dusty as a desert. I'd done the sketch during half-term break, just before I left my village for Kathmandu. Some children had been playing Ludo near me while others played marbles. Still others were kicking balls made of bundled rags, singing, '*Gauncha geeta Nepali...Jyotiko pankha uchali.*'

I pointed to the sketch. 'There was an explosion there recently,' I said. 'I'm sure you heard about it on the news. A girl in grade two was killed. The bomb left another student with a broken leg.'

Siddhartha stared at the sketch in silence.

'Two of the teachers have been killed in the last six years,' I continued. 'There's only one teacher left now.'

'And your point is?' he asked.

'This picture speaks to me about the state of our country.'

'How so?'

I said. 'This school had absolutely nothing. There wasn't even glass on the windows. But now even this little school's been destroyed. Whenever I look at this picture, I'm reminded of the way things are in our country these days.'

'Yes,' Siddhartha said at last. 'I'm sorry. I understand I'm partly to blame, but the ultimate blame rests with the old power centre.'

I looked at him sharply. 'What are you trying to say?'

'I'm underground,' he said, bluntly but softly. 'I'm here to take shelter.'

CHAPTER ELEVEN

'So what do you think?' Siddhartha's voice woke me up. I'd fallen asleep on the couch. 'How did the incident happen?'

I couldn't understand him at first. His presence in my house was disturbing my peace of mind. Remembering our college days, I felt concerned for him, of course, but I was also afraid of him. He'd turned to violence. By giving him shelter, I was inviting trouble from the security forces. If I denied him shelter, I'd be inviting trouble from his people. It was a Catch-22 situation.

He went and looked again at the sketch of my old school. Then he went to the kitchen and made us tea. I followed him. 'What incident?' I asked as he offered me a cup.

'There's only one incident on people's minds at the moment,' he said.

'The massacre at the palace?'

He took a sip of tea. I put down my cup and poured a glass of water for myself. Then I poured us both orange juice and gave him a glass. He put it on the table, pushing aside the newspapers.

'I'm a bit dazed,' I said.

'Because you just woke up?'

'No. I mean, the massacre's so shocking. I don't know what to make of it.'

He finished his tea and started reading one of the newspapers.

Just then the phone rang. It was my landlord calling from the US, asking how things were in Kathmandu. I told him his house was fine. Then he asked how I was. I said I was fine too. Then he asked about the massacre at the palace. I told him as much as I knew.

'I already know that from the internet,' he said impatiently. 'I wanted to hear your thoughts on the subject.'

'I'm at a loss for the moment, Doctor Saheb,' I said.

His daughter came on the line. 'Dai, did you find my puppy?'

All this fool in the US wanted to know about was her puppy! I'd e-mailed her that the puppy had run away, but the truth was I'd given it away before I left for Goa. I'm a busy man. I'm not interested in dogs and cats. Why couldn't the landlord's daughter understand that, right now, my only concern was what was happening to our country?

She told me how sad she was that Princess Shruti had died. They must've been about the same age. When the family had lived in Nepal, the daughter used to talk a lot about Shruti and I'd listened with some interest because Shruti herself was a painter and often opened art exhibitions. I felt especially bad about her death. Maybe she would've survived if they'd taken her to the nearby Bir Hospital instead of the Army Hospital in Chauni. At least then one member of the late King Birendra's family would've survived. When I saw a picture of her two little daughters in a newspaper, I almost wept.

There was static on the line, then it got cut off. After hanging up, I turned back to Siddhartha. 'That was my landlord,' I explained. 'He and his family went to the US on a Diversity Visa but they still won't leave me in peace. They keep calling me to ask about the house. And their dog. They keep pestering me.'

Siddhartha said nothing.

After a while, I said, 'I must be weak. Though I should be happy at seeing an old friend after so many years, I feel uncomfortable having you here.'

In a thoughtful tone, Siddhartha said, 'The massacre at the palace didn't happen just by chance. If you look at it in the national context, you can see many signs that it was planned. I think it was intended to create a crisis in the country.'

'But you yourselves have created a crisis,' I said.

'Think about it,' he said. 'A king who opposed the deployment of the army, a king who wanted a political solution to the issues raised by the People's Movement, a king who wanted consensus among the parties inside the country has been murdered.'

His logic seemed flawed to me. 'But you people want to fight the army, don't you? And don't tell me you admired a king against whom you unleashed a republican insurgency?'

'We should look at things in their totality,' he said. 'We should analyse individuals objectively and judge them on their own merits.'

In front of me hung a painting, a vague image of a woman from Thimi wearing a black sari with a red border. Next to her was a man wearing a *bhadgaule topi*. He had a flower tucked behind his right ear, which meant they were going to a feast. It was a painting about festivals and the change of seasons. I wondered why I'd used so much red in the painting. It looked like it was dripping with blood.

The phone rang again. 'Painter Babu.' It was my landlord again. 'The line got disconnected.'

I hated being called 'Painter Babu', as if I were someone who painted signboards! How did this man ever get a PhD in Social Economics and wind up a professor? How had he worked for so many years as an advisor and consultant in government offices?

'You're not e-mailing any more,' he said, as though I'd been so close to him that we exchanged e-mails every day. His inability to understand my life always irritated me. I had so much work to do, but he always expected me to send him updates on the latest developments in the country. Why had he left the country if he was so concerned about it? And when he did live here, what contribution had he made? Was that why he was suddenly so anxious, because he realized he'd done nothing for the country he'd left behind?

'We came to the US, all right, but my wife's not happy,' he admitted. 'I've found work. I manage a department store. 'Everything's fine but I can't stop thinking about Nepal.'

His wife came on the line. 'Please take good care of my puja *kotha*,' she said.

'Certainly,' I said, though I never set foot in her prayer room and sometimes, at night, heard rats running around inside it.

When the conversation ended, I hung up again and picked up my cup of tea. It was cold. I went to the kitchen to make coffee.

'I want to see the painting,' Siddhartha said.

'Which painting?'

'Have you forgotten? The painting you did of me.'

I thought back—and the memory returned. A long time ago, I'd made Siddhartha sit on a stool for two full days, posing for a portrait. He was a student leader at our college then. I used to watch him taking part in political debates. At first I never talked to him because I wasn't interested in politics. But I was curious about him and his friends, who argued with such fervour during the breaks between classes. Siddhartha was my junior, but he'd caught my attention. Through the painting I'd wanted to show the kind of Nepal our young people aspired to. I called it *What We Want*.

It sold in my first group exhibition. A man bought it just before the exhibition closed. That man no longer lived in Nepal. He'd paid a lot of money for the painting. How could the country make any progress when the well-to-do chose to leave? I'd long ago misplaced his visiting card and heard he now taught in a university in Britain. He was married to a foreigner who'd come to Nepal as a young woman to do post-graduate research. They'd fallen in love and, by the time they'd left Nepal, had already had two daughters. They'd brought their daughters to the exhibition. The little girls were tall for their age, with dark hair and fair skin. The wife had asked me some political questions and wanted to understand the background to the painting. I'd tried to convince her I wasn't a Marxist. 'If I believe in any "ism", it's aestheticism,' I'd told her.

Now I looked at Siddhartha and said, 'I should've given that painting a tragic touch.'

'You said you were painting a figure of hope,' he said.

'I thought I was. If I'd known then what I know now, I'd have painted you as a tragic figure.'

'But you saw me as a representative of the youth movement.'

I shrugged. 'So?'

'So how could that be tragic?'

'I could've painted you dead, killed by a bullet,' I said.

'Then that would be a painting of someone else, not me.'

'What if I told you I have no faith in you people? That I don't think you offer any hope for the future?' I said.

'Then you'd be wrong,' he said. 'If you looked at things objectively, you'd realize that at last our society does have hope.'

'Did I make a mistake in my painting?'

'You were in a hurry. You painted me as you saw me,' he said, 'but you failed to capture me as I really was.'

'You didn't say anything at the time.'

'You never asked,' he said.

'Your expression said it all.'

'That's where you're wrong,' he said. 'You didn't understand. You just went for superficial appearances and painted me as a character, not as part of a larger phenomenon.'

'What difference does it make?' I said, irritated.

'You presented me as a romantic hero, an individual. You lacked the vision to understand I represented more than that.'

'You were immature then,' I said. 'I wouldn't do that painting again. The painting I did was good enough for the times. It was a statement about that period.'

'I never asked you to use me as a character in your painting,' he said.

I agreed. 'No, you didn't. And you've turned out exactly the opposite of the way I painted you.'

He scoffed, 'Then you were deluded. I was always willing to fight for what I believed in.'

'I never imagined you'd turn to violence.'

'Exactly,' he said. 'You created an image and fell in love with it. You never thought about the changes taking place behind the façade.'

'I thought you wanted positive change. And I thought you'd use peaceful means to achieve it,' I said.

'Then that was your mistake,' he said. 'Instead of painting me frozen in time, you should've painted me as a character removed from time and space. That way, you wouldn't have the problem you have now—your inability to reconcile the person you saw all those years ago with the person I've become.'

'Imaginary characters don't make good subjects for paintings,' I said.

'You've finally come to the point, dear artist,' he said. 'You want to paint real characters, but you can't accept that real people change and grow. You're scared of their growth.'

'Is this just a phase you're going through then? A stage in your growth?' I asked. 'A new you?'

'A destructive me, you'd say?'

'I can't disagree.'

'Consider the purpose,' he said. 'Destruction in order to create.'

'Isn't it possible to create without destroying?'

He said, 'The important question is what is being destroyed. To cure this diseased country, its fundamental structures must be changed. And that's what we're doing.'

'But people are being killed.'

'Most of the people who're being killed are representatives of the old power elite. True, some innocent people are getting caught in the crossfire,' he conceded. 'But consider how the crisis first arose. Wasn't it the state which drew first blood? Didn't the state first arrest, torture, and kill unarmed people?'

'And you had to respond with violence?'

'There was no other option,' he said. 'The only possible response was for the oppressed to take up arms. Weapons give us power. Has the state ever listened to the powerless?'

'But our society's being torn apart.'

'People don't need peace,' he said. 'They need justice. People are tired of living in despair under the façade of peace. If there's justice, peace will follow. King Birendra declared

Nepal a 'zone of peace' instead of making it a just country, and that's not good enough.'

I said nothing.

'We shouldn't ask for a peaceful country,' he reiterated. 'We should ask for a just country.'

'Then why is injustice being meted out in the name of building a just country?'

'You should learn to distinguish between justice and injustice,' he said.

'You think I can't?'

'If I'd found the role I genuinely wanted, the events at your old school would never have happened,' he said. 'Nor would this massacre have stained the royal palace.'

'You're talking rubbish. Why drag the palace into this?'

'You see your school as a symbol of the state of the nation,' he said. 'But I see the royal palace as its true reflection. What happened in the palace mirrors the current crisis. Every house in our country is falling into ruins; every family's being torn apart. We have to see the conflict within the royal family as a reflection of the situation in the whole country. That's a scientific approach.'

'But in the case of the palace, the trigger was pulled in madness,' I argued.

'Even if that were true, questions remain. What drove the crown prince to do what he did? Why was he left to rot within the four walls of the palace, with nothing but drugs, alcohol, and guns to occupy him?'

'Obviously, the king didn't have time to give him enough attention.'

'I'm beginning to think you can't understand,' he said, growing exasperated. 'You're talking about an individual. I'm talking about an institution.'

'But institutions are made up of individuals,' I argued. 'I believe in the supremacy of the free individual.'

'You give too much weight to the importance of the individual. That's why you can't grasp the bigger picture. We're fighting to build a new nation.'

'I'm trying to understand you,' I said, 'but I think your policies are confused.'

He said, 'I came to you because I believed you could understand me and what I'm fighting for. You're the artist who inspired me to leave.'

'I did? Leave for where?'

'Leave for a life underground,' he said. 'Ever since I went underground, I've been living on a razor's edge.'

'I was wrong to paint you as a political figure,' I said.

'You're scared of your own shadow!'

'I should've painted you as just an ordinary student.'

'Wouldn't I have become involved in politics in any case?'

'You could've become a lawyer.'

'That would've given me more skills to make my arguments,' he said.

'You could've become a journalist.'

'Then I might've shocked you by presenting harsh truths about this country.'

'You could've become a musician.'

'I would've stirred the people with revolutionary songs.'

'What if I'd painted you as a farmer?'

'I would've joined the rebellion, raising my hoe.'

'I could've sent you to Korea or the Gulf as a labourer.'

'I would've brought all the Nepalis who work abroad back to their country to join the rebellion.'

I said, 'It would've been best to send you to the US.'

'Why do you presume I'd have lost my revolutionary zeal even there? I could organize a revolt from any place on earth,' he said.

'I'm angry that you've resorted to violence,' I said.

'You're responsible for that,' he retorted. 'I was preparing for a teaching career, but the day I saw your painting, I decided to become a good citizen. You gave me the courage to channel the frustrations of the people into revolution.'

'You're wrong,' I said. 'Only the future can judge whether you've become a good citizen. I say you've become a knife that's cutting ordinary Nepalis. You're only sowing bitterness.'

'As an artist, don't you have any urge to change society?'

'Paintings aren't meant to change society,' I said. 'Art isn't politics. Painting's like music, removed from day-to-day life. It's a medium that touches the heart and the mind simultaneously. It seeks only the synergy of brushstrokes and colours. I use colours to express beauty. I'm not involved in politics.'

'Beauty lies in the bitter truths of life,' he said. 'All that your colours express is fantasy.'

'If an artist starts bringing politics onto his canvas, there'll be no difference between him and a politician,' I said. 'The two should remain separate. Art shouldn't become mere propaganda. The professions that are outside of politics give society its depth. Art that's dominated by politics isn't art any more. Art has no life unless it is independent.'

'In that case, I'd like to take you to the countryside,' he said. 'I'd like you to see for yourself the way the country is these days. Then you'll discover that your paintings are meaningless. Then you'll understand that you're lost in a jumble of culture, songs, and dances, a fantasy world of colours.'

I sat down, upset. The coffee was ready. I offered him a cup. He declined. He stayed standing. He was stubborn. He was tough. I pushed aside the curtain and looked out the window. There was a blue flower on a hillock near a neighbouring house. It was one of the last jacaranda blossoms of the season. The monsoon had arrived. For the coming two to three months, Kathmandu would be deluged with rain. Then the cold winds of autumn would blow, clearing the eyes of the city dwellers. Festive processions would flood the streets. If I went to the countryside with Siddhartha, I'd miss seeing the colours, hearing the bands playing music and, most importantly, watching the people enjoying the changing seasons of the city.

Siddhartha wanted me to see the changes he'd brought about. Was it really change or just destruction? 'Where would we go?' I asked.

'If you were a true artist, you'd guess where and why,' he said in a challenging tone. 'Though you fall into the reactionary camp, I feel it's my duty to show you the right path because you're a creative person and I believe there's some hope for you.'

'What if I don't go?'

That'll be your loss. You'll drown in your reactionary quagmire and nobody will be able to save you. History will judge you a traitor.'

CHAPTER TWELVE

On a hillock a girl picked oranges, putting them in a *doko*. Some of the orange trees were taller than she was, though I couldn't say that for all the trees. Was she taller or were the trees taller? She was totally absorbed in her task. At one point she lost her balance and fell onto the mustard field by the hillock. Her basket tipped over, ripe oranges rolling out.

She stood, brushing off the mustard flowers stuck to her dress. On another hillock was a boy, her brother. His basket was almost full. The girl began to hurry, trying to catch up. She had to fill her *doko*, then go home to help cook lunch and wash the dishes.

We'd stayed overnight at her house. She'd served us dinner, then arranged our beds. All the while, her brother was studying by the light of a kerosene lamp. Siddhartha and his friends had chatted with the children's father. Tossing and turning in my sleeping bag I didn't fall asleep till quite late. I could hear Siddhartha's voice, sometimes raised, sometimes subdued. He was explaining history to the old man, telling him why his daughter should participate in the People's War. He and his comrades had already recruited a dozen girls from the village, but the old man was reluctant to let his daughter go. In the end, they gave him a day to make up his mind.

Siddhartha was probably still cajoling the old man even as I watched the girl picking oranges. This might be the last time she'd ever pick oranges in her family's orchard.

'My son and I will be alone if you take her,' the old man had pleaded the night before.

'All us comrades will be your sons and daughters,' Siddhartha replied.

'I haven't even given her a decent education. I feel bad about that,' the old man said.

'Don't worry, Ba. When she joins the People's War, she'll become wise.'

I watched her on that hillock. She was as supple as the stem of a mustard plant, with a cheerful face. Her body was formed of the water which gurgles down from the high jungles and of the sweet juice of oranges. She'd been shaped by the caresses of the sun and the fresh breeze. She was probably wearing the same dress she'd worn to school, a long time ago.

The sunlight was shifting slowly from the mustard field to the hillock. The girl probably had many questions on her mind and much uncertainty in her heart. If she left with the comrades, she'd always be worried about her father and her little brother. She knew she'd meet many girls like herself in the jungle, but still her face was painted with fear. She wasn't the one who'd decide her fate. It was up to her father. I kept on watching her. She kept on picking oranges. Her basket was half full.

The previous night her father had sighed and asked, 'Why did you boys join the war?'

'For people like you, Ba,' Siddhartha said. 'There's no electricity in your house, no telephone, no television. You don't have roads or a market in which to sell your oranges. How long should we look up from the ground at the planes flying overhead, carrying the rich?'

'But it's all according to God's wish,' the old man said.

'That's our biggest mistake,' Siddhartha replied. 'We've been justifying the misdeeds of the rich in the name of God.'

The old man argued, 'We were born and raised in these hills. How can we, who till the land, know anything else?'

Siddhartha replied, 'There's no hospital. The health post's a day's walk away, but there's no doctor there anyway. The primary school has only one teacher. How can he give a good education to the students? If we continue like this, we'll remain nothing but mere peasants for generations to come.'

'That's true.'

'The rich, the powerful, the exploiters, and the bourgeoisie have everything,' Siddhartha continued. 'They can afford any health treatment they choose, all the education they want, and any entertainment they like. They drive expensive cars and indulge themselves in luxury. But what do we have?'

'Anyone can have those things if they become rich,' the old man argued. 'It's only because we're poor that we don't have them.'

Siddhartha refused to give up. 'But who made us poor? No one was rich in the beginning. How can we ever become rich when a handful of people have captured the power of the state for themselves and their relatives, friends, and aides?'

The old man looked lost.

'We'll never get anywhere till the power of the state rests in the hands of the people,' Siddhartha asserted, sensing the old man was beginning to waver. 'Your daughter had to leave school while the children of the high and mighty get to study in America. It's they who'll become the doctors, engineers, members of the Planning Commission, and political leaders of the future. They'll hijack the development of the country. You'll marry your daughter off one day and even after that there'll be no future for her except farming in the hills. Will she be able to send her children to good schools? Generations will continue to live in the hills as you do, as long as the rich keep running the country.'

From where I was standing behind a tree, the girl and her brother couldn't see me. They didn't know I was watching them. I wanted to look at the girl to my heart's content because she was unlikely to be the same person tomorrow. She might end up carrying a gun. Would she plan an attack on a police post one day? I couldn't imagine her as a revolutionary, a martyr! She probably couldn't even imagine being in the midst of such things—this girl so innocently picking oranges and putting them in her *doko*. Tomorrow she could be cut down by a bullet, carried away in a basket, and buried in an unmarked grave. She'd be drenched in blood, far away from her father and brother.

I heard the girl's brother ask, 'Will you go, Didi?'

'I'll do whatever Ba says,' she replied.

'If you did go, when would you come back?'

'How should I know?'

'Do they give holidays for Dashain and Tihar?'

'I don't know'

'You'll have to use a gun, shoot people, make bombs. They say bombs make a very loud noise when they explode,' he said.

She said, 'I've never even seen a gun.'

'I want to use a gun!' the boy declared.

'Have you ever seen one?'

'I saw a hunter's gun once. I saw a hunter shoot a bird. How it fell! That was a long time ago, on the way to school. There aren't any hunters any more. They've taken all the hunters' guns away.'

The girl said, 'That's why there are so many birds in the sky.'

'I love the taste of pigeon!' the boy said.

'I don't like killing birds,' she said.

From this conversation, I realized the children hadn't seen the guns Siddhartha and his companions were carrying. But I'd seen them. They'd made me wonder why Siddhartha had brought me here. Why did he want me to see all this? Why did he want me to see an innocent girl being asked to risk her life? He and his comrades were trying to place a gun in the hands of a girl who was just a budding flower. They were trying to motivate other village youngsters to join up as well. They were emptying the village of its youth, and it upset me.

Again the girl lost her balance and fell amongst the mustard plants. She cried out in pain this time, but her brother, his back to her, didn't hear her. I couldn't help her because that would've put an end to my eavesdropping. So I stayed still and did nothing, like a man devoid of feeling.

'If you go, make sure you come back to see us often,' her brother said. When there was no reply, he looked at the green fields where the wheat was sprouting and towards the terrace planted with cauliflower. Where had the girl gone? He couldn't see her till she stood up again, nursing her bruised knees. Then she went back to picking oranges.

'Bring me a gun when you come home,' her brother said. 'I'll learn how to use it.'

The girl didn't hear him properly. 'Use what?' she asked.

'A gun.'

'Don't you have to study?' she scolded him.

'Is that why you're going, because you don't have to study?'

'Maybe.'

'In that case, I'll quit school too!' he said.

When the boy's *doko* was full, he prepared to go home. The girl went with him. I followed them, still unseen, walking along the elevated ridges separating the fields. The village was beautiful. I took in the cold earth, the morning sun, and the mustard flowers damaged in places by fallen oranges. I breathed in the pure air while the butterflies took flight. I looked at the terraces covered with pale green stalks dancing in the wind. I looked at fallen leaves; the sky, cushioned by fog; the stream that flooded the fields each monsoon, draining the sweat of the hills; the slippery paths where farmers walked each day.

We came upon a group of children returning home with *dokos* on their backs bigger than they were.

A girl asked, 'So are you going, Sanu?'

When she stopped to talk, I stopped as well.

'I won't go,' the other girl said.

'Well, I'm going,' said another.

'How long do we have to keep carrying these *dokos?*' one of the other girls said, her voice turning into the cry of a revolutionary. 'Our mothers did the same thing. Our sisters-in-law do it. Those *dais* are telling us the truth! My father doesn't want to let me go but I said I'm going anyway. Girls from other villages are joining up as well.'

Sanu answered softly. I couldn't hear what she said. I assumed there were many girls there, standing with baskets of oranges on their backs. I strained my neck, but from my vantage point all I could see were a few heads and the tops of *dokos* silhouetted against the sun.

'If we'd studied in boarding schools, we could've become doctors or engineers,' the revolutionary voice continued. 'We could've learned something. We wouldn't have to spend our lives picking oranges, cutting grass, and looking after the mustard fields! Our lives are wasted. Those *dais* are right! If we take part in their struggle, at least our younger sisters and brothers might be able to get a proper education.'

'How stupid you are!' another girl said. 'Do you think we can give the younger ones a good education by killing people or getting killed ourselves?'

'Those *dais* are saying,' the revolutionary voice continued, 'that if we don't take part in the struggle, Kathmandu will never take notice of us. No one will listen and no one will care. Nothing will change if we go on suffering silently and don't try to make our voices heard.'

I heard Sanu's brother say, 'I'll go as well, Didi!'

Many voices chided him. 'You're too small! Go and play marbles!'

Sanu's brother scampered off and the gathering dispersed.

At Sanu's house, the rice was almost cooked. Siddhartha was cooking potato and radish soup. Sanu looked surprised to see him cooking.

We ate lunch in silence. Afterwards, I washed my plate with ash. My hands smelled of it for a long time afterwards. Siddhartha's friends washed the pots.

Sanu's father said, 'That pot was a gift to my wife on our marriage. This is the first time I've ever used it.' He turned towards Sanu and said, 'They want to take you away with them. What do you say, Chori?'

Sanu was silent. She looked at the floor, leaning against one of the poles supporting the house. Her brother sat cross-legged beside her. Finally, she said to him, 'Go to school!'

The old man turned and took Siddhartha's arm. 'From today, you're responsible for her safety,' he said with tears in his eyes.

'Don't worry, Ba,' Siddhartha said. 'Your daughter will be one of our dear comrades in the great struggle.'

Siddhartha's friends had made the rounds of several houses and needed to brief him on the outcome of their recruitment drive. That afternoon he left me to tour the village with them.

I watched Sanu pack some oranges in a bag.

Her father said, 'Leave them. Don't go to the market today. I'll sell the oranges tomorrow'

'But I can sell them and be back by evening,' she said.

'No. Get some rest,' he said. 'Who knows how long you'll have to walk tonight?' After a while, he added, 'Take good care of yourself, Chori.'

Don't worry, Ba. I'll be back soon. Tell Bhai to go to school every day and not loaf around.'

'Don't worry about us,' the old man said. 'Just make sure that when you're walking with them, you don't walk in the very front or at the very back. Always walk in the middle.' In a trembling voice, he said to himself, 'What can we do? We can't protect our children any more.'

I saw a gleam of excitement in Sanu's eyes. She busied herself cleaning the house and washing her father's and brother's clothes. Packing her things in a small bag, she burst into tears when she saw a blouse and shawl which had belonged to her mother and sat sobbing beside them.

Siddhartha and his friends returned in the evening. By then, Sanu's brother had come back from school. It was time for us to leave. Sanu came out of the house, carrying her bag.

The old man asked Siddhartha, 'What if the soldiers punish me for letting my daughter go with you and for giving you food?'

He replied, 'They haven't dared come here since we blew up their post. Don't worry, Ba. This area is controlled by our army, our police, our government.'

As Sanu walked away with us, her brother called after her, 'Come back soon, Didi!'

There were many new faces in our group by the time we entered the jungle.

CHAPTER THIRTEEN

Dear Hajur Aama,
Namaste!

I can't remember what my own grandmother looked like. She probably looked like you. Meeting you opened up a window of happiness in my heart. I feel you've given me many blessings. You have so much experience. I find in you a curious mixture of hope, sorrow, dreams, and life experience. You've lived through an era which, when I look into your face, I feel I understand. For me, you're a book, and every time you speak I turn a new page.

Perhaps it surprises you that someone who's met you only once should write you a letter. I want you to know this is my first hand-written letter to anyone. People don't write letters by hand any more. They prefer e-mails. I use a computer to write my letters too. The computer's become the paper and post for our messages, but writing to you now, I'm beginning to realize how artificial e-mails are. You've given me the desire to write a letter in my own hand, and I'm grateful to you for that.

I could've given you a phone call or dropped by to say all this, but I feel the need to express myself in writing.

At the moment, there's no one in the world who's dearer to me than you. I was smitten the day I met you. I'd never really talked with someone your age. You're as majestic as a mountain, not just because of your years but because you have the wisdom and grace that come with experience. I didn't want to leave your house.

I realized afterwards that I miss parental affection in my life. All human beings need caring guardians.

Right now, in the village I'm in, I see farmers working in their orange orchards. To the north are snow-capped mountains. The contentment I see on the farmers' faces isn't because they have a beautiful view. It comes from their certainty that their orchards will bear fruit. The sun's rays are reflecting off the mountains. They're basking in its warmth. Hajur Aama, you pin your hopes on gods. These farmers pin their hopes on the mountains. They depend on the weather and they read the changing seasons by looking at the mountains.

Your hopes are pinned on gods, the farmers' on the mountains, and mine on you.

I made you dance and you were happy. The day I saw you dance was the happiest day of my life. It was as though the snow on the mountains was melting in the sun and a magnificent rainbow had appeared on the horizon.

You go to temples every day and worship your gods. Depending on your state of mind, you find your gods serious or worried or happy. I wanted to see you elated, full of joy like a living goddess. You have your worries as well as your joys. With hope and happiness you roll the cotton for 'batti' for your gods, while at the same time you worry about your family who are far away from you, just like a farmer who rejoices when his crops bear fruit or despairs when they fail. Similarly, I feel great contentment writing to you. But I also have my worries.

I'm sorry I couldn't accept your lunch invitation. Right now I'm in the western hills, far from Kathmandu. I hope you aren't upset because I had to decline your invitation. I promise I'll come when I get back.

I confess I have one fear, though: I fear I've grown too attached to you and that you might have unreasonable expectations of me. Please remember that I'm an ordinary painter, one of the many book lovers who come to your house.

You're right in saying I'm a stubborn person. I'm willing to be called anything as long as I can make you dance. I'll try to make you dance every time I see you. I don't care if you call me an extremely stubborn person. I have my idiosyncrasies just like everybody else. So, Hajur Aama, you're going to have to dance every time I visit! And you won't be allowed to stop, even if a visitor arrives. I assume your dear granddaughter is reading this letter to you. She'll have to dance as well.

It surprises me I'm saying such an outrageous thing, but why should I lie to you, Hajur Aama? I'm in love. I've fallen in love, though I can hardly believe it myself. But I haven't been able to tell the one I love how I feel. I suppose I don't have the courage. I'm too scared. Why are people afraid when it comes to love? Why am I running away? I'm afraid to face her. I'm not sure how she'll react. What if she rejects me? What if she tells me she doesn't want me? What if she tells me she doesn't love me? Then I'll slide down a slippery slope with no hope of ever getting to my feet again. This is the first serious love in my life. I don't want it to fail. If that happened, my state of mind would be changed forever and I don't think I'd ever recover.

I'm proud. My problem is that the person I love is also proud. She's beautiful, intelligent and, I think, even prouder than I am. She's the loveliest person on earth. She's like a mountain. If she were just physically beautiful, she'd be like the dark side of a mountain, magnificent but never touched by the sun. However, every aspect of her is beautiful. Her intelligence shines like a snow-covered slope in the sun. She leaves me breathless. The snow that melts from her washes over and purifies me. Tell me, Hajur Aama, what should I do?

I began to write this letter at dawn. I pulled back the curtains and was dazzled by the sun as it climbed up the mountain's face. I was coloured by the orange rays of sunrise and bathed in them as I wrote, 'I'm in love.' And just as I wrote that, sunlight poured through the window. So the sun is a witness to my love. With the sun as my confidante, I shed light on my heart's secret desire. You might be able to feel the caress of the sun in my words.

The sun was setting when I first met the woman I love. Now the sun's rising. So I'm writing this letter at sunrise, thinking about a woman I met at sunset. Be my witness, Hajur Aama. I love her. She'll live in my heart as long as the sun rises in the eastern hills and sets in the western hills. Our lives are short. I want you to be the witness to my love.

I must sound illogical to you, like a poet or even a lunatic perhaps. Shakespeare said that poets, lovers, and madmen enjoy absolute freedom. I'm writing on a sheet of paper coloured crimson by the sun. The tip of my pen is dancing while I remember you dancing. It was a strange coincidence, my coming to your house. You switched on the cassette player and I made you dance. I don't really know what led me to you. I came in search of a book and now you've become a witness to my love. It seems books forge strong relationships! I also owe meeting the woman I love to a book, a book that I wrote. If there were no books and if I hadn't written one, and if I hadn't come to your house looking for a book, so much of my life would be empty.

Hajur Aama, the woman I love won't look much different from you when she reaches your age. I'll introduce her to you some day, if she reciprocates my love. You'll be the first to see us together, to congratulate me, and to give us your blessing.

Part of the reason I feel so close to you is your house, which you look after so well. I'd never seen a house like yours. It's a world unto itself, like a piece of heaven fallen to earth. Under your care, anything's possible, it seems. I know you can't read. I hope this letter's being read to you in your library by your beloved granddaughter. But you light the lamp of knowledge. Your house is like a glowing school of wisdom. It's a house befitting a goddess like you. I think of all the other houses in foggy Kathmandu, which even high-wattage bulbs fail to light. The light in your house is brighter than any artificial light. I felt as if I belonged, and wanted to spend months there. I have two habits—I either travel or read. I have the whole world in which to travel and now, for reading, I have your library. It makes me happy to think of you listening to this letter in your library. That's fitting. I hope that my writing is destined to be housed in libraries. That's why libraries appeal to me so much. One day, all that will remain of me will be my paintings and my books. Your bookshelves will house my words.

Along with this letter, I wanted to send a photo of the woman I love to know what you think. I want to show her photo to the world and tell everyone I love her! But I can't do that right now. Love can't be a one-sided thing. I still haven't told her how I feel. I'm yet to find out how she feels. If I find my love reflected in her eyes, you'll be the first person with whom I share my happiness. But for the moment, let me tell you this: the person I love is exactly like your granddaughter. They have the same features and the same characteristics. They are equally proud.

Your loving grandson

CHAPTER FOURTEEN

I arrived on a hill red with rhododendrons. Putting my rucksack down at the teashop, I took off my shirt and wrung out the sweat, a long sigh escaping my lips. Some porters resting nearby took some biscuits out of their packs. Had I asked the shopkeeper for tea? I couldn't remember.

A little girl brought me a glass of tea. I took it and, sipping, looked at the hillside. I was surrounded by the colours of my youth. A new season had arrived. Spring had stripped the sky of the soft, white blanket of winter, which wouldn't return for another year. The rhododendron blooms bore witness to the change of seasons, the flowers looking like flames.

With each sip of tea I felt more light-hearted. I saw a bird take off from a rhododendron blossom, its wings so red it was as if they'd absorbed the colour of the flowers. I wished my eyes could fly with those wings, so I could enjoy the grandeur of the entire rhododendron forest. The snow on the hillside was melting. I wanted to hear the music of that melting. I wanted to follow the path of the melting snow, trickling and splashing against the rocks. Its power must terrorize the deep gorges. I wanted to feel that terror.

Then I heard a girl telling the porters, 'The policemen went up this trail. They died in an ambush half an hour later.'

'Did all of them die?' one porter asked.

I wondered if I'd see any blood on the trail. I decided I wouldn't let it upset me. I'd dismiss it as a reflection of the rhododendron flowers or the play of sunlight and shadow. The people of the hills had been walking up and down these trails for centuries. The footprints of my ancestors were imprinted on these trails. I wanted to touch their footprints, to feel these trails carved from their sweat. If I screamed in loneliness here, the chirping of the birds and the humming of insects would cover the sound of my scream. If I went mad here, my madness would be drowned by the crashing of waterfalls. If I were to weep, anyone who heard me would think it was the cry of a bird.

I'd walk. Siddhartha and his comrades had left me, but I was determined to finish the journey I'd started. I was determined to experience this trail. I could see the prints of cows' hooves. I grew up drinking cow's milk. I wouldn't let my feet stumble. I was indebted to the cows which had nourished my ancestors. I could almost hear the echoes of their bells. This was the trail along which porters had carried black slates all the way to my school. This same trail had taken me to school, where I'd learned the magic of letters, looked through the window of knowledge, and come to understand the language of colour. I'd developed self-awareness on this trail. I'd learned how to dream as I walked on this trail. I owed my dreams to this solitude, this forest, these flowers, these hills that shaped the sky, and this trail that shaped the hills. I wanted to find again the tears that had dropped from my eyes when my mother dragged me to school, pulling me by my ears.

After so many years, I was back.

I heard the girl tell the porters, 'The school closed after the teacher was killed. The children don't go to school any more. They herd cattle now.'

A porter asked, 'Isn't this the same village where a political leader was killed some time ago?'

I left the teashop, scared about what I'd find.

Further on into the forest, I heard a noise it. At first it sounded like a monkey jumping from tree to tree, but then my mind gave the sound new shapes. I heard footsteps and thought it could be a person, a jackal, a deer. The noise grew louder and the things in my mind grew larger. I started to imagine leopards and bears. I tried not to worry and quickened my steps, but my heart was pounding. I told myself it was nothing.

Suddenly there was a crashing sound and I screamed, 'Oh God!'

It was some cows who had burst out from a dense grove of rhododendrons. Behind them came a cowherd, wielding a stick.

Relieved, I walked on.

The cowherd called after me, 'Be careful, Dai! There might be mines on the trail! One exploded a few days ago. Just there,' he said, pointing with pursed lips. 'They say there are more mines under the bushes. Be careful.'

I started to walk very slowly, looking carefully at the ground before every step. But I wanted to enjoy the sight of the rhododendron flowers. These messengers of spring were blossoming so beautifully. The slope beside the trail was covered with flowers, red masses topping every bush as if to say 'namaste'. Just seeing them thrilled me. I was overwhelmed by the riot of colour. My heart took flight at the sight of flowers everywhere, above me, below me, to my right, to my left, in front of me, behind me. The whole forest was ablaze with colour. These were the same blooms, stems, bushes, forests, and trails I used to pass so many years ago. But I saw them differently now. I was the same person, but my consciousness had changed.

From a distance, the cowherd called out to me, 'Don't worry too much, Dai. Just be alert.'

I looked at him. It was amazing. He was standing at the edge of a cliff, guiding his cattle. He was so close to danger, yet he was concerned for my safety. I was touched. That cowherd reminded me of my childhood. He was still tending cattle, while I'd become a painter. We were separated by a span of two decades, but at his age I'd been no different from him. I spoke like him, I even looked like him. The only difference was that this boy's mother didn't drag him to school by his ears. A bomb had ripped his school apart. After that, forty of his classmates had been abducted and held for two days. The headmaster had been killed. The cowherd came every day to these forests littered with mines. Now, lost in thought, he looked at me, resting his head on his stick.

Some distance ahead was a rhododendron tree completely covered with flowers. I stood in its shadow. I wanted to pick a flower. I felt blessed to have returned in this season. After ten years, I'd come back to the rhododendron village, my village, the village which gave birth to me and raised me, educated me, and sent me out into the world. I'd become a painter and now I was returning in search of colours. None of my relatives lived here any more. But, for me, this village contained everything. Didn't my paintings carry the reflections of these hills and the shadows of this trail? The colours on my canvases came from this village. The rhythm in my paintings came from the waterfalls nearby. These hills gave me my beliefs. These flowers shaped my character. The fog that drifted over these hills shared my secrets. My whole being was made up of the ground on which I was standing, the air I was breathing, and the sunbeams that were bathing me.

I took out my notebook and read aloud a poem I'd written for my darling Palpasa. I wanted the air to hear it.

Let me take you to the village
Where I was born, behind that hill
To the fields where I played.
Slippery rocks
Rivers filled with fishermen's nets.
Let me show you the field
On which fluff from the trees falls.

Should thick fog cover the village,
We shall wake up with the rooster's crows.
Should dense mist cover the trails,
We shall follow the waterfalls.
Should clouds cover the sky,
We shall weave them into an umbrella.

We shall chase deer
Along slippery heights
Along slopes beneath cold shadows.
Wiping sweat off our brows
We shall fly with the pheasants.
I shall braid wild orchids into your hair
And take you to my hills.

Many have left their birthplaces.
Some have deserted the places that loved them.
Everywhere I see
People have left their villages.
Everywhere I see
Those who betrayed love.

My village now is like a widow.
May spring come
May the rhododendrons colour my village.

I will take you to the village
Where I was born.

Hearing me recite the poem, the cowherd came up to me. 'Are you singing a song, Dai?' he asked.

'I'm reading a poem,' I said.

'Can I copy it?'

I gave him a pen and a piece of paper and he started copying my poem. I watched him in wonder. When I was his age, I'd drawn the hills with pencils in just the same way. I'd also written poems back then and written down the songs of the shepherds. I'd given them my own rhythm and sung them in school.

'You have the hallmarks of a poet,' my teacher said to me once.

I replied, 'I'm going to be an engineer, Sir.'

My friends had laughed.

Pointing to the classmate who laughed the loudest, the teacher said, 'And you'll be a cowherd.'

The classmate replied, 'No, I'll be a schoolmaster, Sir.'

This time the teacher had laughed. 'Oh, you'll be a master all right. A master tailor!'

The class erupted in laughter.

A girl called Urmila had asked, 'And what am I going to be, Sir?'

The class laughed again.

'What do you want to be?' the teacher asked.

'I want to be big.'

The laughter grew louder.

'Don't worry. You won't stay small much longer,' the teacher said, fuelling the laughter.

Urmila had blushed profusely. She'd been married off before she'd actually grown big, though. We all watched her leave the village in tears, with her bridegroom.

From that day on, my classmates called me 'Engineer Sa'b'. All except the boy who wanted to be a teacher.

I laughed, remembering those days, and my laughter fell to the ground like a rhododendron flower.

'Why are you laughing, Dai?' the cowherd asked. 'Have I made a mistake in copying the poem?'

'I'm laughing for no reason,' I said.

He went back to copying the poem.

'My handwriting's bad, isn't it?' he said.

'No, no. It's better than mine,' I said.

'Not a lot better though.'

'Is your school closed?' I asked.

'Yes.'

'When will it re-open?'

'It's wide open. A bomb blew it up,' he said.

I asked, 'Do you like the poem?'

'It's good. Which book did you copy it from?' he asked.

'I wrote it myself.'

He looked at me quizzically. 'But who gave you the ideas to put in it?'

'I thought of them myself.'

He looked surprised. 'Can anyone write a poem by themselves?'

'Anyone can be a poet if they want to be,' I said.

'I don't want to be a poet,' he said. 'I want to be an engineer.'

I was stunned.

Soon I had to move on. As I left, the cowherd again warned me to be careful. Then he went back to the edge of the cliff, where he stood reading the poem out loud. He didn't know the metre, so he gave it a new one, creating a rhythm inspired by the beauty of his surroundings.

CHAPTER FIFTEEN

From behind the wall at the entrance to the village, someone shouted in English, 'Who's there?'

I caught sight of a shadow and recognized it immediately. It was Rup Lal Ale, a former soldier. He was wearing a cap as usual. And apparently he hadn't lost the habit of speaking in English. He was the only former British Gurkha who insisted on speaking it. With schoolchildren and educated people from Kathmandu, he never used Nepali. I'd tried to avoid him as a boy, afraid I'd have to speak English with him. He also spoke in a very loud voice which always sounded like a reprimand.

His voice still had a stern ring to it. 'Who's there?' he said again.

I felt a pang of pity when I saw him. His cap had faded. He was wearing a ragged shirt and threadbare shorts. It would've been different if he'd returned after qualifying for a pension. What good was it to be a British Army man without a pension?

'Good evening, Lahure Kaakaa,' I said.

He didn't recognize me. He was wearing very thick glasses and, as I approached, I saw that the left lens was cracked. I remembered that his left eye had been injured when a leopard had attacked him. After that, he'd walked around for several years with a bandaged eye.

He'd almost lost his life in that mauling. It was the year he'd returned from Malaya. Hearing that a leopard was asleep near the village, he'd led the villagers into the forest. Then, simply to show off, he'd fought the leopard, wrestling it single-handed. It was a miracle that he hadn't been killed and that he'd lost only an eye. The story of his fight with the leopard soon became legendary and spread to all the neighbouring villages. People from far away came to our village just to see the man who'd fought a leopard.

After he recovered, Lahure Kaakaa had two stories to tell. The first was about an experience he'd had in Malaya and the second about his fight with the leopard. He told everyone these two stories. He even developed his own style of story telling. His Malaya story invariably began with 'I got into position with my rifle.' And his story about the leopard always started with 'The bastard was hiding in a bush.'

A dog was barking nearby. I saw a heap of cow dung near the wheat fields. The sun had moved towards the hills above the village. The old man was staring at me intently, struggling to recognize me. His confusion was understandable. I'd left ten years ago.

Finally, appearing to remember, he pointed his walking stick at my face. 'Ah, yes!' he exclaimed. 'Are you the same young chap?'

'Which chap, Kaakaa?'

'The young chap I used to tell my war stories to.'

I wasn't sure he really recognized me. All the youngsters in the village used to listen to his war stories. Now many of them were probably in the British Army themselves, fighting in some war or another. Many others would've joined the Indian Army or gone to Malaysia, the Gulf states, or South Korea in search of work. Only the children of Bahun families went into other professions, mostly teaching. I wondered whether any of my friends were still in the village.

I asked, 'Do you really recognize me, Kaakaa?'

'I think you're the son of my good friend,' he said.

All the men of my father's generation were his good friends. I still doubted he knew who I was. But at least he knew I'd grown up listening to his stories.

Finally, he said, 'I still get so emotional when I remember your father.' And I realized he did recognize me after all.

'Let's not talk about my parents, Kaakaa,' I said. 'Tell me about yourself.'

'I'm all right,' he said. He embraced me and let me in. When I was a child, he'd noticed I was taller than my friends and suggested I apply for a job as a clerk with the British Army. When I grew even taller, he exclaimed, 'You could even become a traffic policeman!'

I followed him into the village. The field was dotted with heaps of cow dung. We took a detour, climbing along a trail that snaked up to the village centre. Ahead of us were several women, carrying *dokos* full of grass which they must have cut from the banks of the river below. I still remembered the rocks on the river bank. Those rocks had made me an artist. In their shapes I'd seen the forms of people, animals, and birds. The birds that landed on them had intrigued me. I'd become so fascinated with birds that once I even tried to fly off the top of a haystack. That flight had kept me in bed for two days.

Everything in the village brought back memories. I remembered the harvest season, when I used to sleep on a bed of hay beneath a blanket of hay. We used to whip our ox to make it walk faster on the grain and to jump on a *koal* to produce mustard oil. In winter, we used to drink hot sugarcane juice. I looked at the mound where the *koal* used to be. The last of the sun's rays were creeping over it. Tears came to my eyes.

‘That Bhanu bastard put a corrugated tin roof on his house,’ Kaakaa said. ‘His son sent him money from Malaysia.’

I asked, ‘How’s your health, Kaakaa?’

‘All right’

‘I think about you.’

‘Oh? What do think about me?’

‘I remember your stories,’ I said. ‘No one can forget the man who used to gather together all the children or the village and tell them stories.’

‘Well, I’m glad to hear that.’

‘If it weren’t for you, Kaakaa, this village wouldn’t hold anything for me any more.’

He looked at me fondly. ‘That makes me happy. It’s like my own son has come back.’

‘I am like your son,’ I said. ‘Tell me about the situation in the village.’

He glanced around, then came close to me and whispered, ‘Take care, my son. I hear a big group’s coming today. They take away anyone who’s young and strong. They don’t give old folk like me much trouble. We just have to give them food, cooking utensils, and plates. They cook the food themselves, eat, wash the dishes, and leave.’

‘Do you speak English with them?’ I asked.

‘I can easily tell who’s a Maoist and who’s not,’ he said. ‘First, I speak in English. If someone tells me not to use the language of the capitalist, I know he’s a Maoist and I stop speaking English.’

It was Kaakaa who’d badgered my father to send me to Budhanilkantha School in Kathmandu in the fifth grade. My father had agreed, but when we reached the district headquarters, the entrance exam was already over.

'Your son's an intelligent boy,' Kaakaa said to my father. 'Send him to a good school, at least to the Aanp Peebal School in Gorkha or the Gandaki Boarding School in Pokhara.'

'He'll study in the village,' my father said. 'If he works hard, he'll do well anywhere.'

My father was a very strict man. He'd threatened to throw me over a cliff if I didn't go to school. I still get goosebumps when I think about it. 'Go to school,' he'd boomed, 'or I'll throw you over. Do you hear the growl of the leopards?'

Stubbornly, I refused to go till, finally, my mother dragged me to school by my ears.

'How's the school these days, Kaakaa?' I asked.

'There's no school any more,' he said. 'A bomb exploded when the children were studying.'

We climbed a hillock in silence. Someone came towards us, holding a radio. My father bought a radio from a British Gurkha before I was born. It was the first radio in our village. My father gave the soldier a milch cow for it. All the villagers used to gather in our house to listen to it. 'After the batteries ran down, that radio didn't say another word, no matter how hard I twisted its ear,' my father told me once. In the end, he'd exchanged it with the same soldier for an ageing cow. 'I knew the cow couldn't bear calves but at least it could still produce dung,' he'd explained.

The smell of cow dung grew stronger as we approached the place where my house used to stand. I wasn't sure if there would be anything left of it.

I said to Kaakaa, 'I guess my house must be a wreck by now. Can I stay with you?'

'Silly boy,' he said, 'do you have to ask?'

From Kaakaa's house, I looked over to where my house used to be and was surprised to see it still standing, the slate roof intact. But the verandah and the wooden pillars supporting it were awry. I walked over and looked at its decrepit façade. The courtyard was a shambles, as though packs of village dogs had run through it. The peach trees were either dead or dying. After a while I returned to Kaakaa's house.

Darkness gradually enveloped the village. Someone somewhere started playing a flute. I remembered Krishna Lal who used to wander through the village playing his flute. He could never stay still while he was playing.

'Who's playing the flute, Kaakaa?' I asked.

'Have you forgotten Krishna Lal?'

'Krishna Lal still plays the flute?' I beamed in joy. 'Does he still roam around while he plays?'

'He can't walk,' uncle said. 'They took the bullet out of his leg but it didn't help. He was caught in crossfire,' he explained. 'He was wandering around, playing his flute, and didn't hear the firing when it started.'

I looked away, towards Shubha Shanker's house. There was no sign of life. Shubha Shanker used to go to Kathmandu once a year, walking seven days each way, just to watch the Indra Jatra. 'You won't go to heaven if you haven't seen it at least once in your life,' he used to say. 'And, even if you do get to heaven by mistake, they'll ask if you've seen it and, when they find out you haven't, they'll send you straight to hell.'

I learned from Kaakaa that Shubha Shanker had gone to heaven a few years earlier.

Kaakaa offered me a glass of hot water. 'Here, have some water.'

The village felt unnaturally quiet. It seemed as if there was no one else in his house. I wanted to ask but didn't know how to phrase the question. I just looked at the verandah of my old house, the verandah where I used to draw as a child. Once I'd even drawn Kaakaa as he told us his stories under the tree.

I'd also made many drawings of the mustard field next to my house. I still remember how the pollen in the mustard flowers looked. Drawing in the mustard fields was the beginning of my love for colour. One day, I stole money from my father's shirt pocket and bought coloured pencils in the market. I still feel guilty about it. My father beat a shepherd, whipping him with wet nettles, thinking he'd stolen the money. I'd heard the shepherd lives in India these days. I would like to meet him and apologize.

I took a sip from the glass. 'This tastes like coffee!' I exclaimed.

Kaakaa looked surprised. 'What do you mean it tastes like coffee? It is coffee.'

'I mean, this is good coffee,' I said, correcting myself. The smell was unmistakable. It was indeed coffee.

Kaakaa noticed my confusion. 'What do you take us villagers for?' he said. 'I've had a coffee plantation for two years now. I planted coffee on your family's fields as well. They weren't being used for anything and you never came back, so I thought I'd put them to good use.'

That's fine,' I said.

'I look after the plantation by myself,' he said. 'It keeps me busy all day. Then, in the evening, I go down and stand by the wall where I met you.'

'Why do you do that?'

To wait for my son.'

'Why? Where did Belu go?'

'If I knew, I wouldn't wait for him every day,' he said.

I put the empty glass on the floor. Then, realizing there was no one else to clean it, picked it up, washed it, and put it on the table.

'That coffee was great,' I said.

'The climate gets into everything we grow here,' he said proudly.

Just then, a group of girls and boys walked past the house in total silence. Clearly, Kaakaa had given up the habit of talking to everyone. He just looked at them warily as they walked by. I was also watchful. A girl at the tail end of the group glanced at me. She looked very determined. The boys and girls looked like they were all about the same age. They all wore similar clothes, which might've been uniforms. They all walked at the same pace.

'Who are they?' I asked.

'People of the New Power,' Kaakaa whispered when they'd gone.

'What do they say to you?'

'They say under their system the country will be transformed.'

'Do you know any of them?'

'Yes. One of them.'

'Which one?'

'The girl walking at the back.'

'Who is she?'

'My daughter,' the old man said as he walked into the house. 'I had one daughter and now she's gone.'

My God! That girl was Yam Kumari? How she'd grown! But then ten years is a long time in the life of a child. I remembered her as a little girl, always crying and holding onto her mother's sari. When I left the village, she was playing marbles. I thought she might've recognized me, but maybe she was just wondering who the stranger at her father's house was.

‘Do they come past regularly?’ I asked.

Kaakaa began to light a lantern. ‘You never know when they’ll come and when they’ll go,’ he said. I only pray she doesn’t get killed.’

‘With those people...’

‘At least she’s not alone,’ he said, reassuring himself.

‘Are the others from this village as well?’ I asked.

‘What? Didn’t you recognize anyone?’

‘No.’

‘Neither did I,’ he said, disingenuously. ‘My glasses aren’t so good. If I focus on one, the others go blurry.’

‘How many from the village have joined them?’ I asked.

‘Birkhe’s son,’ he said, ‘and Bhanu’s daughter, Mori’s son, Khuile’s eldest son, Kumale’s second oldest son, Bikhe Bishokarma’s son, Kaila’s daughter and Pundit Homnath’s. They were probably all there.’

‘So how come you let Yam Kumari join?’

‘She was going to school, preparing for the School Leaving Certificate. Then one day, out of the blue, she came home wearing their uniform. She showed me a gun and I taught her how to use it. What was I to do? I thought she’d be safer that way.’

I left the house. The group was out of sight. I walked a little way in the direction they’d taken. Darkness was falling, but I could still see the path. The moon hadn’t risen yet. I looked at my old house. At this time of day, I used to sit on the verandah reading by the light of a lantern. But tonight the house where I’d spent so many happy hours as a child was totally dark.

When I returned, Kaakaa said, ‘When I look at your house, I want to leave the village myself.’

I said nothing. What could I say?

'Come back when you have some time to spare,' he said. 'We could develop a trekking route. If we could establish a route to the base of Dhanchuli Himal, it would attract people from all over the world.'

I thought about it and realized he was right. Walking west from the village to the base of Dhanchuli Himal was like entering a different world. The landscapes were rich and varied. It'd be a fantastic trekking route. If we could develop it, tourists would go to Dhanchuli Himal via Kotgaon and spend a night in our village on the way. The village would be transformed. It could be the perfect place for me to build the resort of my dreams.

With a bit of landscaping, my own land, with its gentle slope, could also be transformed. My house was on a hillside a little way out of the village. It would be the perfect site for a resort. In the middle of the coffee plantations, I could build a centre where artists could come and work. I began to dream how this beautiful transformation could be achieved.

The hills could be different in the future. People would start coming back. We were living in the age of global communication. Communicating was becoming easier and cheaper every day. Thanks to microchips, satellites, optical fibres, and the net, I could live in this village and still be a part of the global village. Trekkers who wanted to experience the hills alone would always come, but these days everyone wanted access to the Net. I knew the thought of combining the hills and the internet was strange, but I was fascinated by the idea of bringing them together. It intrigued me to think that my village, though remote, could be part of the global village. Was it possible? A satellite dish above the gourd vine could usher in a new age.

'You look lost in thought,' Kaakaa said.

'One day my house will change,' I replied quietly.

The old man looked at me curiously.

'I've got a sketch in my mind,' I said. 'And I'm going to hang it right here in this village.'

'Keep dreaming,' he said, laughing.

'But I'm not kidding, Kaakaa. This isn't just an idle day-dream.'

Someone knocked at the door.

The old man leaned out the window and asked, 'Who is it?'

Yam Kumari said, 'Ba, it's me,' and shone a flashlight towards the window.

I went down, lifted the cross bar, and opened the door. 'How are you, Rolypoly?' I joked.

She shone the flashlight in my face. 'Oh, hello, Dai!' she exclaimed happily. 'I saw you earlier but I didn't recognize you.'

'So are all you girls carrying guns these days?'

'Well, we couldn't study,' she said, 'and we couldn't go abroad to work.'

'I was thinking of marrying her off,' the old man said from his bed upstairs, 'but no such luck!'

'I've decided to make my own destiny,' she said huffily.

By the light of her torch, Yam Kumari opened a chest in the corner and took out some clothes. Then she took some rice from a container in the kitchen. I watched silently, wondering what the old man, listening from upstairs, must feel.

'Are you going already?' I asked.

'We're taking shelter in the next village tonight,' she said, 'I hope we'll meet again, Dai.'

I couldn't sleep the whole night. Before leaving, the girl had said 'Please don't call me Rolypoly any more, you skinny Dai!'

'All right, I'll call you Comrade Rolypoly,' I'd said.

The next morning, Kaakaa opened my rucksack and stuffed a package inside it. 'Take it,' he said. When I hesitated, he said, 'It's just coffee, a token of my appreciation for letting me use your land.' Then he added, 'I hope you won't forget us.'

'Don't worry, Kaakaa. I'll come back.'

'You will?'

'Yes. I'm going to come and develop that trekking route with you and build my resort,' I said. 'You may not believe this, Kaakaa, but I have an idea which will change the face of our village. It'll create jobs for our people and a market for our produce.'

Sarcastically, he said, 'You sound like a member of the Planning Commission.'

'This hill is special,' he said as I prepared to leave. "You have to understand this hill.'

I looked at him. He was wearing the same cap, the same shorts, and the same shirt he'd always worn. 'This hill is special,' he said again. 'It's neither too high nor too low. Near the top, you can pick kafal. Here, we have coffee. Kafal needs a cold climate and coffee needs warmth. Oranges grow near the top and bananas near the bottom. You can go uphill and pick oranges, then downhill and pick bananas. Do you get my point?'

"I understand, Kaakaa,' I said.

He stood, like my village, upright but facing an uncertain future.

I walked around my village one last time. Then I walked downhill. There was *saag* growing everywhere. I could smell it. In some places it had been picked and left to dry in the sun. I wanted to pull a white radish from the ground and eat it. I could see masses of millet plants swaying in the wind.

My village was looking for a future. It deserved prosperity, and I could help bring it. I wanted to give new life to my village. The fields of mustard had taught me how to draw. I'd borrowed colours from these hills and wanted to pay them back with interest. I'd been given so much by the earth, the wind, the water, and the life and culture of my village. The rows of *saag* had taught me about straight lines, the hills had taught me the upward strokes of my pencil, and the streams had taught me how to bring them back down. The head straps or the *dokos* on people's backs, the broad-brimmed hats on farmers' heads and the sickles they carried in their hands had taught me curves and circles. The heights of the hills and the depths of the valleys had taught me the essence of life. The place in the hills where I was born had turned into a coffee plantation. I wanted my art to contribute to the transformation.

CHAPTER SIXTEEN

Past the hill, I came upon a band of armed Maoist guerrillas. A girl was leading them. She ordered a male cadre to conduct a thorough search of me. He found nothing objectionable on my body or in my rucksack. The leader put a white flower in the barrel of her gun. Her comrades did the same. One boy couldn't find a flower, so he used a piece of paper instead. 'You're entering our area of command,' the girl said to me. 'You don't need to worry now.'

I wasn't scared, but a tour guide walking along the same trail looked nervous. He was guiding five Austrians from Salzburg. He'd assured them they'd be safe and was trying to appear calm. He didn't want them to worry. Talking to him, I discovered he wasn't really a guide but an environmentalist from Kathmandu. He was taking this group to his village to inaugurate a school they'd donated a million rupees to build.

For a while we walked with the Maoists. Out of their earshot, the environmentalist said to me, 'You look like you've been travelling in these parts for quite some time. Do you think there's trouble ahead?'

'They've put white flowers in their guns,' I said, trying to reassure him.

'Even so, there's still the possibility of crossfire.'

'That only happens when they try to take new territory,' I said.

'So this area is completely under their control?'

'Yes. Did you pay the entry fee?'

'Two thousand rupees per person,' he said. 'I have the receipts in my pocket.'

The Austrians looked uneasy. One middle-aged man took a bottle from his belt, drank some water, and passed the bottle to another man. The rest were wiping sweat from their foreheads.

'Your friends are brave,' I said to the environmentalist. 'The girl who's leading us...'

'The one in uniform?' he asked.

'Yes. She's a friend of a girl from my village,' I said. 'Have you talked to her?'

As he nodded, the girl came up to us. The barrel of her gun was pointing, inadvertently, at my cheek. So what if there was a flower in the barrel, I thought. It's still loaded. It could still go off!

She asked the environmentalist, 'I hope you're not guiding American spies?'

'No,' he said.

'Get their passports. All of them,' she said

Looking worried, the Austrians handed over their passports.

The environmentalist said, 'I hear you give visas to enter your territory.'

'We don't do that,' she said. "How long will you be staying?'

'We're inaugurating the school tomorrow and we'll go back to Kathmandu the day after that.'

We were walking along the trail I wanted to develop as a trekking route. A little further on, it looped to the west. I walked ahead. The environmentalist said something to the Austrians and they quickened their pace. Why the rush, I wondered. It'd be far more pleasant to rest for a while and let the sweat dry.

Soon the guerrillas had moved far ahead, as if taking part in a rally. I introduced myself to the Austrians. 'I'm an artist,' I said. They seemed more relaxed once they knew who I was.

That evening, we stayed together in the newly constructed school building. One of the Austrians, a school teacher, explained that many of his students had contributed to the building from their own pocket money.

'Dear guests, don't be concerned,' said the chairman of the school's management committee, trying to put the Austrians at ease. The environmentalist translated what he said. 'The children of this village will be able to study in proper classrooms at last, thanks to the generosity of Austrian children.'

I was beginning to think about a new painting when the chairman turned towards me. But it turned out he wanted to talk to the environmentalist, who was sitting beside me.

'What should we do?' he asked. 'Some representatives of the People's Government have turned up. You do understand what the People's Government is, don't you?'

The environmentalist stole a glance in my direction, as if for guidance. Then he said, 'Ask them to come in.'

Three youngsters came in. They introduced themselves, shook hands with the environmentalist, and told him, 'We want to put on a short cultural performance during the inauguration tomorrow.'

The environmentalist glanced at me again, miserably. They controlled the area, after all. The school couldn't function without their cooperation. And what harm could there be in a cultural show? He agreed.

The youngsters left and we had dinner. The Austrians ate rice pudding for dessert.

After dinner the youngsters came back. 'We asked to do one performance but allow us to do two,' one of them said to the environmentalist.

What could he say? He agreed.

The youngsters left. We were about to go to bed when they came back again. 'We asked for two performances but allow us to do three,' one of them said.

The environmentalist said helplessly, 'If the chairman agrees, I have no objection. But we were hoping to finish the programme quickly and get away early.'

The next day, a large group of guerrillas were present at the inauguration ceremony. They sang a song of welcome. Then the chief of the People's Government of the village gave a speech. Then they performed a military drill. Then they sang a 'people's song'. The school students, standing as spectators, applauded after each performance.

To a guerrilla standing next to me, I said, 'What if the army arrived now?'

Scratching the ground with a splinter of wood, he said in a low, confident voice, 'We provide total security.'

The 'people's song' ended at last. Then the Maoists performed a dance, raising their guns in the air.

'What kind of security do you provide?' I asked.

'Around the school is the first cordon,' he said. 'A bit further out, there's another. The next one's outside the village, then there's another a few miles out.'

'So you have cordon after cordon?'

'Yes. That way we know well in advance if any security patrol's approaching.'

'But what if they come by helicopter?' I asked.

'We don't fight the enemy in our area of command,' he said. 'If they come, we disappear so there's no confrontation. You're our guests. We're responsible for your safety.'

'Really?'

'But outside our area of command, in the areas we're still fighting to control, who can say?'

A local Maoist leader stood at the rostrum to make a speech. Before beginning, he pumped his right fist in the air. The Austrians looked on impassively. They had garlands of flowers around their necks, and one of them was taking photos of the Maoists with a digital camera. I noticed he was careful not photograph their faces so as not to arouse their suspicions.

The Maoist leader began to explain the origins of the world order according to dialectical materialism. It took him over an hour to get through this, as though he were stringing prayer flags across a wide river. Only then did he touch on Nepal's history. He took another fifteen minutes just to arrive at the era of Prithvi Narayan Shah. While explaining the abuses of the parliamentary system, he suddenly remembered Che Guevara. Then he declared that, under the leadership of COMPOSA, all of South Asia would become a red fortress. Before ending his 'two words,' he asked everyone present to chant revolutionary slogans.

Then there was a break in the programme. I stretched my legs as tea was served and, before we realized it, almost all the spectators had gone. I told the environmentalist I needed to leave as well. He looked unhappy. The Austrians also seemed to want me to stay. But I knew the environmentalist had asked members of the People's Government for permission to order a helicopter to take the Austrians out, and they'd agreed. The Austrians would reach Kathmandu the next day and I'd be on my own in any case. So why shouldn't I be on my way?

I headed off towards the district headquarters. Now that I was alone, I walked faster. I could feel the breeze, even in my heart. My steps quickened to the rhythm of the breeze. Tramping along the dusty trail, I reached a settlement by evening. It was a settlement of displaced people. They were considering moving on, to the plains, if the situation didn't improve. I walked on.

Soon I reached another village. At a house near the entrance, I saw a woman hiding her face in her shawl. All I could see was her nose. She was wiping away tears. This is what happens when people had no one to comfort them, I thought. Seeing me, she called out as though we knew each other. Then she broke down.

'That shoe,' she said, pointing to a canvas shoe lying on the ground outside her house. 'That shoe!'

I couldn't understand what she was talking about.

Finally, a boy came over and explained that the shoe was a message from the guerrillas, ordering the family to send someone to join their ranks. The woman had seen it outside her house that morning. After that, she hadn't drunk a drop of water or eaten a morsel of food all day. She'd just sat there weeping.

The boy told me that one of her sons was in the police force and the other had left for the district headquarters to take the School Leaving Certificate exam. The Maoists were obviously asking for the second oldest son.

I sat down not far from the woman, took out a piece of paper, and started to sketch her. She grew self-conscious, as though I were taking her photo. The boy watched my pencil move.

'You remind me of my elder son,' the woman said to me. Then she started babbling to herself. 'If I don't send my younger son to the jungle, I'll have to go myself. Or I'll have to give them a hundred thousand rupees.' She looked devastated. 'Even if I sell all my oxen, I'll get only ten thousand. And who'll buy my oxen in this village?'

The boy who was watching me sketch explained, 'Her husband's in India. She's got no one to turn to.'

'What do her neighbours advise her to do?' I asked him.

'They've told her to promise to pay the money when her husband gets back.'

'A hundred thousand rupees?'

'If not that much, then whatever she can afford.'

At this, the woman thundered, 'Did my husband go to work in India just to feed these greedy pigs?'

The boy tried to reason with her. 'You also have a son who's earning money.'

'Who knows if he'll ever come back,' she said. 'He can't even come here during the holidays. He's probably already married and settled down somewhere else. Who knows? Maybe he's already been killed in combat.'

'Don't talk like that, Aama,' I said.

The boy teased her, 'Why don't you go yourself? We'll call you Comrade Aama.'

'Don't be stupid,' I said.

'She's just weak,' he scoffed. 'She's not the only one in this position.'

My sketch was complete. I showed it to the woman. She didn't seem to recognize herself, but she'd stopped crying when I left.

The boy followed me. 'If you want to reach the district headquarters before dark, you'll have to hurry,' he said.

I thanked him.

'Hey, you didn't draw me,' he said.

'If I did, I wouldn't be able to reach the district headquarters before dark.'

'You could stay here tonight.'

'But what if someone puts a shoe in front of the house where I stay?' I asked.

'Visitors don't have to go,' he said. 'The worst that could happen would be that someone would steal your shoes.'

'One shoe or two?'

'Why only one? The thief would need both.'

'So he can deliver messages to two houses?'

We parted ways.

CHAPTER SEVENTEEN

The lodge owner was worried. Her cat was yowling upstairs. The lodge owner was sure this boded ill. She was standing at the door of her lodge, looking out fretfully. She didn't even hear me say 'namaste'. Her young son responded, though, joining his palms politely, He took me to the room next to the one in which the cat was yowling. Giving me the key, he said, 'Come down for dinner. Curfew will start soon.'

The cot was narrow and the blanket dirty. The walls were decorated with posters of film stars: Amitabh Bachchan, Manisha Koirala, Rajesh Hamal, Bruce Lee. Pasted on the window were the covers of audio cassettes of Nepali and Hindi film music. There was a feminine scent in the room. It probably belonged to the lodge owner's daughter, not that I could see a daughter anywhere.

I opened the window and looked out on the main market of the district headquarters. Evening had set in. There were very few people on the street. The shops were closing.

I went down for dinner.

'I hear they've gathered near the hills,' the lodge owner said, serving me potato curry. 'They might be planning an attack.'

I was the only guest. The owner's son was eating at a nearby table. On the wall was a menu listing prices for noodles, momos, fried chicken, chowmein, *chhoila*, mutton *sukuti*, rum, vodka, beer, and Khukuri Filter Kings.

I heard the sound of marching feet outside. It must've been an army patrol, but I couldn't tell in which direction they were heading. I finished my meal and washed my hands, glancing at myself in the small mirror by the basin. As I chewed some betel nuts, the lodge owner's son began to do his homework.

'The sound of boots is a bad sign,' the lodge owner whispered.

'Why are you so worried?' I asked.

'A lot of strangers have come here in the past few days,' she said.

'It's probably nothing,' I said.

I headed upstairs. Behind me, I heard her bolt and bar the main door of the lodge. As I climbed the stairs, the cat darted away in the darkness. I went into my room. Manisha Koirala smiled. I opened my rucksack and took out a novel, *The Bridges of Madison County*. Folding the blanket into a pillow, I started to read. If I'd read the novel before seeing the movie, I might've enjoyed it more. Whenever I read about the character called Robert, I pictured Clint Eastwood. When I read anything Robert said, it seemed to me that Eastwood was speaking. If I hadn't watched the movie, I would've been free to imagine for myself what Robert might look like. I would've found him more interesting. But, as it was, it seemed to me the novel had been written about Clint Eastwood.

But soon I was engrossed in the book. Love transforms a person, I thought. When we fall in love, we become different people. Otherwise, how could Robert be filled with such passion? His love was mature.

Suddenly, the lights went out. The film stars on the walls retreated into darkness. I got up and opened the window. The market was silent except for the sound of the river below. It was so dark that even the stars were invisible.

The lights came on again. I went back to reading the novel. Francesca had fallen in love with a stranger despite having a middle-aged husband and children. Even at her age, she was still capable of finding love. Tired of the monotony of her life, she'd re-discovered herself through her relationship with Robert. Every love story has its absurdities. Francesca loved her husband and children, yet she couldn't resist the embraces of a stranger. Would she leave her family for this nomadic photographer?

The lights went off again. Again I opened the window. There was no candle in the room. The shadows of houses loomed over the market.

Outside my door, I heard the lodge owner say, 'This isn't good,' while locking another door.

'The telephones are dead,' said a voice from a neighbouring house.

I lit a match. The room was bright for a moment. The film stars came into view as though to reassure me that everything was fine. I could hear the lodge owner muttering outside. I threw the lit match out the window. Suddenly, it seemed as though the whole market had gone up in flames. I heard a sound like hail pouring onto the tin roof above me.

The attack had begun.

Across the river, I saw a giant fireball explode and disappear instantly. A loud bang drowned out the gurgling of the river. I shut my window. There was another loud explosion and the house shook to its very foundations. The cat started miaowing piteously in the next room and I heard the lodge owner scream. In another room, her son cried, 'Aama!' My bed rattled as though there was an earthquake. A ray of light peeped through a crack in the window.

Over the sound of the explosions, I heard a voice on a loudspeaker: 'We've taken the headquarters. Lay down your arms and surrender.'

Silence descended over rhe market. The cat's cries became louder. The lodge owner and her son were whimpering.

Then a second round of attacks began. I heard a deafening noise like a landslide. Several houses nearby seemed to collapse. The terrified voices of the neighbours rose to a scream.

Again there was sudden silence, followed by the voice speaking through the loudspeaker, then another attack. Again the earth seemed to slip and slide. My bed rattled violently. I tried in vain to steady it.

'Oh, God. God.' The women's voices scared me more than anything else. In the cool night, I was sweating as though it was a hot summer's day. I put my fingers in my ears and held on to my cot for dear life.

'This is your final warning!' the voice boomed through the loudspeaker. 'If you still don't lay down your weapons and surrender, we'll show no mercy. This is your final warning!'

There was a commotion outside. It was impossible to guess what was going on. I could hear people wailing in the neighbouring houses. There were footsteps somewhere. A sea of humanity was flowing. Suddenly, there was complete silence, then the sound of the sky exploding. Someone cried out in pain. I held on tightly to my cot. 'Shoot! Shoot!' Myriad noises assaulted my ears. The cat yowled. It was as though a baby was being born, a mother writhing in labour, a funeral procession chanting dirges, a bride weeping, a wounded bird cheeping—it felt as though a swarm of bees was inside my head.

Calm descended at last. Unbelievably all the noises ceased at once. For a long time there were no explosions, no sparks, no wailing. Even my cot was stable.

The roosters hadn't crowed, but I knew it was morning. Cautiously, I got up and went to the window. No one had come out of his or her house. There was no movement in the market. I could see smoke swirling up from several burned buildings and the smell of soot was in the air. My eyes hurt. It was as if I'd woken up from a nightmare. I was still holding on to my cot, unable to believe the attack had ended. In the dim light of dawn, I could see the film stars in my room. Bruce Lee looked ready to fight, Manisha Koirala was smiling,

I noticed several spent bullets on the floor of my room. I looked down and saw a hole in the leg of my trousers. A bullet had just missed my right knee. I picked up the shell, put it in my pocket and opened the door. Tentatively, I called for the lodge owner. There was no response. I went towards her room and saw the cat lying dead in a pool of blood. I stood in front of her door. I heard incomprehensible mumbling inside.

Outside, a helicopter appeared in the sky. Another landed across the river. I went out onto the verandah. A group of police, fresh arrivals, were swarming around the police post. Some were carrying away dead bodies dressed in uniforms like theirs. Others were searching through the wreckage of houses.

The lodge owner finally opened the door to her room. She was trembling violently. Her son also appeared, holding her hand. He'd wet his pants.

I went out of the lodge. The road was now crowded with security personnel. The bank had been blown wide open. The jail had been broken into and the prisoners released. None of the government offices had escaped attack. Every house with a signboard had been hit. The road was littered with bullets, shells, and bombs. As I walked through the market, some people opened their doors and cautiously peeked out. Everyone looked weary. They looked at each other as if surprised so many people were still alive.

Someone asked me to move but, dazed, I didn't even look at him.

'It's over now,' someone else said.

'I hid under my bed all night,' a man was telling the bank manager.

The manager was holding his head in his hands. The bank had been looted. 'They pointed a gun at my head and asked for the keys,' he said. 'What could I do?'

'Kathmandu's created this problem,' the man told him. 'We're facing the problems Kathmandu can't solve,'

The jailer scurried towards the Chief District Officer. 'Two prisoners refused to go with them and three have come back. The rest are still at large,' he said.

People were watching from doors and windows, from their compounds, and from the sides of the road.

I passed a temple in which there was a stone idol of a god that never spoke a word. There were no worshippers. The bells were silent, incense sticks unlit. Only the smell of explosives scented the air. I looked at the idol. Elegant and mysterious, it was the work of an accomplished sculptor. God stared at me and I stared back. I'm sure the idol was still looking in my direction as I left. I'm also an artist. My works were also watching this battered country.

'Everything's finished,' a woman said, sighing. A helicopter took off. Another arrived and landed beyond the suspension bridge. There were no birds in the sky. People gathered in small groups, telling each other how they'd survived the night. Heading back to the lodge, I noticed that several trees had been hit. Their bark had been ripped off and many of their branches stripped bare. I passed a garden in shambles. A little further on, several policemen in dirty uniforms were resting against a wall which was half destroyed. From behind it, a number of dead policemen were being carried out and laid beside the living.

One of the policemen resting against the wall stretched his legs and saw an unexploded bomb. He looked anxious but didn't move. Beside him, two police officers lay dead, sprawled like drunkards with their faces to the ground.

A group of journalists decended from a helicopter and ran towards the market, aiming their cameras at the devastation. A journalist with a tape recorder came up and took me by the arm. A photojournalist took pictures of the bullet hole in my trousers. I took the shell out of my pocket and showed it to him. He took more pictures.

'How many people died?' he asked.

'Ask the CDO,' I said.

'What do you have to say about the attack?'

'It was a nightmare.'

'Could you elaborate?'

'The police will be able to tell you more.'

'Why aren't you injured, despite being hit by this bullet?'

'I didn't even realize it'd gone through my pants.'

'Were you sleeping?'

Several other journalists had surrounded me by then. 'Look! There are some police officers,' one of them said, and they all rushed away before I could answer the last question.

A policeman resting against the wall opened his mouth to say something, but before he could say a word, another journalist said, 'Look! The police inspector.'

And all of them rushed towards the inspector.

The inspector, tired from the overnight battle, tried to get up off the ground but, before he could say a word, the journalists saw the CDO and rushed off to interview him.

I went back to the lodge and prepared to leave.

'I don't want to do any business today,' the lodge owner said. 'Stay another day. Won't charge you anything.'

The lodge owner's son started to weep, holding on to my trousers.

'They might attack again,' the owner said. 'We'd feel safer if you stayed.'

I looked at the little boy. He was crying and looking at me hopefully. He wanted me to stay. But I had to go.

CHAPTER EIGHTEEN

I was disappointed when Miit Ba didn't offer me a place to sleep. He didn't say 'Stay' and Miitini Aama didn't even come out of the kitchen to greet me. Bhai and Bahini weren't at home. It was odd. Miit Ba said absolutely nothing, though I kept looking at him expectantly.

It was a long time before he finally told me that Resham, my *miit*, my best friend from childhood, had been killed a month earlier.

Miit Ba began to cry as he told me this. I heard Miitini Aama sobbing in the kitchen. The house, which was so familiar to me, suddenly felt cold. My childhood fights with Resham, our games of marbles, and our football games with balls made out of bundled rags were all things of the past. Miit Ba used to give us bananas and Miitini Aama used to feed us yoghurt and *chiura*.

I'd made a mistake in coming.

'Seeing you reminds me of my son,' Miit Ba said, turning away from me. He clearly didn't want me to stay. I looked at his back. He was wearing a tattered vest. I could see hair peeping out from under his cap. There was no longer a single strand of black. His heels were dry and cracked like a field that hasn't seen rain. He was looking at the barley in the fields by his house and wouldn't turn towards me. I felt a surge of love for him. He didn't have the strength to look at me.

'Miit Ba,' I said, 'I'm your son too.'

'But we aren't your biological parents,' Miitini Aama said from the kitchen.

Her words pierced my heart like a knife. She had once loved me more than she loved her own son. She used to feed me milk with honey, saying a Brahmin's child loves sweet things. She used to beam with happiness when she saw me and would tease me, saying 'Look. A Bahun bird has landed in a Magar's nest.'

I used to tell my *miit*, 'Resham, you go and live at my house and I'll live in yours.' Resham used to kick me. There were times when he'd hit me hard, leaving me writhing in pain. Miitini Aama would sympathize with me and punish Resham. Once he kicked me in the balls and I nearly fainted. Miitini Aama had grabbed him by the hair, shaking him back and forth. I'd only stopped crying after Resham began crying too. I'd said, 'See, I got back on you!' Then, infuriated, he'd chased me. Another time, while chasing me, he fell off a terraced field and hurt his knee. Miit Ba worried then that his son would never become a soldier. After I left for Kathmandu, Resham joined the Nepal Police. He'd forgotten about me by then, but Miit Ba wrote, 'Resham's a policeman now.'

'Hey, skinny Bahun,' Resham used to tease me. I used to tell Miitini Aama when he called me names and she'd smack him. Resham hated it when I snitched to his mother. Sometimes I'd hit him, too, on his thighs, but he was so strong, it was like hitting a rock. I never won any of our fights. Once, after losing a fight, I stopped going to his house. After several days, Miit Ba came to my house to ask why I wasn't visiting them. 'The bananas are ripe and we have some tasty yoghurt for you,' he said, trying to lure me back. 'Miitini Aama's worried about you.'

'I won't come,' I said, suppressing a strong urge to go. 'I'll never come!'

Miit Ba left, frustrated. But I took a shortcut and reached his house before he did. 'Where have you been, Miit Ba?' I asked as he arrived.

'I've been to the market,' he said, disguising his surprise.

'But you haven't brought anything back,' I said.

'Oh, I've brought something,' he said.

'What?'

'Some smacks.'

'Really? How much did they cost?'

Two rupees per smack,' he said. 'Come here and I'll show you.' And he gently hit my cheeks.

Resham and I stopped fighting as we grew older. We learned that best friends shouldn't fight.

'Miit Ba,' I said now. He still stood, facing the fields of barley. Miitini Aama was still in the kitchen. Neither of them reacted.

So I left and went to Miit Kaakaa's house nearby. The front door was closed. I knocked but no one answered. The house was falling apart. It hadn't been painted for a long time. It appeared to have been empty for years. The kitchen garden was overgrown with nettles.

I walked down to a teashop.

At first, the shopkeeper didn't look pleased to see me, but he offered me a stool to sit on anyway. I put down my rucksack. Then I recognized Hari Lal Damai. He'd sewn vests and shorts for Resham and me when we were children. He used to play music at all the marriage ceremonies. When he played his *narasimha*, the veins in his neck used to swell as though they were going to burst. He used to blow the instrument so loudly that even people in the neighbouring villages could hear it.

With a long scarf, clean trousers, and cap, Hari Lal used to be the best-dressed man in any marriage procession.

'Your Miit Ba's terribly unhappy,' he said to me.

I didn't say anything.

'His eldest son's dead. The younger ones have joined the Maoists and there's no telling where they are,' he said. 'The two old folk never leave their house any more. They just sit there and listen to all the conflicting stories passersby tell them.'

I asked if he could make dinner for me, hoping I could stay there for the night.

'I don't have a spare bed,' he said.

'I've got a sleeping bag.'

He agreed.

He started a fire. 'I've been hoping to move to the plains,' he said. 'This village is so empty now. Sometimes the old couple weep, sometimes they mumble strange things. There are days when they don't say a single word and days when they never stop talking.' He asked, 'Do you want some bananas?'

'No, thanks.'

'Yoghurt?'

'No.'

'You loved bananas and yoghurt as a boy,' he said. 'You used to eat lots of it at Resham's house. Do you remember how we used to tease you?'

I remember that every time they saw me heading for Resham's house, people used to say, 'So, off to eat bananas and yoghurt?'

'When did you open this shop?' I asked.

'Two years ago,' Hari Lai said. 'I'm glad you feel you can stay here.'

'It's good there's no discrimination any more,' I said, referring to the low status of his occupational caste, tailors, in our society.

'Still, not many people come to my shop. It's mostly other Damai,' he said. 'But after people wearing pants and shirts like yours started coming, the discrimination has reduced.'

I was glad to see that Hari Lal had become a teashop owner. His shop wasn't particularly well organized but he sold tea and snacks as well as *daal bhaat*. In one corner of the shop was a sewing machine, the same hand-operated sewing machine I remembered from my childhood. He probably still used it in his free time.

'I'm sure you have to pay tax?' I asked.

'Yes. The people of...what do they call it? The People's Government. They collect taxes.'

He put more wood on the fire and blew on it to stoke the flames. 'I really pity the old man,' he said, going back to Miit Ba. 'Sometimes he comes here asking for a box of matches. Then, after I give him one, he gives it back to me, saying he has one at home already.' I looked at him as he went back to stoking the fire. 'Sometimes he comes and asks for rock salt and when I tell him I have some, he just turns and walks away.' I helped him, blowing on the fire as well.

He lit an unfiltered cigarette and was smoking quietly when we heard a noise outside. Some people had arrived. They called for the shopkeeper.

He went out.

'Did anyone stay here last night?' someone asked.

Hari Lal asked, 'Why? What's the matter?'

'Just answer the question.'

'No. No one was here.'

'Then did you hear anyone walking past your shop last night?'

'No,' said Hari Lal. 'I would've woken up if I'd heard anything. I'm a light sleeper these days. I wake up even if just a dog goes by.

'Are you sure you didn't hear anyone?'

'Why would I lie? What's this about anyway?'

'Listen, you nosey old bastard,' a man said. 'One of the prisoners the Maoists let out of jail in the district headquarters was a thief. He'd stolen a statue from a temple. A night later, the son of a bitch came back and stole the same statue again. They say he went this way.'

'Not the old statue of Lord Shiva?' said Hari Lal.

The men left, telling him to stay alert.

'Once a thief, always a thief,' Hari Lal said, coming back into the shop. 'That bastard couldn't break the habit even after going to jail!'

He began to cook some *dhido* and potato curry.

'You're not saying anything,' he said. 'Am I talking too much?'

'I'm just feeling sad,' I said.

'Did you want to stay at your Miit Ba's house?'

'No.'

'It's for the best. He's lost his senses. He says things he doesn't mean.'

'It seems like there's no one else in the village,' I said.

'There's another old couple. They're no better off than your Miit Ba and Miitini Aama. They have poor eyesight and can't go anywhere. They're waiting for their sons to come back. One's in the army and the other's joined the rebels. The one in the army sent them a message saying that if they wanted to see him, they should come to Kathmandu because it's too dangerous for him to come back here. But the old folks can't go to Kathmandu.' He sighed. 'Their grief's going to kill them one day.'

He served me *dhido*. The potato curry was over-cooked. I took a few mouthfuls, washing them down with water.

There was a noise outside as I ate. It was Miit Ba.

'Hari!' he called loudly.

'Yes?' Hari Lai went out.

'Have you seen my Miit Chora?'

'No, I haven't seen him,' Hari Lal lied to protect me.

I wondered if I should say something.

'Don't lie to an old man, you bastard,' Miit Ba snapped. 'He went this way. Were your eyes snatched by a monkey?'

'I swear I haven't seen him,' Hari Lal said. 'See. My eyes are fine.'

'Bastard!' Miit Ba said, annoyed. 'You think I don't know your tricks? You can spot a cat in the dark. You're the first one to know who's eloped with whom. And now you're trying to tell me you haven't seen my Miit Chora?'

'Why would I lie to you?' Hari Lal said, adding one lie to another. 'I did see a shadow go by. But that was a while ago. Don't you think I'd recognize your Miit Chora if I saw him?'

'Maybe it was just a dream,' the old man said softly. 'But I thought our Miit Chora came to see us. Hari, if he should drop by, ask him to come to our house. We'd love to see him.'

Miit Ba left. Hari Lai came back in.

I decided I couldn't stay away. I washed my hands and rinsed my mouth. Then I followed Miit Ba back to his house, leaving a hundred rupee note on the bench for Hari Lal.

'But I don't want your money!' Hari Lal called, running after me with the note in his hand.

CHAPTER NINETEEN

I was walking on my own. A few people walking on the same trail had already passed me. I saw a little girl sitting on a stone beside the path, picking burrs off her dress. I was about to walk by when she stopped me.

'Your friends have gone. Why are you so late?' she said crossly. I was surprised to hear her reprimand a stranger old enough to be her father.

I just smiled, but she stopped picking the burrs off her dress, waiting for my answer.

'Why didn't you make them wait for me?' I said.

'How could I do that, old man?'

I was amused at being called an old man. It made me laugh.

She went back to picking the burrs off her dress. I sat down beside her.

'What are you looking at?' she asked crossly.

'I'm trying to figure out what you look like,' I said.

'What do I look like?'

'An apple.'

'Can a person look like an apple, Uncle?'

'I just mean you're cute.'

'Nonsense,' she said. 'Apples aren't cute.'

I was taken aback for a moment. Hearing the word 'nonsense' made me think of Palpasa. It cheered me up.

'You're right,' I said. 'Apples can be tasty but not cute.'

The little girl had a runny nose. The snot was running down to her upper lip. She tried to sniff it back up, still intent on picking the burrs out of her dress.

'How did your dress get so many thorns?' I asked.

'I went into the bushes to pee. I didn't know there'd be burrs. Why don't you help me pick them off?'

I picked some burrs from her dress. She wasn't paying attention to anything else.

'What's your name?' I asked.

'Nanu,' she said.

'That's a pretty name,' I said.

'Nonsense. Names can't be pretty,' she said.

'I'm sorry. You're right. Flowers can be pretty, not names.'

She agreed, still sniffing.

'I like flowers. I like marigolds,' she said.

I tried to help her pick the burrs off her dress, but it was difficult.

'You don't even know how to pick off burrs,' she chided me.

'I've never done it before,' I admitted.

'Who picks them off for you?' she asked.

'I've never had burrs in my clothes.'

'You never go into the bushes to pee?'

I burst out laughing. 'I do. But my clothes have never picked up burrs.'

'That must be because you wear pants.'

Once again, I burst into laughter. 'Such naughty burrs,' I said, 'troubling a little girl!'

'Burrs don't have eyes,' she said. 'They don't know whose clothes they're sticking to.'

'But people have eyes,' I said. 'Why didn't you use your eyes when you went into the bushes?'

'My eyes are too small.'

'Because you're a little girl?'

'I'm not a little girl,' she said, standing as tall as she could on the rock I was sitting on.

'Where are you going after this?' I asked.

'To my *miitini*'s house.'

I felt as if a thorn had pricked my heart. 'What have you brought for your *miitini?*' I asked.

'A banana,' she said. 'Are you going to your *miit*'s house?'

'I'm just coming back from my *miit*'s house,' I said.

'What did they give you at your *miit*'s house?'

'Bananas. My Miit Ba gave me bananas.'

'Are you hiding them so no one else will eat them?'

'Would you like one?'

'I eat only one banana a day,' she said, 'and I ate one this morning.'

'Why don't you have one more today?' I said, opening my rucksack. 'And here's one for your *miitini* as well.'

I gave her two bananas. She peeled one and ate it. 'It's sweet,' she said.

'That's because I put sugar in it.'

'You're silly!'

'How else could it taste so sweet?'

'Oh,' she said, confused.

'They sprinkle sugar on the banana fields. Don't you know that?'

She smiled. ' I don't believe you.'

'You're right. I'm only kidding,' I said.

'But why do bananas taste sweet?' she asked, growing serious.

'Go to school. You'll learn things like that.',

'Did you go to school?'

'Yes.'

'But you don't know the answer to that question.'

'Some fruits are sweet, some are sour, and others don't have much taste,' I said. 'And even the sweet ones have different flavours. If you go to school, you'll learn lots of different things.'

'Our school's closed,' she said. 'Is yours open?'

We started walking together. She took my hand. In the other, she held the banana for her *miitini*.

'Do you know what?' she said. 'It's my birthday today.'

'Today?'

'Yes. Mummy says so.'

'How old are you today?'

'Five.'

'Since it's your birthday, your *miitini* should be giving you a gift,' I said.

'There aren't any bananas in my *miitini*'s field.'

Just as I smiled we heard a loud noise. I stopped walking. 'What was that?' I asked.

' I think a rock fell down a cliff,' she said.

'No, it sounded different.'

'The further a rock falls, the louder the noise it makes,' she said. 'Don't you know that?'

We started walking again. She said, 'Your friends must have gone a long way by now.'

'They're not my friends,' I said.

'Good,' she said. 'Then you can come with me to my *miitini*'s house. You can stay there tonight.'

I was surprised by her invitation. 'Stay in a stranger's house?' I asked.

'I'll ask my Miit Ba,' she said.

A thorn pierced my heart again. 'What will you tell him?' I asked.

'That you've come with me.'

'What if he asks you who I am?'

'I'll tell him I met you on the way.'

'Well, what if he says no?'

'We'll give him the rest of your bananas.'

I smiled. The night before, at Miit Ba's house, I hadn't slept a wink. I'd spent the whole night attending to the old couple, who seemed to have become children in their grief.

I asked the little girl, 'What if your Miit Ba still says no, even after we give him the bananas?'

'He'll agree.'

'But what if he doesn't?'

'I'll tell my *miitini* to start crying. Miit Ba will have to agree just to make her stop.'

I laughed.

'Do you ever want to go to Kathmandu?' I asked.

'No,' she said. 'That's a scary place. Even kings get killed there.'

'Aren't you scared here?'

'Sometimes. My daddy listens to the radio and says people are being killed. Do you know where people go when they die?'

'No.'

'You don't know anything!'

'Where do they go?' I asked.

'How would I know?'

'Are we near your *miitini*'s house?'

'It's just nearby,' she said. 'Why? Are you tired?'

Suddenly, at a fork in the road, she stopped. Below us, people were gathered in front of a house. It looked like there'd been some kind of accident there. A man with a sad expression on his face came up and took my little friend in his arms.

'Nanu,' he told her. 'your *miitini*'s dead. She picked up a bomb when she was playing, and it exploded in her hands.'

Oh my God! My whole body began to tremble. I stood there shocked. That was the noise we'd heard.

Nanu dropped the bananas and dashed towards the house, crying. She ran like a kite being pulled by a string.

CHAPTER TWENTY

This climb never used to be so difficult. I'd climbed this trail a hundred times when I was a boy. Now I wiped the sweat from my brow and took a deep breath. From a teashop, two strangers looked at me with open curiosity. Past the teashop, the trail forked. For the first time in my life, I didn't know which way to go.

The stares of the strangers needled me. The lady who owned the shop had aged a lot since I'd last seen her. She set a kettle of tea to boil. The strangers were talking to each other. 'Her husband died a senseless death,' I heard one say, referring to the owner. I heard the tinkle of a teaspoon against a cup as the teashop owner stood in a corner with a shawl over her head, mixing sugar into the tea. 'They took him to the cliff over there and shot him. The radio said that he was a terrorist.'

The teashop owner gave me a vacant look. I gave up the idea of having a cup of tea. I couldn't stay there. I wished the sun wasn't so hot. This hill shouldn't have been so hard to climb. It wasn't that steep, but my legs felt weak. I didn't know why I felt so drained of energy. I felt as if I was walking in a funeral procession. Though I was wearing shoes, I felt as if I was stepping barefoot on hot rocks. My rucksack wasn't really heavy, but it felt like a bag of stones a drill instructor might make a recruit carry for punishment.

'Where do you think that man's from?' one of the strangers whispered to the other as I was leaving. 'It's difficult to tell these days. They dress in disguise and speak other people's languages perfectly, even copying their accents. If you let someone sleep in your house, thinking he's from the army, the next day your house's destroyed. The same thing happens when you give shelter to someone you think comes from the jungle.'

I turned and looked at them one last time. They were still staring at me.

I walked on, feeling weary at the thought of perhaps not being able to sleep well for a second night in a row. No one here believed I was neutral. I'd become a stranger in my own home district. Who was I? My identity was linked to my profession, but who'd respect my profession here? What had my paintings done for these hills? No one knew my art. My identity as an artist wouldn't win anyone's trust.

I realized Siddhartha had done me a favour by bringing me back to these hills. He'd persuaded me to come back to face all the fears of the world.

The air was different from the way it was when I was a boy. The flowers had taken on different shapes. Everything had become discordant. The hills were the same but they were tense. Even the rocks seemed aggressive. Siddhartha had urged me to come here, had challenged me to come, but he hadn't accompanied me all the way. He'd shown me the way, then left. It was as though he'd blindfolded and abducted me. When I took off the blindfold, he was gone. Of course, I was in my home territory, walking my trails, touching my earth, and looking at the forests where I'd whistled as a boy, but there was a difference. Now I was scared.

I thought I heard someone cough nearby, but perhaps it was just my imagination.

I was walking uphill, but it seemed I was sliding downwards.

I stopped, not knowing what was happening.

A man came towards me from above though it seemed as though he was also coming towards me from below. I was facing south, yet I could see the Himalayas. I rubbed my eyes and looked at the man.

Impossible! He looked exactly like me. His physical appearance was exactly like mine. He was wearing my clothes and carrying my rucksack. He, too, had a sleeping bag tied to the bottom of his rucksack. He, too, was unshaven. When I stopped, he stopped too. I looked at him. He looked at me. I took a step forward. He did too. I stopped. He stopped. I took another step forward and we bumped into each other.

'I've come back to my village after ten years,' he said, as if we knew each other.

Frozen with terror, I couldn't say anything:

'It looks like I won't find a place to sleep again today,' he said. 'No one believes I'm an artist.'

I still couldn't say a single word.

'I reached my village but realized I couldn't stay there,' he said.

Why was he saying these things? Who was he? Was he trying to frighten me? Was he playing some sort of game by wearing my clothes and copying my behaviour?

'The night I was in the district headquarters, there was an attack,' he went on, telling me about my own experiences. He was looking straight at me. It was like looking in a mirror. I pinched myself. 'The worst thing was finding out my *miit* had been killed,' he said. 'I spent the night at Miit Ba's house, but I didn't sleep a wink all night.'

I grew truly frightened. I stammered, 'And did you meet a little girl along the way?'

'How do you know that?' he asked, growing suspicious.

'I'm just guessing.' I said.

'She was going to her *miitini*'s house. She had no idea her *mittini* had just died.'

'She was carrying a banana,' I said.

'Yes,' he said. 'But how do you know that?'

'Just guessing.'

Before I knew what was happening, the man took out a pistol and aimed it straight at me. 'Tell me who you are,' he said, menacingly.

Trembling, I looked at him helplessly. 'I'm an artist,' I said.

'Liar!' he thundered.

I racked my brain for something to say but nothing came. He put the gun to my temple. I had no idea what to do.

'You can't scare me,' I said at last. 'There are no bullets in your gun.'

That confused him. For a moment he looked vulnerable. He lowered the gun.

Summoning all the strength I had, I kicked him. He fell. I grabbed the gun and ran some way off. Then I turned around. He was standing in the same spot, looking at me like a child. I aimed the pistol at him. He crouched as though trying to dodge a bullet. Then, as if remembering there were no bullets in the gun, he stood up again. I pointed the gun at the sky and pulled the trigger. The gun was loaded and went off with an incredible bang. The man looked very upset. I aimed the gun at him again. He ducked. Then I threw the gun at him. He picked it up and ran downhill.

'Thanks,' he called out. I watched him go. Even from behind he looked exactly like me.

After the shock wore off, I started to laugh. How absurd the whole thing had been! I reached a teashop and stopped, trying to suppress my laughter. But it was as though I were a child. I couldn't stop chuckling. Finally all my laughter burst out in one loud guffaw.

'Do you want tea?' the shopkeeper asked warily.

'No,' I said, between laughs.

Laughing, I moved on.

'What a strange person,' I heard the shopkeeper say behind me. 'He laughs alone.'

A customer said, 'He must have lost his mind.'

From a distance, I saw a man I'd met on the train from Goa to Gorakhpur. He was in the Indian Army. When he recognized me, he greeted me but with a dejected expression. I was hoping he'd invite me to drink rum with him as he'd done on the train. We'd had to keep it hidden from the conductor. Instead, he continued to look morose.

'Where are you heading?' I asked.

'I'm on my way back to India,' he said. 'I only stopped because I saw you.'

It was good to meet someone with whom I'd once shared some light-hearted moments. He followed me along the trail without saying anything. I was still giggling now and then, thinking about the strange encounter.

'Why are you laughing, brother?' he asked.

'Because of this unexpected meeting with you,' I said.

But this didn't seem to lighten his mood. He wiped the sweat from his brow with a handkerchief and let out a long sigh. Then he said, 'I couldn't persuade my son.'

'Did you meet him?' I asked.

'Yes. He talked to me about politics. I tried but I couldn't convince him to leave the rebels and come back with me.'

Just then, his youngest son came running up behind us. The man stopped to talk to him. It looked like they'd be a while so I bade him farewell.

There was a cliff ahead. As I walked along the edge, I thought again about the absurd encounter and chuckled. What a stupid man I'd met. He'd taken out his gun with such confidence but completely lost his presence of mind when I told him it wasn't loaded. He'd believed me. What a fool!

I was full of self-congratulations at having saved myself. If it hadn't been for my brilliant idea, I'd probably have been dead by now. I remembered the kick I'd given him and guffawed. The kick had landed right in his stomach! He'd fallen like a stone and I'd immediately grabbed his gun. It was as though he'd given it to me, like an obedient child! The fool! Why carry a gun if you don't know whether it's loaded or not? He'd even aimed it at me. How gullible of him to believe what I'd said off the top of my head. He'd even thanked me when I tossed the gun back to him. He was the biggest fool I'd ever met.

I suppose he was frightened of me. That's why he'd taken out the gun. He might've wanted to pre-empt an attack, in case I had a gun as well. Thinking about the whole thing, I just wanted to laugh and laugh and, because I was alone, there was no need to hold back. I chortled to my heart's content and afterwards felt lighter for it. But even then I kept laughing. The fool! Why had he taken out that gun? And how could he have believed me when I said it wasn't loaded? I laughed and laughed.

'Hey!' someone shouted.

I turned around. It was him again. He was coming towards me with the same gun pointed at me.

'What are you laughing at?' he asked. My laughter died.

'Nothing,' I said.

He came right up to me and held the pistol to my forehead.

I started to tremble.

'Were you gloating about how clever you were?' he asked.

'No. No, I wasn't.' I was close to tears.

'What were you laughing about then?'

'Nothing.'

'Get ready. I'm going to shoot you now,' he said. 'Look the other way.'

Obediently, I did exactly as he told me, my whole body shaking like a leaf.

'Don't tremble so much,' he said. 'I might miss.'

At that, I burst out laughing again.

'Why the hell are you laughing?' he snapped.

In between gasps of laugher, I said, 'The thought that I'll never be able to laugh again makes me want to laugh.'

'Then laugh,' he said. 'I'll give you one minute to laugh.'

I seized that opportunity to kick him in the stomach. And he fell down exactly as he'd done before. I grabbed his pistol in exactly the same way. I took a few steps back and fired it in the air. The shot created a deafening noise. He stood up. I threw the pistol back at him. He thanked me again and ran downhill.

Continuing uphill, I turned and watched him go. He was a pitiful sight. I wondered again why a person like that would carry a gun. Why point it at someone? And then why worry you might miss? Why allow someone a minute's reprieve for laughter? And why thank your quarry for returning the gun at the end of it all?

I burst into laughter again.

The man I'd met on the train from Goa caught up with me some time later. 'You're laughing a lot today,' he said.

'Sorry,' I said

'No. It's good to laugh sometimes.'

'There's plenty of time to cry.'

'Very few people live their lives laughing,' he said.

'I doubt there's anyone.'

He nodded. 'Even the king died crying.'

'So many people are dying; so many people are killing.'

'I came home laughing,' he said. 'But I'm going back in tears.'

'Life's funny,' I told him. As we parted, I said, 'I hope we meet again on a train some day.'

But before he could say anything, a crowd of rebels appeared out of the blue and surrounded him.

'What's this?' he cried out, frightened.

'You can't go back to India,' one man said sternly. 'You have to come with us. We'll give you guns and bullets. Everyone dies some day. We want you to die for your country.'

The man tried to get away but in vain. One of the rebels signalled for me to move on, but I stayed where I was, watching. The rebel again signalled for me to leave. They didn't want me, only the other man. 'You're experienced in the art of war,' one of them was urging him as I left. 'We'll put you in charge of a company.'

I moved on. Eventually their voices became inaudible. Again I was alone. What if my double were to reappear? What a fool he was! I began to laugh again. There wasn't far to go.

CHAPTER TWENTY ONE

Walking ahead of me was a woman who'd been widowed the day after her wedding. I felt as if I were stepping on her tears. To one side of the trail was an injured bird that had fallen from a tree. One of its wings was caught on a branch. The flapping of its wings devastated me. That and the sound of the widow's breathing were the saddest music I'd ever heard. This was the last climb of my trek and the hardest one yet.

Kathmandu was far away from this fog-bound hill. There was no way I could return to the capital dressed in my ragged, stained shirt. It would be dangerous to do so. I'd raise too many questions. I needed to clean myself up and clear my vision before I returned. But I was beginning to think I would only reach Kathmandu as a news item about another casualty of war.

Walking behind the widow was an elderly man. He was on his way to claim his son's body. His sighs had become the sighs of the hills. He was leaning on a walking stick, but it was hard to tell whether the stick was supporting him or he was supporting the stick. Still, he walked more quickly than me. There were flowers around us, but they had no perfume. They'd been picked, thrown down, and trodden under foot. A small flowering bush by the side of the trail was covered in dung. As we climbed, the hill grew steeper, adding to the woes of the stooped old man. The hills in which he'd invested his sweat, blood, and tears had become a burden to him. Now he was in a hurry to claim his dead son.

'I just buried one son,' he said. 'Now I have to identify the body of another.' He hobbled along, bereft of hope.

Behind me was an old woman. She was also on her way to claim a body, the body of her daughter, which had been crammed into a basket and placed on a riverbank across the hill. The old woman was now forced to identify her own flesh and blood, though the blood had long stopped flowing from the body. She'd identify her daughter by her face, the same sweet face she'd held to her breast all those years ago. She'd never have to worry now about getting this daughter married. She'd never see her wearing bangles, a *pote*, or *sindur*. The old woman had managed to send her daughter to school so she could learn to read and write. But she hadn't been able to teach her the difference between right and wrong.

The old woman was almost running as she climbed the foggy hill with her shawl covering her face. I didn't have the courage to look at her. She was like an arid, sun-scorched hillside without even one drop of water. No streams flowed. Even her eyes were dry.

I was climbing surrounded by bereaved people. But when we came to the crest of the hill, I'd take a different path.

I wanted to meet Siddhartha before I went back to Kathmandu. How long had it been since I'd last seen him? We'd walked together for a few days, then he'd left me, saying 'You'll be safer walking without me.'

'I want everyone to be safe,' I'd told him. 'You're talking about a temporary, artificial thing,' he replied. 'You need permanent peace for everyone to be safe. And for permanent peace, the state must negotiate with the people.'

'But if you want negotiation, why are you and your people trying to bring the state to its knees by killing these innocent villagers?' I'd asked angrily.

'Who's killing them? How and where are they being killed?' he'd said, turning to go. 'You're an artist. Go and see the situation with your own eyes. That's all I want. My best wishes go with you.'

Where was Siddhartha now? What had he been doing all this time? How could he bear to be responsible for these widowed hills? How could he stand to see these innocent people being turned into widows or orphans or losing their children? Or was he only thinking about the next attack on a district headquarters? What was he doing? How and when could I meet him? Which path should I take?

At a pass, I came across some people gathered in a group, listening to a small transistor radio. They looked afraid when they saw me. Why? I didn't have a gun. I had only a few sheets of paper, some pencils, and a paint brush. Why be afraid of me? I was just an artist. I wanted to meet Siddhartha. Was he somewhere nearby? I wondered. One man stiffened. He took me by the arm and led me into the bushes, away from the group. All I could see was the sky, with a bank of clouds drifting northwards.

'Are you really who you say you are?' he asked, eyeing me suspiciously. He frisked me and searched my rucksack. He even searched inside my shoes and made me unzip my sleeping bag.

Suddenly, he pushed me down so I was crouching in the undergrowth. A helicopter had appeared overhead. When it disappeared behind a hill, the man took me by the arm again, saying, 'Follow me.'

He took me back to the path and handed me over to someone else. The other man said, 'Please don't ask me any questions. But I must warn you: if there's a confrontation, you're on your own. Come on.'

I followed him. We entered the woods, brushing past thorn bushes and low branches and jumping over gullies and ditches. Eventually we came to a solitary house where the man handed me over to someone else. This man looked me over, then started walking. I followed him, assuming that was what I was supposed to do.

The trail narrowed, like a pencil line on paper, a trail easily erased by rain. In some parts it didn't even look like a trail.

'If you make any trouble, I'll shoot you,' the man said without even looking back at me.

'Who, me?'

'Yes, you,' he said, still not turning back. 'Don't talk so loudly.'

'Why not?'

'Even the plants here have ears.'

I babbled, 'I've never seen a plant with ears!'

'Act your age,' he snapped, pushing aside a branch in his path.

'I've just turned thirty two,' I volunteered.

'I didn't ask your age,' he hissed. 'I was just reminding you that you aren't a child.'

'Okay. I'm reminded.'

'Good,' he said, or maybe I just thought he did.

He stopped near a cliff. I stopped as well. I wondered if we were supposed to jump off. Across the gorge was another cliff face and, far below us, I could see some thatched huts in a forest. There was also a school with a corrugated tin roof. The reflection of the sun on the tin flashed in my eyes. The man whistled. The sound echoed along the gorge. A similar whistle answered, but there was no accompanying echo.

'Do we have to jump down?' I asked.

'Do you want to?' he replied, without even bothering to look at me.

'Just asking.'

'Don't ask any questions,' he snapped. Moving left, he jumped over a log. I realized I hadn't even seen his face clearly. I guessed he was in his mid-twenties. If we ever met again, I thought, I wouldn't be able to recognize him. His voice was distinctive though. He spoke very quickly and softly.

I followed him. We heard another helicopter nearby but couldn't see it. It seemed the security forces had intensified their patrolling of the area.

As we walked along the edge of the cliff, the man said, 'If you fall from here, not even the eagles will find you.'

Further ahead, we met a girl. She pretended not to see us. The man hung back and I realized I was supposed to follow the girl. The man disappeared before I even realized he was leaving. The girl led the way without so much as glancing at me.

'Are you married, Bahini?' I asked, curious about her.

'Does that matter?' she asked in return.

The trail sloped downhill. She walked fast, as if to make me sweat.

'Those pants suit you,' I said, unable to control my babbling.

With quiet composure, she said, 'It seems you've never seen a bullet.'

'What makes you say that?'

'It you had, you wouldn't talk about such trivial things.'

I saw a gun tucked into the waistband of her pants, covered by a shawl. We arrived at a stream. An old log served as a bridge. She stepped onto the slippery log, planting her sports shoes confidently on it, and walked across quickly.

'You should be the heroine in an action movie,' I said, trying, stupidly, to make light conversation.

'Didn't my friends tell you to be quiet?' she growled.

'They told me not to ask questions.'

'Then why...?'

'Why what?'

'Why are you talking to me?

'I can't seem to help it,' I confessed.

'Remember, I'm not responsible for your safety,' she said threateningly.

'Is there danger ahead?' I asked.

'That all depends on how you behave.'

She crossed a wheat field and entered a forest as any woman looking for fodder might. But she was carrying a modern weapon in her pants. An instrument of death had become an extension of her body, a snake embracing a flower. She was a simple village girl. But she was also a rebel. I needed to be careful what I said to her.

She walked so quickly and lightly that it was hard for me to keep up. She might have been a doe. Where was she taking me? She didn't seem to care if I was following or not. I quickened my pace as she scampered up a hillock.

'The man who marries you will be lucky,' I said.

She stopped and put a hand on her gun.

'Are you in love?' I blurted out and immediately regretted my words.

She took out her gun, glaring at me.

I trembled. I apolozised profusely, 'Sorry! Sorry!'

After that, I followed her in dutiful silence, as if I were in a mediation centre where all conversation was banned. But then I began to think: whole villages are in mourning, hundreds of houses have been abandoned, thousands of people face an uncertain future. And this girl's pointing a gun at me. Who does she think she is? Does she have the courage or the capability to solve our nation's problems and create a prosperous future for us? No. All she had was a gun, and she was using that gun to intimidate me.

'You know, you can just tell me what you want,' I said. 'You don't need to threaten me with your gun.'

'Where words don't work, bullets do,' she said simply.

'So you've taken up arms because no one listens to you?'

'What other choice do we have?' she asked, then added, 'I wish our words would work with you.'

'I've seen bullets,' I said, pointing to the hole in my trousers. 'I survived a bullet, see?'

'You might not be so lucky next time.'

'Can I tell you something, Bahini?' I said, 'Don't get angry, but that gun doesn't look good in your hands.'

She said combatively, 'You mean only bangles look good on a woman?'

'Well, at least bangles don't kill,' I said.

'This gun's for my protection,' she said. 'I'm strong because I have this gun.'

'But how long will that last?'

'I'll live courageously as long as I can.'

'But why are you so intent on cutting your life short?'

She said, 'A long life without purpose is a waste of time.'

'And life becomes purposeful when you carry a gun?'

'It's better than wearing bangles just to show I'm a slave to some man!'

I ventured, 'Please don't be angry but...I...Are you a virgin?'

At this, she took out her gun and pointed it straight at me. And I couldn't help myself: I laughed like a lunatic.

In sheer frustration, she fired a bullet in the air.

My laughter died immediately, like a balloon which had suddenly burst. I raised my hands, closing my eyes.

All of a sudden, some men appeared from nowhere. They grabbed me and blindfolded me. They also frisked me and searched my rucksack.

At one point I could tell we were walking uphill. When my blindfold was lifted, I found myself in a stunningly beautiful valley. I was surprised to see the girl beside me with a gag in her mouth. Were her comrades punishing her for some reason? There was an orange grove in the distance and I could see someone walking through it. It was Siddhartha, I couldn't see his bodyguards. He was alone.

'Look! Siddhartha!' I said excitedly, pointing towards him. The girl wriggled around. She tried to say something through the gag. Her hands were bound. I couldn't understand it. 'Hey, Siddhartha!' I shouted. 'Siddhartha!'

One of the men who'd blindfolded me said, 'Shut up!' He took out a gun. I saw Siddhartha reach up to pick an orange. He saw us and I waved to him. But instead of waving back, he threw the orange to the ground, turned, and began to run. The men began to run after him with guns in their hands. I couldn't understand what was happening. I just stood there beside the girl, watching them run. The girl kicked me and tried to say something again. I untied her hands and she pulled the gag from her mouth. By then, the men had caught up with Siddhartha. He was completely surrounded. I heard three shots and he fell.

I was speechless with shock. The girl covered her face and sank down onto the grass. I couldn't believe what had happened. A helicopter appeared from nowhere. It hovered just above the ground, its engine still running. The men got in. The dust thrown up by the spinning of its rotors temporarily blinded me.

As the helicopter disappeared behind a hill, I looked at the girl. She was writhing on the ground, crying inconsolably. I ran towards Siddhartha.

He was lying in a pool of blood but was still breathing. He held my hand and opened his mouth to say something.

'I'm so sorry, Siddhartha,' I said with tears in my eyes. 'This is my fault! I didn't realize who those men were!'

He moved his lips. Blood was pouring out of his mouth. I couldn't understand what he was trying to say. I looked into his eyes. They tore my heart out. They were still so perfect and still so bright. His eyes found my face. But as he stared at me, the light behind his eyes flickered and died, like a candle snuffed out by the wind. I sobbed. I screamed. I wept like a child.

I closed his eyes, laid him down among the mustard plants, and sat by his body beneath an orange tree, my tears falling onto him as his blood soaked my clothing.

CHAPTER TWENTY TWO

There was no suspension bridge over the river any more. It'd been bombed a while earlier. How, then, could I get across? Clueless, I looked around. There was no one in sight, though there was a boat on the far shore.

I was still soaked in Siddhartha's blood. I washed the blood off my hands, shirt, and trousers. The river didn't look the same. There wasn't a single person around.

'Hello,' I called towards the boat.

Only the cold breeze answered.

'Hello!"

The boat lay motionless.

'Hello! Hello!' I screamed like a madman.

Why was I here on the shore of this river? I should never have come to these hills! Why had Siddhartha brought me here? Why had he brought me back to the place I was born, where I grew up and made friends, to the same forests, hills, and cliffs I remembered from my childhood?

'Hello! Hello!'

I began to feel feverish. I felt as if I were drowning in a sea of sand. I whistled loudly, but there was still no answer. 'Hello!' I screamed in agony. All I heard was the echo of my own voice.

Near evening, a boatman finally appeared on the opposite shore. He rowed the boat towards me, using all his strength. I finally felt better. I'd soon be back in Kathmandu. The person who'd brought me here was dead and I'd helped his killers identify him. He'd been unarmed and alone in that orange grove. He didn't even have his bodyguards. He'd been helpless, like a deer surrounded by hunters.

Had Siddhartha really been killed because of me? The girl wouldn't have fired her pistol in the air if I hadn't babbled so inanely. Those men wouldn't have ambushed us, and if I hadn't called Siddhartha by name, they wouldn't have recognized him. Was I an accomplice in his death? Was I a murderer?

Reaching me, the boatman said, 'You look lost in thought. Climb in.'

I sat in the boat. With every stroke of the oars, ripples rose in the ocean of my thoughts. Would Siddhartha still be alive if I hadn't tried to find him? No, I didn't think so. He'd told me he lived his life on a razor's edge. But that was his choice. He'd chosen to put aside his fears and walk through fire, but he'd also forced others to walk through fire with him. He would've been killed anyway, even if I hadn't come looking for him. The helicopter was there anyway. If not then, he would've been killed some other day. He'd accepted the possibility of an untimely death. He wasn't afraid. But then I remembered that moment: he'd tried to run like a deer but was surrounded immediately.

They'd shot him in the stomach and in the head. And he'd fallen like a log. He'd tried to tell me something but didn't have time. If he'd been shot one fewer time, perhaps he would've been able to utter one word. I still felt the warmth of his blood. The river was deep, the boatman was rowing mechanically. We were heading eastwards.

While travelling with Siddhartha, I'd come to see our country with new eyes. I'd seen the potential for restructuring society. I'd felt I could produce a new painting, write a poem, or create a melody.

Siddhartha had chosen to walk on the edge of a knife, but he'd also turned the hills into a knife. So many young people had followed him mindlessly and taken up arms without understanding the consequences. They were exhilarated by the power guns gave them. But such power brought nothing but devastation.

'I heard a leader was killed up there somewhere,' the boatman said. As he spoke, some water splashed from his oars into my face. 'Have you heard anything?'

I couldn't say anything. I couldn't speak. I couldn't express myself at all. Siddhartha had been close to my soul, but now I was stained with his blood. How could I reveal that? Had anyone else been through what I'd suffered?

Siddhartha had said he'd joined the movement to give a new tune to the times. Today he was nothing but ashes. No, today he lay buried somewhere in an unmarked grave. In a while, he'd be nothing but bones. But I'd always have the memory of his life and his dreams. He'd been out of tune with the times and was dead as a consequence. And I was the one who'd felt his last heartbeat.

Dry leaves floated on the surface of the river, symbolizing the end of life. But somewhere in the hills, the tree from which they'd fallen was probably still standing, waiting for the season to change and new leaves to grow.

The boatman strained against the current. 'It's so sad to see war in our country,' he said. 'It's terrible to see our own people die. Don't you think so, Bhai?'

His words shook me. I hadn't just seen the war: I'd been through it, and now I was escaping it. His words brought so many scenes back to my mind. He made me think of the girl picking oranges, the little girl going to meet her *miitini* with a banana in her hand, old people grieving for the loss of their children, the owner of the lodge and her son, people who'd seen bombs explode, children who'd stopped going to school, villagers who'd advised me to walk carefully, and exhausted policemen leaning like logs against a crumbling wall. I felt dizzy. Was I waking up from a nightmare:'

How could it be that I'd met a shadow who looked like me, had my name, wore my clothes, shared my experiences, and even aimed a gun at me? How afraid I'd been. I'd been haunted by my own thoughts as I climbed that hill. I'd been surrounded by images of widows, orphans, and old people who'd lost their children. I was falling apart. Even when I saw a real person, I saw the face of a widow, painted by my fear. I was losing my balance as I walked, sometimes in silence, sometimes laughing for no reason. I must've lost my senses; otherwise, I'd never have said such idiotic things to the girl who led me to Siddhartha. My thoughts had been all over the place. I'd had no equilibrium. It was the warmth of Siddhartha's blood which had brought me back to reality. I'd been walking through a war zone.

'I don't want to talk,' the boatman said, 'but it just comes out, even though it doesn't make sense to speak.'

'What do you mean?' I asked.

'I don't have a clue who you are,' he said. 'If I say one thing, you might take out a gun and shoot me. If I say something else, you might still take out a gun.'

There he was, steering the boat which was taking me across the river. But he looked so worried. He was doing me a service, but I was making him feel nervous. He was helping me to cross safely but saw me as a possible threat to his life. I'd lost my identity. No one knew who I really was, I was making people uneasy. Still, the boatman was rowing the boat.

'This boat's my livelihood,' he said. 'I feed my wife and children by rowing it. But I fear this boat might get me killed some day.'

'Why do you say that, Dai?'

'Someone will ask, "Why did you take that person across the river? Who was he? Why didn't you report it?" and one day I won't have the right answer.'

There was nothing I could say to that. I watched him cut through the water with his oar, the marks it left disappearing in a swirl. He'd been doing this work for years, but the water flowed on, undivided.

Siddhartha had tried to divert these waters. 'We're creating a new flow,' he'd said. But now, like a bubble, he'd floated to the surface and disappeared. Or perhaps he'd been sucked down into a whirlpool.

This river marked the end of a phase in my life. I reached the far shore thinking that I'd left Siddhartha on the other side, that the only things travelling with me now were memories. I'd left Siddhartha at peace on the other side.

I was returning to Kathmandu after going through this strange phase. I'd have to tell people about my friend who'd become a rebel leader and was killed as a result. He lived on only in my mind, as formless and fluid as water. How could I capture his shape and sound? Now this journey, a month-long dream, was going to end. I was about to begin a new phase.

Before leaving, I wanted to reassure the boatman. I'd tell anyone he chose who I really was. I didn't know to which side the checkpoints ahead belonged. If I didn't convince them about my identity, the boatman could be in trouble. I decided I'd disclose my full identity but never, of course, my relationship with Siddhartha.

I was in danger from both sides.

CHAPTER TWENTY THREE

Where the river widened, I reached the last valley of my journey. I leaned on a simal tree and looked at a rainbow arched across the sky. It was raining in the hills. There was a dark cloud above me. The western horizon was red and rain-bearing clouds were rolling in. Their movement reminded me of a Newar woman hurrying to the marketplace, wearing a *haku patasi*, a black sari with a red border. Nature's the greatest artist. Humans communicate only a tiny fragment. The sky was always creating new forms, their shapes as changeable as the times in which we lived.

I felt the heat of the sand even through my shoes. But the river looked cool and the breeze was soothing. 'A golden day will rise...' I hummed. The long walk and my disjointed thoughts made me feel a bit giddy. I saw a bird taking off from a bush. I'd have to trek another full day to reach the bus stop. I'd be all alone on this stretch. My only companions would be the gentle breeze, the river's gurgle, the sound of my footsteps, and the cold fear inside me. That fear pricked me like a needle. At one point, I thought I saw a statue ahead of me. But no, it was just a dead tree. A wave rose from the river and crashed onto the shore. I bade it goodbye.

Then I heard someone coughing behind me. I turned around and saw a young man carrying something on his shoulder. Seeing me, he came to a halt and looked me straight in the eye. Then, he walked on without saying a word. Soon he'd passed me.

I followed him. He was walking very quickly. What was he carrying: food, weapons, or both?

'Did you say something?' he asked at one point, turning to face me.

'No.'

He turned back and walked on.

I hummed again, 'A golden day will rise...'

Then I heard another person behind me. I turned and saw another young man, also carrying a bag on his shoulder. I grew jittery. He also looked into my eyes, said nothing, and moved on.

So I followed him as well. He also walked very quickly. What was he carrying: grains, guns or both?

At least he didn't ask if I'd said something.

I continued humming.

Eventually, I reached a teashop. 'Who are you?' someone there asked me.

'Who, me?'

I recognized the speaker. He was one of the young men who'd passed me. The other man was sitting next to him on a bench made of freshly chopped wood. I could smell the aroma of pine. I put down my rucksack and saw my sleeping bag had come untied. They watched me tie it back on.

'I'm a traveller,' I said at last. 'At least for the moment.'

'Be a bit more specific,' one of them pressed me.

'I came to visit my village,' I said. 'Now I'm going back to Kathmandu.

'What do you do?'

'I paint.'

'What kind of paintings?'

'Modern art.'

'Can you show us?'

'I'm too tired.'

'Well, have some tea first.'

'Okay.'

I ate some biscuits dunked in tea. It'd been a long time since I'd had anything like biscuits. They were the most delicious thing I'd ever eaten.

'More biscuits?' one man asked.

Before I could answer, both of them turned and looked away. I looked in the same direction and saw a group of young people coming towards us, carrying the same kind of bags. There were three or four girls among them. They came to the teashop and sat down without saying anything.

I ordered another cup of tea and another packet of biscuits.

The youngsters weren't talking, even among themselves.

'Can you do a painting now?' one of the men asked me.

I glanced at the shopkeeper. She'd been staring at me for a long time. Three of the youngsters went into the teashop. The shopkeeper went in, too, and busied herself attending to them. I heard a commotion inside. Things didn't look good.

As I took out a sketchpad and some coloured pencils, a few village children came up to us. One of them tried to touch the pencils. The others gathered round to watch.

'I can make a drawing. What do you want me to draw?' I asked the men.

They didn't know what to say and simply looked at each other. I thought in the meantime I'd make a sketch of the youngest child in the group gathered around me. The children looked at my pencil moving on the paper like a butterfly dancing. They were delighted by the emerging figure. I liked to sketch the people I met while travelling. They provided me with raw material when I sat in my gallery painting, reminded me of the shapes and colours I'd seen. They were like diary entries, acting as notes on which to base my work.

The boy I was sketching began to giggle, amused at the way my pencil moved. The other children giggled as well. The young people, now surrounding the table, also had their eyes glued to my sketchpad.

The figure of the boy emerged on the paper. He blushed as the other children recognized him and began to tease him. He ran away. The young people stared at the drawing.

'Okay. Here's something you can do,' one of them said, taking out a gun and putting it on the table. 'Draw our Comrade Chairman.'

'I've never seen him,' I said.

'What?'

'I mean, I haven't seen your Comrade Chairman.'

'Haven't you seen his photograph?' he asked.

'Yes. But I only remember him vaguely,' I said, 'All I really remember are his moustache and his hair.'

'So what else do you need?'

'I need to see his photograph again.'

They glanced at each other sharply. One of them produced an old newspaper from his pocket and showed me a photo of Comrade Chairman.

'That's too blurry,' I said.

He said, 'Your sketches aren't any clearer.'

'True, sketches are less clear than photos. But if I'm going to base my work on a photo, it has to be clear.'

'Just do the best you can,' the man said.

'What if I don't do it right?' I said.

'It doesn't matter.'

'But I'm afraid,' I said, 'that if I don't draw his face right, you'll punish me,' and I handed the newspaper back.

They looked at each other again.

Soon, the mother of the child I'd sketched approached. She said, 'Can I see it? They tell me you've made a photo of my son.'

'It's not a photo, Aama. It's a sketch,' said a young comrade.

The child was holding the edge of his mother's sari and looking at me shyly, with a finger in his mouth. I gave the woman the drawing of her son. She looked at it and laughed.

'The nose is twisted!' she said. 'It looks like him but the nose is twisted.'

As she left, I saw a man coming towards me, his young son in tow. 'Can you draw his picture as well?' he asked. 'My son really wants you to.'

Before I started sketching him, I saw a little girl with her aunt and decided to draw her first.

'How much should I pay you?' the aunt asked.

'This is my gift to your niece,' I told her. I turned to the little girl and said, 'I'll give this to you if you promise me you'll go to school.'

'I promise,' she replied, and ran off joyfully with the sketch in her hand.

Her aunt didn't thank me with words, but she looked so happy I knew she was grateful.

'How much do you charge for a sketch like that in Kathmandu?' one of the comrades asked.

I laughed. My profession required so much explanation. I tried to explain as best as I could, and most of them seemed to understand, or at least pretended they did.

'Which school of thought do you belong to?' one of them asked.

'What do you mean?'

'Which school of political thought?'

'I only have a passing interest in politics,' I answered. 'My life revolves around art.'

'What do you think of the war we're fighting?''

'I don't disagree with your demands,' I said. 'Some of them are justified.'

'But what?'

'But I'm not happy with the means you've chosen to achieve them. I don't believe in violence under any circumstances. I don't think I need to say more.'

At that point, the shopkeeper came out and asked what I wanted to eat. I ordered *daal bhaat*. 'Some fresh green vegetables would be wonderful,' I added.

She headed back to the kitchen. Some of the comrades began to cook for themselves. As evening fell, they switched on the radio and listened to the news. 'It might be on the BBC,' one of them said. I didn't know what they were waiting to hear.

The shopkeeper put a kerosene lantern on my table. By the dim light of the lantern, one of the young men read a newspaper. Several others shared the pages. They were old newspapers. I overheard a discussion between two young men in a corner and worried they were talking about Siddhartha. My heart pounded.

'Where are you headed?' I asked one of them.

'Far away,' he replied.

'Hello...'

I saw a young man trying to get a connection on a satellite phone. 'Hello? Hello? Hello?' Finally, he got through. He spoke in a code which I couldn't understand. If he's carrying a satellite phone, he must be a high-ranking cadre, I thought.

I was still sketching but didn't have a clue what I was drawing. In one sketch, the face suddenly developed a resemblance to Siddhartha. I quickly scribbled over it. That could've been disaster. I took out another sheet of paper and started sketching the girl who'd been going to meet her *miitini*, but I couldn't draw her well. I tried again and failed again. It hurt to remember her. Should I make sketches of Miit Ba and Miitini Aama? I knew I wouldn't be able to do those either.

A cool breeze was coming up from the river. The sound of the water was soothing music. A river is an eternal traveller. It always makes the same sounds, but we hear them differently at different times. The river we hear in the afternoon is different from the river we hear in the silence of the night.

These young people had taken up arms and were risking their lives at an age when they should've been in school or college. The fate of the children I'd sketched would be the same.

At one point, a girl whose sketch I'd done came and tugged at my shirt. 'Sir,' she said, 'come to our house. My father says you have to come and eat with us.'

'But I've already ordered food here,' I told her.

'No. You're to be our guest today,' she insisted

'I'm sorry. They've already cooked food for me here. But I'll come tomorrow morning for tea, all right?'

'All right,' she said and ran back to her house. It was dark but she knew the way.

The cool breeze caressed me. One of the youngsters started to play a *madal*, giving the music a revolutionary beat. Another took out a flute and began to play. The river seemed to become quiet, sending only the cool breeze to remind us of its presence. The leaves of a banana plant danced to the music. A papaya tree stood behind us at attention. The shopkeeper brought a plate of fresh pineapple. I picked up a slice as the whole night came alive with music. Many of the men, and even the women, were singing in chorus now. It was too dark for me to see their faces. Besides, not all of them were there. Many were making a round of the village, collecting food. They'd need provisions for tomorrow, when they'd spend the night in the jungle.

Eventually, a group of youngsters returned with sacks full of grain.

From the kitchen came the smell of saag frying in mustard oil. Coriander chutney, black daal, green beans cooked till soft. These would go well with rice. To the beat of their *madal*, I ate my meal as quickly as a flock of birds devouring grain laid out to dry in a farmer's yard.

'Do you want some more?' the shopkeeper asked.

Embarrassed, I told her I'd had enough. In any case, I'd heard it was good for the health to stop eating while still hungry. But the young people obviously hadn't heard that. They ate heaps of food, serving themselves one helping after another. As they ate, the shopkeeper took my plate and told me she'd put a mat on the balcony for me to sleep on.

From the balcony, I looked down and saw one of the young men tuning a radio. Then I heard the familiar jingle of the BBC Nepali service. I lay down on the mat, wondering why these youngsters gave such importance to the news. Why were these people, who lived in constant danger, so interested in knowing what was happening elsewhere? I could hear the man with the satellite phone talking to someone. I wished they'd asked me to sketch him, but they weren't interested in my sketching them. Putting a coffee flavoured candy in my mouth, I slipped into my sleeping bag. I started humming.

Would they shoot me? Would anything happen to me while I slept? I'd told them I didn't agree with their ideology. I'd even refused to make a sketch of their Chairman. Maybe I shouldn't have done that? I could've done it in seconds. Many questions swirled in my mind. What was the worst they could do to me? They might shoot me. But what would they get from that? Bullets weren't cheap. How much did a bullet really cost? I'd heard it depended on the type of gun.

I saw one of the young men open a sack and take out a few packets of rice and a gun. Food and guns! How big was a bullet? Some were no bigger than a kernel of corn. But the bullet which ripped through my pants was quite long. Where had I put the shell? I felt around in my pockets.

I hummed again and turned over in my sleeping bag. I caught a glimpse of white flowers by the river, veiled in darkness. Eventually, silence descended, and I felt relieved when all I could hear was the whisper of the river.

CHAPTER TWENTY FOUR

The horn of the night bus sounded loudly, calling the last passengers. I looked out the window at a small roadside market. The village on the distant hills was covered with mist. Tomorrow morning I'd see Palpasa. I wanted to tell her about the villages I'd been to, the orange groves, the mustard fields, the rhododendron forests, the little girl who'd been on the way to meet her *miitini*, and the boy who'd stopped going to school. I wanted to tell her about everything I'd seen in the hills in these last few months.

The driver honked the horn one last time. The conductor climbed in through the rear door next to me.

The bus was packed with passengers. It was leaving for Kathmandu, where I'd see Palpasa again. She'd see the hills through my eyes as I told her my stories. She'd hear the villagers crying, the sounds of suffering growing louder as the chirping of the birds faded away. She'd cry when she heard my stories. She'd understand for herself that the soul of the country was suffering. Then she could contemplate her own future and the challenges which lay ahead. She'd have to choose her own path, of course, but I had to make her understand our country and our troubled times. She'd embark on her own journey but I could share that journey with her. I could give her my support. I could motivate her. I'd capture the vista of my experiences on canvas and she'd grasp those images in her mind. I'd give her my images and she'd bring them to life. I'd give my voice and she'd provide a melody. I'd give my colours and she'd provide a rhythm. Together my beloved and I would tell the world the stories of our country.

The bus starred with a jerk.

Though I was still far away from Palpasa, she was close to me in my thoughts. She understood my book and my paintings; she understood me. She'd studied my paintings deeply, page after page, and the feelings I'd conveyed in my book were now an integral part of her. She'd touched me through my book. When I told her about my experiences in the past few months, she'd understand me even better.

I had no doubt she'd be fascinated by the places I'd been to. She'd travel to them through my art, following my brushstrokes. She'd see the restlessness of those places, the rivers and their crashing waves, and she'd understand the source of this restlessness. Palpasa would see the tidal wave sweeping away village after village.

Siddhartha was at peace. I was free from the bonds of that friendship. I'd left it behind. Now Palpasa and I would start a journey together. When she understood everything about me, my past and my present experiences, our journey together would begin.

The woman sitting next to me nudged me.

'Namaste,' she said. It was dark. I couldn't see her face properly but her voice was familiar. 'Don't you recognize me?' she asked.

'I don't,' I said. 'Sorry.' I looked at her more carefully. I sensed she was smiling.

'Palpasa!'

'Oh my God!' she said. 'How amazing to meet like this! After all these months! How are you?'

'I've had an incredible journey,' I said. 'I can't believe the things I've seen but meeting you here like this is the most incredible thing that's happened so far!'

'You just disappeared,' she said sadly. 'I told myself all artists must behave that way. That helped me to forget about you. It was just too painful to remember.'

'I couldn't help it, Palpasa.' I tried to explain. 'A friend convinced me to go with him to the hills, and I'm returning with my hands soaked in his blood.'

'Why? What happened?'

'He was a friend from my college days. I hadn't seen him for years. He'd become a Maoist leader. He took me with him, but he was hunted down and slaughtered like an animal.'

'How?'

'He chose to risk his life,' I said. 'The fact that he was killed doesn't really surprise me in itself, but the horrible part was the way he died. I was partly responsible for his death and I can't get over it.'

She studied me intently in the darkness.

'He left me early in our journey,' I said. 'Eventually, I went looking for him. A girl was guiding me. Because of me, she fired her gun in the air and that alerted the security forces. They captured us and took us to the place where my friend was waiting. Then I called out to him, I called him by name and that helped them identify him. They shot him and he died in my arms.'

Palpasa sat in silence, looking at me. As the bus went round a bend, a truck passed from the opposite direction and I saw her face for a fraction of a second in the light of its headlights.

'Getting on with your life is the important thing now,' she said. 'You shouldn't allow the death of a person who lived by violence to devastate you. Remember, he'd probably killed other people.'

'But what about the sacrifice...'

'How can you improve the lives of others by sacrificing your own life?'

'But I feel responsible...'

'How are you responsible?' she asked. 'Your friend came and went like a breeze. The times didn't accept him or he failed to understand the times.'

'His death's affected me so much I can't think of anything else,' I said. 'He took me out of Kathmandu and I saw my country in ruins.'

'But it must give you inspiration, as an artist?'

'I don't know. At least I came back alive.'

'And thank God for that.'

'But what about you?' I asked. 'How come you're here?'

'Remember I once told you I wanted to make a documentary?'

'Yes?'

'I've been filming.'

'What?'

'It doesn't matter. I couldn't go where I wanted,' she said.

'Where was that?'

'The security personnel at the district headquarters advised me not to go to the villages. But I didn't listen. I was on my way there from the district headquarters—I'd only gone a little way—when some people stopped me.'

'And then what happened?'

'They interrogated me, asking my father's name, my grandfather's name. They searched my bags, shouting at me, asking why I'd come there without their permission.'

'Oh.'

'After I'd answered all their questions, they wrote down my name and description. They said they needed to ask their leader what to do with me. They kept me in a house in a village for two days. They didn't hurt me but I was their prisoner. In the end, they told me I had to leave. I'm really furious. I can't believe the way they acted.'

'That is strange,' I said.

'They've made the villagers their prisoners! No one can go anywhere without their permission. It's simply a dictatorship. It shows how they'd run the country if they ever came to power. And that could only be achieved at the barrel of a gun, not with the support of the people.'

In the dark of the bus, I stole a glance at her and she stole a glance at me, as though we were taking turns looking at each other. Her long, dangling earrings suited her. She seemed both tense and relieved to see me.

On the dark highways of Nepal, night buses generally move at very high speeds, as if they're competing in an Olympic race. These days drivers are afraid that their vehicles might be ambushed or that there might be a strike somewhere, blocking the road. Our bus was also speeding madly and this kept me and Palpasa from having an in-depth conversation. Each time the bus turned, we'd fall against each other. It was like a dance. We tilted to the right, then to the left, and we rose off our seats together at every jolt. Though we tried to keep a respectful distance, the movements of the bus kept throwing us together.

I wanted to hold her hand. How would she react?

She started to talk again. 'I saw fear and tension in everyone's eyes,' she said. 'When people feel like that, what can really be achieved? They're even afraid of a girl with a camera! Such cowards.'

'Cowards?'

She was livid. 'What else would you call people who are scared of a camera?'

'You're right. They're cowards.'

'I couldn't explain anything to them,' she went on. 'They weren't even willing to listen to me.'

'Were you on your own?'

'I went with my camera;'

'Where did you want to go?'

'Wherever my camera took me.'

'You haven't changed,' I said.

'But you have,' she said.

I said, 'But I haven't forgotten you.'

'You came like a flower in the spring,' she said, 'and the next season, you were gone.'

'And in the next season, I came back,' I said.

After a while, the bus slowed down and stopped after several jolts. The conductor shouted, 'Anyone want to pee?'

I got up.

'No one else?' the conductor asked.

A few more people got up.

As I brushed past her legs, I said to Palpasa, 'I can't tell you how much I've missed you.'

I heard her say, 'And how could I have forgotten you? Grandma keeps talking about you all the time.'

'All my problems are forgotten, now that I've met you again,' I said as I got off the bus. 'You have no idea how much I need you.'

Outside, a few passengers were relieving themselves behind bushes. I moved further away for more privacy. The driver honked the horn. Why was he suddenly so impatient? Then I realized it wasn't the bus which was sounding its horn but a jeep approaching the bus. The bus driver started the engine and began to pull out to make room for the jeep.

I hurried towards the bus, thinking it might go without me. As I did so, I heard an incredibly loud bang and found myself thrown to the ground. I tried to turn my head. All around, I heard people shrieking. I didn't know what was happening. Dazed, I ran my hands over myself to see if I'd been hurt. The road was lit up. Everything seemed to be on fire. I heard people groaning. A few people were running wildly, tripping over me. When I got up, the bus was on fire.

'Palpasa!' I screamed.

Through the blaze, I could hear the horrible shrieking of the passengers trapped inside the bus. I thought I could hear Palpasa's voice above the rest and the sound almost drove me insane. People were running away, but I stood there helplessly, unable to move, unable to think. Then I noticed a row of torches moving up the hill. Our bus had been caught in an ambush, laid by the people carrying those torches. The jeep, however, was safe. It was a police jeep. Several police officers got out and started firing in the direction of the lights moving up the hill, ordering us to stay where we were. Two passengers from the bus lay beside me unconscious.

'Palpasa!' I screamed again towards the inferno.

But no one in the bus could've survived. With a shudder, its metal frame collapsed like a dead tree struck by lightening. It was still burning. In no time, all that was left was a charred skeleton. No one inside was screaming any more. The few survivors were standing like ghosts on the highway. My whole body was shaking like a leaf. All my dreams and desires were suddenly gone, as swiftly as a bird flying off the branch of a tree. I'd survived only because I'd got off the bus. And Palpasa had been killed only because she hadn't. It was absurd—the reason I'd survived and the reason she'd been killed. There was no logic behind it. It's not that I'd survived because of some act of courage and she'd died because of some weakness. None of it made sense.

It was a crime. It was cowardice. All logic and all common sense were gone. Why was I alive and Palpasa dead?

I heard one policeman say to another, 'It was us they were trying to ambush. We survived by a matter of seconds. If the bus's headlights hadn't come on, we'd have been dead!'

The other said, 'Our driver must've sensed something. He swerved just in time; otherwise, it would've been us.'

I'd looked at Palpasa for the last time ever as I got off the bus. It was just the briefest of glances; I'd hardly seen her. Now I realized it would be the last time I'd ever see her. I thought about her lovely eyes, her soft skin. I wiped my eyes. Why had I gotten on the same bus as Palpasa? Why had she gotten on the same bus as me, a journey that brought her life to an end? Why? Why? These questions came into my mind again and again. I felt as if I were going mad.

Journalists arrived in the morning, like a swarm of hornets. Their lenses were everywhere. A cool breeze was blowing over the stream by the road but I felt hot and feverish. I was still shaking like a leaf. As the sun came up, I wished I could wake up from this nightmare.

A group of journalists surrounded me. 'How did you survive?' one asked.

Weakly, I said, 'I got off the bus to pee.'

'What did you see?'

'I saw the bus on fire.'

'How did the explosion happen? How did the police jeep escape?'

They flooded me with questions.

'Were you travelling alone?' a journalist asked from the back of the crowd. The question rattled me. Should I answer him? Why should I? Was there any reason to tell him who'd been sitting beside me and what she'd meant to me? Was there any sense in making that public? I said nothing. The camera lenses zoomed in on me as I wiped away my tears.

'How did they detonate it?' another reporter asked. How could I answer that? All I'd seen were torches moving up the hill. There'd been an exchange of fire between them and the police, then silence.

'Were any relatives of yours in the bus?'

I said nothing.

'Were you able to rescue anyone from the bus?' a journalist shot at me.

'Don't you have anything to say about the incident?' another asked.

I was silent.

The person who'd brought happiness to my life was gone. Oh God, I couldn't believe it. Palpasa had become the sweetest picture in my life. I had fallen in love with her dreams. I'd felt we'd travel together to a wonderful destination. Now she was gone. She'd disappeared in flames before my eyes.

The poor girl. She'd struggled so hard against her family and tradition to live her own life. Now time had taken her in those cruel flames. I stood there, where that terrible thing had happened, feeling that time was testing me.

I sat down. I stood up. I stood a while, then sat down again.

Oh God. How could I just have witnessed the death of my love?

CHAPTER TWENTY FIVE

The first thing I did when I reached Kathmandu was to go to Palpasa's house. I was sure her grandmother would be inconsolable. She'd surely faint upon hearing she'd lost her cherished granddaughter. It'd be difficult for me to tell her the news, but I felt it was my duty. I had to tell her what had happened, as gently as I could. I'd have to remind her we were living in a time of war, and that she and I were alive and that Paipasa was dead only due to the vagaries of fate.

When I reached Palpasa's house, I found Hajur Aama rolling *batti*, sitting beside the statue of Buddha—a statue of Buddha in a house in the capital of a country at war with itself. I looked at the statue and felt its eyes were saying something to me. But I had nothing to say in return. I turned away. The Buddha's eyes struck me as ironic. I didn't want to chant 'Om mani padme hum': this mantra had brought no peace. Were the Buddha to be born today, even he'd raise a gun. That's what someone in the hills had told me.

Hajur Aama smiled when she saw me. She smiled just as I was imagining the Buddha raising a gun. Maybe that's why her smile took on a sardonic, mocking twist. With some effort, I smiled back. Then her face became truly joyful. She obviously hadn't heard yet. Some of the dead were yet to be identified. Many would never be. They'd be listed among the disappeared forever.

My eyes filled with tears. Through her thick lenses, Hajur Aama didn't notice.

She took me into the house. She was talking, but I couldn't concentrate on what she was saying. My attention was drawn to a new painting on the wall. It was one of my paintings, the one called *Rain*. When had Palpasa gone to my gallery to buy it? I felt cold inside. I couldn't speak.

'Sit down,' Hajur Aama urged me. 'Why are you standing? And where have you been for so long? Were you lost?'

I still couldn't say a word.

'Palpasa left a letter for you. She went away with her camera and I haven't heard from her since. But she told me she'd be gone for a while. She took a lot of clothes with her. She was complaining that she couldn't find good walking shoes in her size.'

Still I said nothing.

'She was angry with you,' Hajur Aama went on. 'I was so delighted to get your letter! But she looked very thoughtful after she read it. Then she kept asking me all the time whether you'd dropped by or telephoned.'

'That wasn't possible,' I said. 'I'd gone to the hills. The situation there was terrible. All the communication towers had been destroyed. There was nothing but bombs and bullets everywhere.'

'But you should've told Palpasa you were leaving,' she chided me. 'She's very interested in you, you know.'

I still couldn't say anything.

Hajur Aama said, 'You wrote you're in love with a girl like Palpasa. Is she really like her? I'd like to meet her. You said she even behaves like Palpasa. How strange! What a wonderful letter that was! I wept as I listened to it. And Palpasa cried while she was reading it too.'

'But it wasn't a sad letter,' I protested.

'You don't have to write something sad to make people cry. It was very touching.'

'What was so touching in it?' I asked.

'I can understand why Palpasa cried,' she said. 'She realized how fond you'd grown of this house. In fact, she didn't just cry, she sobbed. It was Palpasa who made this house, you know. She had the old house dismantled and then rebuilt according to her own design.'

Hajur Aama went out of the room. I looked again at the painting on the wall. I remembered Palpasa saying that she saw herself in the female figure. Hajur Aama came back in with tea.

'What inspired her to renovate this house?' I asked.

'She told me there was a house like this in one of your paintings,' she said. 'Is that true?'

'I'm amazed, Hajur Aama.'

'I think she was falling in love with you.'

'Why do you think that?'

'Maybe it was after she found out you love someone just like her. Her tears fell onto your letter while she read the parts about this house and about your love. I saw her wipe away tears at least twice.'

Hajur Aama gave me Palpasa's letter. I looked at *Rain* one last time. That one painting had added new character to the house. Outside in the garden, I tore open the envelope, avoiding the Buddha's eyes. Those eyes could ask me questions I didn't want to answer. I didn't want to look into those peaceful eyes, but avoiding them felt more difficult than dodging a bullet. If this Buddha were made today, he'd carry a gun in his hands. If I ever created a Buddha image, maybe that's the way I'd make it.

Dear Artist,

Unknowingly, you stole my heart, then disappeared. You've been gone such a long time. I have absolutely no idea when you're coming back. I'm so worried. Without you, Kathmandu's like a frying pan. I stepped into it, you lit a fire underneath, and then you left. How long can I stand this?

A car honked at me and I realized I was walking down the middle of the road. I let the car pass. On the sidewalk, I bumped into someone. I let him pass too. Then I went back to reading the letter.

Why have you done this to me? If you had to disappear, why steal my heart beforehand? Why did you inspire me to dream? You put a small child in the sun and left her without caring whether or not she could endure the heat. Why don't you respect other people's feelings? Couldn't you have told me you were leaving? Couldn't you have told me where you were going? Why did you leave me alone to worry about you? And who are you anyway to disappear like that, leaving everyone to worry? I've begun to doubt whether you're the same person, the same dear artist I knew. I'm beginning to wonder whether it's the same you who wrote the book I love so much.

I'd reached the main road. On the sidewalk, several passersby were waiting to cross the road. I stood with them.

I wouldn't have worried so much, if you hadn't written that letter to Hajur Aama. I was crying to open up to you. But you disappeared, hurting me, for reasons I can't even guess at. This is deception. If you'd intended to disappear, why did you write that letter to Hajur Aama and create in me a desire for love? Why did you mention the word love in your letter at all if you weren't sincere, if you don't even understand what the word means? If you wanted to play this game, why did you have to involve Hajur Aama? That really annoys me. I've noticed a change in myself. I'm getting angrier every day.

The people around me crossed the road. I folded the letter and followed them. It was sunny, but I felt cold. Was the sun really shining? Why were the people around me walking so slowly? Being Nepalis, surely they know how to walk? Their forefathers must have come from the hills, yet it seemed they hardly knew how to walk. Such stupid people.

I'm an ordinary girl with a few dreams. I want to do something meaningful and make something of myself. I was just a blank sheet of paper drifting in the wind before you caught me and coloured me. You gave me coloured feathers and I started to fly. I was scared when I met you. The writer of a book I loved came into my life and destroyed my peace of mind. I was happily in love with your paintings, but then you appeared in person and inspired me to fly. You came like a strong breeze, disturbing the dry leaves on a riverbank, and I flew across the river.

I had to face the fate of the yellow leaf in your painting. All along, I was trying to escape from you and put my feet on solid ground. I wanted to be still, like a plant with its roots set deep in the earth. I ran away from you, but you came to my house in Kathmandu and forced me to take flight on your dreams. You even worked your magic on Hajur Aama. When I came to deliver Hajur Aama's invitation to lunch, you treated me like a lover. Did you ever take time to wonder what I thought of you?

Someone on the sidewalk elbowed me. What a rude fellow! Why was he in such a rush? Where are you headed, fool, and why are rushing to get there? You live only once. Why are you pushing people around?

The evening I read your letter to Hajur Aama, I felt completely unsettled. I still feel myself seesawing from one emotion to another. I want to say something, I want someone to hear what I have to say. I want to bare my feeling. I want to go around my neighbourhood, my city, carrying your letter and the feelings it gives me. But you're nowhere to be found. You've been gone for so long now that my feelings are beginning to turn to bitterness. I would've been so relieved just to be able to say one word to you, but you left me with no clue how to contact you. You've hurt me; you've made me sick.

Now I need to heal myself by telling myself you were just an apparition. Why did you come into and go from my life, disappearing, then reappearing to upset my equilibrium? And why are you afraid of seeing the ripples created by the stone you threw into a still pond? I wish I'd never met you. I used to be at peace with myself. I was content. No one had ever been so close to me. Is this a punishment for falling in love with your book? I wonder why your paintings meant so much to me. They spoke to me so eloquently that, after I met you, the artist who made them, my perspective on life changed. Even the very first time we met, I felt close to you. I want to rewind time and go back to the days before I met you.

I was like a clean sheet of paper then, one without a single splotch of ink. I could've made any picture on it I wanted. But you took me by surprise. You smeared colours on that paper and stained me. Someone has robbed me of my mornings. My days no longer have dawns.

I've never felt such agitation, even in the States. I had a few relationships there. They were more about lust than love, but I have no regrets. Of those experiences only memories remain, and those memories mean nothing to me now. I was glad to come back to Nepal. I was full of self-confidence when I came back. But you came into my life and destroyed my peace of mind. I wasn't able to resist you. You hijacked my will, then left me alone to suffer.

You're a good artist. I'm not the only one who appreciates your work. I'm sure you have many admirers. I'm beginning to feel you're not the person I took you for. You must be dear to many and many must be dear to you. You're very far away. If I can't reach you, I'll just rot here alone. But I don't want to rot like this. Thanks to your inspiration, I want to blossom like a flower. I want to begin my work.

'Drishya!' someone shouted from a car, honking the horn. Who was it? Why wasn't he giving me some privacy? Couldn't he see I was reading a letter?

I looked up and saw Tshering. 'Idiot,' I called out to him. He was grinning at me, but I didn't smile back. The traffic light turned green, but Tshering didn't drive on. Why did he want to spoil my day? I waved him away and went back to reading the letter.

I want to disappear from your life in exactly the same way you've disappeared from mine. I have to go far away from you to find peace. I want to be out of the reach of your lies and deception. I know you'll tell me you left for something to do with your work. I'm also leaving for something to do with my work. You'll tell me you didn't have time to let me know. I want to tell you the same thing. I'm leaving with my camera the way you left with your paintbrush. I want to go where you can't find me. That'll heal my pain. I'm sure you know I'm not a girl who can just remain passive. I also want you to know I'm not motivated by revenge.

Yours truly,
Neglected Reader

Folding the letter, I put it in my pocket. My shadow moved in front of me as I walked towards the rooftop restaurant where I'd once had dinner with Palpasa. She'd been in a combative mood that evening and we'd debated. I took the table we'd shared and sat on the same chair I'd sat on then.

'Do you know why I came back to Nepal?' she'd asked.

'Why?' I'd asked.

I was absorbed in a long article, analysing the western world's obsession with Spiderman and Harry Potter. Fascination with Harry Potter hadn't sidestepped the east either. It was a fact worth pondering that the mother of a little girl had become the world's richest author by writing children's books. Her books had been translated into sixty languages and published in two hundred countries. The article was beginning on its argument that the author's greatest achievement was diverting children from television, computers, and video games and bringing them back to books. I was just getting into it when Palpasa interrupted me.

'I didn't like my parents' attitude,' Palpasa said.

Putting the article aside, I looked at her. She was looking straight into my eyes as she spoke. It was clear she wanted my full attention. She wanted to make me understand. And it was possible I could misunderstand her. After all, we'd grown up under very different circumstances, in different countries, and surrounded by different cultures. I wasn't in the mood to give her my full attention, but I guessed she was trying to make the point that understanding each other could be the first step towards love.

I asked, 'Why didn't you like your parents' attitude?'

'They were always asking me why I went around with certain men.'

'Which men?'

'Whenever I had a male friend, they'd question me about his background. They were so possessive. They believed no daughter of theirs should have relationships with anyone less educated than she was.'

I looked at her more closely.

'They believed that friendship with a less educated person would demean me somehow,' she said.

'What did you tell them?'

'Nothing. They wouldn't have understood. If I'd found a friend who was better educated than me, his parents probably would've discouraged him from seeing me.'

'That's true.'

'And how would my parents feel then?' she asked.

'But you never told your parents these things?'

'It's as if we speak different languages.'

'Don't they understand English?'

'I'm not talking about Nepali or English. I'm talking about the way we think. The gap between the way we think is so wide that it doesn't matter which language we use. We can never communicate.'

'You came back to Nepal just because of that?'

She said, 'They wanted me to marry someone with a PhD. Tell me, does a person look at the other person's qualifications before falling in love? My parents put people into boxes. I couldn't go on living with them.'

'It's just the generation gap,' I said.

'No. In Kathmandu, I've found so many people of my own age who think exactly like my parents do.'

'Really?'

She'd told me how, wanting to get to know how Nepalese society was these days, she'd once gone into a sari shop, thinking that people in sari shops had time to chat. In vegetable markets, in contrast, everyone's in a hurry. Palpasa had talked to a man from outside the capital, A female friend with her didn't approve and whispered in her ear, scolding her.

'What did she say?' I asked.

'She said it was unbecoming of me to flirt with a man like that,' she said. 'Why should anyone tell me whom I should or shouldn't talk to? Did I need to identify the social status of a person before even talking to him? Should I never talk to people from outside Kathmandu just because they might be less affluent than I am? It's not the generation gap,' she insisted. 'It's an attitude problem.'

I'd agreed, then teased her, 'If the attitude problem exists here in Kathmandu as well, will you go back to the States?'

'You don't want to understand me," she snapped. 'What I'm trying to say doesn't relate to geography; it relates to human nature.'

Wanting to provoke her, I said, 'So, are you saying that Nepalis in general have this attitude problem?'

'Let me give you an example,' she said, ignoring my question. Then she told me about her experience after September 11. She said the attitude of some white Americans towards foreigners had become clear. One day, she had been riding on a bus when an Asian man got on and sat down beside a white American. The white American had moved to another seat.

'Do you get my point?' she said.

'Was it really like that?'

'Can you imagine such blatant discrimination?'

She told me how uncomfortable she'd felt being around conservative Americans who looked askance at Asians. She spoke very passionately.

'I understand,' I said, sipping my coffee.

She stared at me intently. I wanted to look away from her, but she was holding my gaze, wanting to control me.

'The place I came from isn't the US,' she said.

I looked at her, surprised.

'I didn't come from the States. I've never lived in the States,' she said.

'Well, where did you come from then?'

'New York. And New York isn't the US,' she said. 'If I'd lived anywhere else in the country, I would've faced discrimination from ultra-conservatives who live in very narrow worlds.'

'What strange things you're saying,' I said.

'Look. Compare it to the situation of someone living in North Korea. Their horizons are limited.'

She said that every place had its own unique character. People from every corner of the world lived in New York. Almost every language on earth was spoken on its streets. Every day New York restaurants served food from all over the world. Its population was a human rainbow and no one there would dream of discriminating against someone because of the colour of his or her skin.

'Tell me,' I said. 'I live and work in Nepal. I like being here. Does that mean my worldview is limited?'

'You don't get me,' she said.

'Maybe you have preconceived ideas about places,' I said.

'No. They're based on my experience.'

I said, 'I'm starting to see a problem in your attitude.'

'No,' she said, defending herself. 'I'm trying to say that people are products of their environment.'

'But don't your parents live in New York?'

'They live there, but only physically,' she said. 'Their thoughts belong somewhere else, in another time. I'm not trying to claim that all the people living in New York are sophisticated. I'm arguing that generally places shape people. But there are always exceptions. A person living in Kathmandu could be just as sophisticated as a person living in New York.'

'Am I sophisticated?' I asked.

'It's not your fault,' she said breezily, 'but I do see some shortcomings in you.'

'Shortcomings?'

'Just small ones.' She shrugged. 'Everyone has some. For example, you don't take things seriously enough. I don't believe you take my opinions seriously.'

'What makes you say that?' I asked.

'You've never had a serious conversation with me. You've never discussed serious issues with me.'

'That's not true!'

'You probably think you've impressed me,' she said. 'But I'm an admirer of your paintings more than anything else.'

'But I never...'

'You don't take me seriously,' she repeated. 'I've never had the feeling you see me as your equal'

'How can you say that?' I asked, stung.

'Every time we meet, for example, you compliment me on the way I dress. You did that today as well,' she said. 'You think all women love to be complimented on their appearance.'

'I'm an artist! I'm drawn to colours and textures.'

'No, you're a male chauvinist. Your idea of what makes a woman happy comes from your sexist preconceptions. You've never tried to understand the real me.'

I was wondering how I could convince her otherwise when she got up and left.

I watched her walk away, thinking she'd turn and come back. But she didn't.

And today she wasn't there, sharing the table with me. The girl who'd stormed out that evening would never come back. I'd never be able to convince her.

I asked for the bill. The waiter who brought it always wanted to talk to me. He always wanted to ask me questions. Today, just the sight of his face made me angry.

'Sir, are you religious' he asked.

'No,' I said.

'Why not, Dai?' he asked.

Paying the bill, I said, 'Religion promises good things in the next life. It doesn't teach you to fight for what you want in this one.'

'I understand.'

'What do you understand?' I snapped as I turned to go.

'I understood what you said,' he called from behind me.

'You can't understand me!' I said.

'But I've understood,' he said.

Climbing down the stairs, I shouted, 'Anyone who says he understands hasn't understood a damned thing!'

He followed me down the stairs. 'Why?' he asked. 'Why are you saying that?'

'What's left to understand when you understand everything?'

'But I understood you!'

'Then you're the Buddha,' I said. 'So close your eyes and shut up!'

I heard him laugh as I went out into the alley.

CHAPTER TWENTY SIX

Someone had opened a flower shop below my gallery. Some important event must've been happening because a lot of people were there buying flowers. Climbing the stairs from the parking lot, I felt like I had arrived at a different gallery. I remembered the fragrance of the hills, the perfume of flowers overwhelmed by the smell of explosives. Human memory is so fallible. Only yesterday, we'd lived in a beautiful place where sunbeams mingled with the perfume of flowers. A new openness in society and better communications were leading to progress. But now...

The day's newspapers lay bundled on the table like discarded flowers. I like reading a newspaper only if I'm the first person to read it. Then it seems fresh to me. If someone else has read it, I find it stale. Newspapers give me a sense of a new day, they raise new possibilities. For me, the best way to start the day is discovering the meaning in their words, paragraphs, and pages. They open up my country and beyond. They make me think. They broaden my horizon. Even if it's afternoon, I wish people 'good morning' when I'm carrying a newspaper.

There was another old newspaper on the table. It said the prime minister had gone to Belgium to buy weapons. From the window I saw the shopkeeper below arrive in a van filled with flowers. After the prime minister came back, even these flowers would smell of explosives. I kept staring out the window until, suddenly, I saw people running wildly along the street. A bomb had exploded nearby. Just that morning, another small bomb had gone off on a street close to my house.

I climbed up to the roof. As the clouds cleared, a structure spiralling towards the sky came into view. It was a monastery. Palpasa had told me someday she'd become a nun. I kept looking at the monastery till it started to drizzle and the view became hazy.

Despite the rain, some pigeons were playing on the wires hanging above the rooftops. The sky was blanketed with thick cloud. It was a melancholy day. But the streets were full of cars rushing to and from unknown destinations. I could hear music from a CD shop. At the grocery store across the road, a man was trying to tune in to an FM station. There was a new cyber café on the other side of the road, but the old language centre, boutique, and 99 rupees shop were still there. It was amazing that, while life was being squeezed out of the villages, Kathmandu was thriving. I saw a crowd of people lined up in front of headhunting agency. Where did they want to go: the Gulf, Malaysia, South Korea, Afghanistan, or Iraq?

How long was it going to rain?

Going downstairs, I saw Phoolan had left a letter for me.

I'm surprised by your behaviour, Dai. Please contact me when you get back. I couldn't keep running the gallery on my own. With you gone and me having no idea where you were, I didn't feel comfortable in the gallery.

But I sold one painting, the one called 'Rain'. Palpasa insisted I sell it to her. She paid a lot of money for it. She even tipped me. She came to the gallery several times after you'd left. She never seemed to tire of looking at your paintings. And she was always ringing to ask if you'd come back or contacted me. Even when I told her you hadn't, she'd still come to the gallery and spend hours here. We talked a lot about you. She asked about me as well. I told her that if it hadn't been for you I'd still be herding goats in my village.

I don't remember anyone caring about you so much. Palpasa. Didi is beautiful and genuinely fond of you. I'm like your 'bahini', so please don't get angry when I say this, Dai, but I have to tell you: you and Palpasa fit together. You'd make a good pair. She never talks about herself, only about you. She wants to know everything about you.

I want the best for you. You're alone, you don't have any family, I'm the only one who's close to you. You live a solitary life, that's why you can wander off when you feel like it. Now you need to lead a practical and organized life. I haven't asked for anything from you so far. With your permission, I have to say one thing to you—marry Palpasa. I know you're an introvert and things like this embarrass you but I could deliver your proposal to her if you want. I'll be really disappointed if you say no. I'll leave your gallery forever and go back to my village. And even if you come there and ask me to come back with you, I'll say it'll only be on one condition—that you marry Palpasa. I'm sorry if what I've said makes you feel uncomfortable. Take care of yourself and think about what I've said.

Her letter was signed '*Your Secretary*'.

I hadn't realized Phoolan had grown so smart working in my gallery. She'd always loved to speak in English with visitors. 'This'll improve my English,' she used to tell me. 'And I'll learn foreign ways as well.' Later, she'd become fond of art. She wanted to understand it. She'd been furious when Kishore proposed to her. I wanted her to become someone, to do something worthwhile with her life, and my gallery had been the best place for it.

I tried to phone her. A friend of hers at the girls' hostel recognized my voice and asked, 'Where have you been?' Then she said, 'Phoolan's left.'

I froze. 'Where did she go? To her village?'

'No, I mean she's left for college.'

'Oh.' Relieved, I hung up.

Later, as I was drawing some outlines for a new painting, Kishore came in.

'Hi, Dai,' he said.

I'd just started a series of works dedicated to Palpasa's memory. I also intended to dedicate to her the art centre I planned to build in my village. People who were interested in art could come trekking through the beautiful hills, enjoy being close to nature, and then spend a few days immersed in art. Outside, the world would continue just the same, full of struggle and conflict. Inside the small world I'd create, my guests would lose themselves in a different world, a world of creativity, a world of flowers and the changing seasons.

I'd make a painting of the confluence of two rivers festooned with flowers as it is during Thulo Ekadashi. The new bridge over the river had been blasted away. Seeing it gone brought back childhood memories and tired my imagination. Christina had told me, 'Our part of the world's been through this already and moved on. That's why the west is ahead of you.'

What the Dutch and other westerners had gone through long ago was happening in our country right now: we were fated to go through a painful phase in our history. If we could navigate through these dangerous waters, perhaps we could arrive at a safe destination. Where was the tree on the other side of the river to which we could tie our garland of flowers?

We could tie it securely at the other end in Kathmandu, a modern, civilized, and safe place.

'I said "hi",' Kishore reiterated, startling me.

Sitting on my comfortable sofa lost in thought, I'd forgotten he was there.

'I haven't seen you for ages,' he said.

'How are you?' I asked.

'Do you know anyone at the American Embassy?'

'Why?'

'I need a visa.'

'Won't they just give you one if you just apply?'

'No, they don't trust me'

'Why not?'

'They don't believe I'll come back.'

'Just tell them.'

'What?'

'That you'll come back.'

'They won't believe me.'

'Why not?'

'But what if they don't?'

'Then don't go.'

'You don't understand!' he said crossly. 'All my friends have gone.'

'If they've let all your friends go, why would they stop you?'

'But what if they do?' he asked. 'The visa section lets some people go and refuses others. So many people come back from there in tears. One man was granted a visa but his wife wasn't!'

'My advice to you is to answer their questions with a smile. Tell them you don't want to stay in the US, that you like Nepal. Say, for you, Nepal's just as good as the US and, besides, you have to come back here to work.'

'That's what I told them in my interview for a Schengen visa,' he said. 'But they rejected my application anyway. What they said was, "With so many problems in your country, why would you want to come back? Many Nepalis have applied for political asylum in Europe." '

I wanted to change the subject. How could I be responsible for things beyond my control? 'Aren't you bringing out a new album?' I asked.

'I'm in the middle of rehearsals now,' he said. 'Two of my songs on the first album were big hits. Did you know I was asked to do some live performances? I did three! And I can't even remember how many interviews I've given on FM radio!'

'Good for you.'

He was excited. 'And I've been receiving so many fan mail. After I did a live show at the BICC, I even autographed people's t-shirts and hands. Some of them took off their t-shirts and made me autograph their backs!'

'Fantastic!'

'That's not all!' He was getting really worked up. 'I get so many phone calls. Some people call at midnight to say "I love you". I even got a letter written in blood! It scares me that some of my fans say they'd be willing to die for me. That's part of the reason I want to leave.'

Trying to calm him down, I said, 'Why leave when your fans love you so much? Stay in your own country. One day you'll be a very famous singer.'

But he didn't want to listen and left, annoyed. All he wanted was to go to the US at all costs. He told me he had friends everywhere, from Boston to LA.

As he was leaving, he said, 'There are very few houses in Kathmandu without at least one family member in the US.'

'Well, maybe.'

'My family will think I'm a failure if I can't get a visa,' he called as he went down the stairs.

'So let them,' I said, but he'd already gone.

Peace returned to my gallery once more.

I looked out the window and saw the crowd of young men still milling around in front of the headhunting agency. If I went down, I'd be sure to meet someone who'd ask me if I could give him work or get him a job by pulling some strings. Coming to the gallery today, I'd talked to a young man who said, 'I've just filled out the application form to go abroad. I sold all my land to do it.'

Another young man I'd met earlier was so desperate for a job that he said he'd do anything.

'What would you do?' I asked.

His simple answer haunted me: 'For just a few rupees, I'd stand outside your gate all night and guard you with a *khukuri* in my hand.'

I turned away from the window and went back to the couch. But I couldn't sit still. I went to the window again. I wanted to be where I could hear the sound of waterfalls. I wanted to transfer that music onto my canvas. I wanted to capture the shapes and songs of birds and the gentle contours of terraced fields. There used to be a time when I couldn't even afford paint. I'd felt desperate. Now I had all the paints I needed, but I wanted to run away from them.

I switched on my computer and got a surprise. My e-mail account was overloaded with messages. Among the messages were innumerable e-mails from Christina. I wondered if she was all right. Her last message had arrived only yesterday. She'd written, threateningly, 'If you don't reply, this will be my last e-mail to you.'

I counted her previous e-mails. There were at least a dozen. No wonder she'd lost patience.

I opened each of her e-mails and read them carefully. She wrote about my art and expressed concern about the changing situation in Nepal. She also wrote she was coming back to do some reporting.

'Nepal's my first international war-reporting assignment,' she wrote.

War reporting!

I wrote back: 'Welcome to Nepal, my dear art lover, my dear journalist.'

Then I replied to all her e-mails.

Afterwards I poured myself some wine, but it smelled like vinegar. It was a bottle I'd uncorked before leaving for the hills. I poured it down the sink and looked around for another. Where was all the wine I used to have? I found a bottle inside a paper bag. It was the bottle Palpasa had brought to my party.

I couldn't open it. I put the corkscrew aside and looked out the window again. To my surprise, I saw Christina coming down the street towards the gallery. She was already in Nepal. When had she left the Netherlands? And when was she going back? Was she coming to visit my gallery one last time?

I met her at the door. 'Hello, Christina,' I said. She punched me in the chest exactly the way Palpasa had done at the church in Goa.

She put down her bag and looked around, pleased to see I'd done exactly what she'd wanted with the walls.

'Do you know how many e-mails I sent you?' she said. 'How many times I called the gallery? How many times I came here to see if the door was open?'

'I've got some idea,' I said.

'You don't,' she said. 'I know artists in general aren't reliable but I'e never come across such selfishness even in European artists. In the beginning you were so good about sending me e-mails and now you don't even reply!'

I said, 'I'm sorry, but you don't know where I've been.'

'I'm going back to the Netherlands tomorrow,' she said.

'No!' I said, pretending not to believe her.

'Yes.' She was adamant. Looking straight into my eyes, she said. 'Mr Artist, this is my last evening in Kathmandu.'

'So? What can I do about that?'

'I'm telling you,' she said, starting to sound angry, 'that I'm leaving tomorrow'!'

'Am I trying to stop you?' I said.

'Did I say that?'

'I thought maybe you had that impression.'

'That's the last thing I'd think,' she said. Then she turned to my paintings and looked at each one carefully.

It was rare to find someone who appreciated art the way she did. I wanted to make her feel welcome. I went out to the flower shop and came back with a bouquet. Handing it to her, I said, 'You've honoured my gallery with your visit.'

'Thank you,' she said, softening. 'I didn't expect this.'

'I didn't intend to surprise you.'

'The biggest surprise was finding you here at all.'

'For me, too, having the chance to meet you again is a wonderful surprise,' I said.

'Why should it be such a surprise?'

'People like you who love art show me the way to go.'

'Really? I'm flattered.'

'But I'm not just flattering you,' I said.

She punched me playfully in the chest again. I took her hand and said, 'I'm telling you the truth. I'm really glad to see you.'

'But I'm going back tomorrow;' she said, raising her eyebrows and waiting for my reaction.

I asked, 'So what do you think?'

'About what?'

'About the colour of the walls.'

'It's perfect, dangerously perfect.' Then she said jokingly, 'You know, I think I'm falling in love with this gallery.'

'Good,' I said. 'That'd save me. If you fall in love with my gallery, you won't need me.'

Another playful punch.

After a while, I closed the gallery and we drove to a nearby hotel. The bar was almost empty. In one corner, an elderly foreign man was playing the piano. He caught Christina's eyes and nodded in greeting.

'It's easy to play the piano,' Christina said to me, 'but hard to play well.'

'Everything's like that,' I said.

'You mean, for instance, paintings?'

'You catch on quickly.'

'No. You're quick to notice I've understood,' she said, waving to the old man who was playing the piano.

'When are you really leaving?' I asked.

'Tomorrow.'

'There's the problem,' I said.

'What?'

'You journalists are always in a hurry. You're so impatient that you can't wait for things to take their natural course.'

'What do you mean?' she asked.

'Why are you in such a hurry to go back to your country?' I said. 'If you journalists weren't always rushing, things wouldn't happen so fast.'

'But my assignment's over.'

'What kind of assignment was that? There's so much happening here. The situation's getting more complex with each passing day. How can you say your assignment's over? That's the attitude of a parachute journalist, who covers a crisis, then disappears.'

'But there's nothing to write about at the moment,' she said.

'I'll give you a story,' I said.

'What story?'

I took a sip of wine and said, 'My experiences will make a good story for you.'

She looked at me sceptically.

'I went to the hills recently,' I said. 'I was virtually kidnapped and taken back to my home village, where I discovered everything had changed. Just the thought of what happened after that leaves me trembling. I lost a friend. Then I lost the woman I loved.'

As I told her everything, it seemed like a dream, even to me. I let go of all my inhibitions. Maybe I shouldn't have drunk so much wine. While I was telling her about Palpasa, she comforted me, putting her hand on my arm. She cried when I told her about my visit to Palpasa's grandmother.

The piano music grew louder as the evening wore on. A candle was placed on our table. I talked on and on, Christina comforting me all the while.

I don't remember our parting. The next morning, I found a wilted rose in my shirt pocket.

CHAPTER TWENTY SEVEN

'Christina, go and have a coffee.'

'No, thanks,' she said, not moving an inch from her chair.

'You could sit in the reception area,' I suggested.

'I won't budge till the painting's finished,' she said.

We were in my gallery. I was working on the sixth painting in my Palpasa series, but I was having trouble with it. I just couldn't find the right colours. The brushstrokes didn't seem to suit the shades I'd given them. I wanted to put hope into the figure of Palpasa. At first, I'd painted her in vermilion, but it looked like blood. I couldn't even distinguish between vermilion and blood! This canvas was taking all my energy. And I was getting annoyed with Christina. I wanted to work freely without hindrance. But she kept interrupting all the time.

'That's a perfect combination of light and shadow,' she said, like an expert. 'I feel like I'm in the hills.'

'Could you do me a favour?' I asked at last.

'Sure.'

'Please go out for a while.'

'I promise I won't disturb you,' she said. 'Just pretend I'm not here.'

'Look, my dear lady,' I said in exasperation. 'I need to forget even my own existence when I paint. I can't have someone hanging around. Please!'

'All right, my dear artist,' she said, getting up. 'I don't want to be a nuisance.'

I didn't notice her leave, but I was finally alone. I was trying to capture the moment I'd touched Palpasa for the last time, when I'd touched her in passing as I got off the bus. That had been our last moment together. This series was my biggest challenge. If I could do it successfully, I'd be portraying a page in both the history of my country and the story of my own life.

The day before, Christina had asked me, 'The language of colour is universal, but there seems to be a distinctly Nepali touch to the way you use colour. How's that possible?'

'The unique Nepali use of colour was developed by our artists centuries ago,' I told her. 'I'm just borrowing it.'

Artists don't leave empty spaces on a canvas just to save paint; all spaces are determined by the maths and science of the paintbrush. Empty spaces in a painting can make it more mysterious and even tell their own story. The impact of my paintings depends on the relationship between the colours I choose and the spaces I leave.

Every artist creates his own style, and that style's a statement. Through my paintings, I was trying to convey my views on contemporary Nepal. Christina understood the political message in the works I was creating. That was why she asked so many questions.

These paintings were a reflection of my journey and my sufferings. I couldn't be objective. The language of time was brutal and could easily defeat me. I was one lone man battling overpowering forces on the small stage of his gallery, with only a paintbrush in his hand. My paintings had energy; they had a kind of power. But at times I felt helpless, like a warrior whose only weapon was colour.

Violence is a demanding subject for any artist. An artist needs courage to paint violence; an artist must be fearless. While trying to create a painting of the girl whose *miitini* had been killed, I hadn't been able to sleep for two nights. A little girl and her best friend—such a delicate relationship. Their innocence suggested soft shapes and gentle colours. But the event that ended their friendship forced me to use sharp edges and harsh colours. I mixed my tears into that painting; they mingled with the colours. Tears exist for only a few seconds. What was wrong with an artist using them as witness to his feelings?

Some canvases in this series looked like I'd made collages, incorporating press photographs into my paintings. But that wasn't the case. The distance between the two was too great. Press photographs capture an immediate event. A painting shows the same event but with more depth and with the perspective only the passage of time brings.

Still, despite my sufferings, hope was the ultimate message of the Palpasa series. Had my brush done justice to that? In places, vermilion looked like blood and blood like vermilion, yet, in reality, the two represented complete opposites. Vermilion stood for hope, while blood stood for failure and despair. The message of my paintings was that I wanted vermilion. The warmongers wanted to see a blood-soaked canvas stretched across the country. They wanted the piles of weapons to grow higher, seeing in them their ultimate victory. I was trying to give their cowardice a colour.

'The thing that makes me love these works is the way you've managed to show courage on innocent faces,' Christina had said.

'That's why they're being sacrificed,' I'd said. 'I'm trying to show how cowards continue to live, while the innocent are sacrificed.'

She said, 'Defining one action as courage and another as cowardice is tantamount to making a political statement. You've done that. Your own courage comes from making a clear statement about which side you're on. That's so important, especially today.'

The stand I'd taken was that of people who resisted the warmongers on both sides. I belonged to this, third force. People who felt as I did could be targeted by either side because we opposed both. I'd protested against both warring sides in these paintings, my colours showing my support for the third camp. This was my strength. But would I be safe in choosing this path?

'Excuse me.' It was the annoying Christina again.

I continued working, paying no attention to her. I was, trying to paint a tika on Palpasa's forehead, but it looked crooked. I could change a line in my painting by covering it with colour but sometimes that made the paint too dense.

'You're pretending you didn't hear me,' Christina said.

'You're right.'

'I'm leaving.'

'I'm not stopping you.'

'Are you going to give me that painting or not?'

'Which one?'

'You're pretending you don't understand again.'

'I don't understand. Which painting are you talking about?'

'That one.'

She pointed, but I didn't bother to turn around. I already knew which painting she wanted. It was the one called *Palpasa Café*. Café-gallery-resort with internet facilities. I'd decided that each room in the resort would be a gallery in itself. I'd hang my art in these galleries. I wanted my guests to feel they were living in a gallery. But it was difficult to say whether the painting *Palpasa Café* showed me more as a painter or as a designer.

I was going to build two types of rooms: studios and the suites. Those who preferred luxury could stay in the suites. But in both types, my guests would be close to nature. The instant they opened their curtains and looked out the window, they'd see the flowers and trees and feel the seasons come into their rooms.

My resort would have lots of empty space. Empty space is as essential for a good room as it is for a good painting. The walls would be hung with paintings. That was how I wanted my resort to be: white-washed walls, the natural perfume of flowers, the warm rays of the sun, and the breeze coming in through the windows.

'When your resort's finished, I'll be your first guest,' Christina said.

I said, 'You'll have to trek for days to reach my resort.'

'You think I couldn't do that?' she said in a challenging tone.

Turning to her, I playfully stroked her cheek with my paintbrush, smearing her with red paint. For a while, it looked as if she'd decided to be friends again. But no, she was still angry. Sometimes Christina could be as demure as a Nepali woman. If she stayed long enough in Nepal, no one would guess she was a foreigner. She had long dark hair. The only problems were that she was too tall and that she had blue eyes. Still, people could easily mistake her for a Nepali.

'This was the first painting I ever saw created in front of my eyes,' she said. 'That's why I'm not leaving without it.'

I didn't want to give it to her. It showed the gallery resort I wanted to build in memory of Palpasa. It represented my future. There'd be a courtyard, walled with red brick and floored in grey slate. It would all be dedicated to Palpasa. I knew how difficult it'd be to make Christina understand how special that painting was to me, but I had to make her understand. That painting wasn't for sale.

'I'm going to disturb you for a while,' she said. She took out her mobile phone and took my picture with it. Many visitors had taken pictures of my paintings while pretending they were talking on their phones. What was this, a photo studio?

'Did you have some coffee?' I asked.

'Don't change the subject,' she said. 'You still haven't agreed to give me that painting.'

'When are you going back?' I asked.

'Where? To the hotel?'

'No, to Amsterdam.'

At this, her anger turned to fury. I wanted to make her go away, but not too far. I wanted her to stay in Kathmandu for a while. She stormed out of the gallery without even wiping the red paint from her cheek.

I wondered where she'd go. I didn't think she'd leave the country. I knew she'd planned to go back to the Netherlands several times but kept changing her ticket. I didn't believe she'd even filed any stories. She was happy just to spend time with me. That's why she got paranoid over small things. She'd lied to me when she said she'd come to report on the war. She'd come here to write a long story about modern eastern art. Otherwise why would she have tried so hard to get close to me?

As for me, I was obsessed with the Palpasa series. When it was finished, I'd finally be free. Only then would I be able to look at Christina with clear eyes. Since I'd come back from the hills, I hadn't spent one day without painting. Every moment was devoted to images. Even when I didn't have a brush in my hand, lines and colours danced in my mind. I needed to keep working on the series to remind myself I was alive. Losing Palpasa had left me in great distress, but I had grown used to the agony. I breathed in pain and breathed out painting.

It was close to dawn now, but I was in no hurry to end the night. I'd recuperated somewhat from my journey. The ironies of life had become normal; its absurdities no longer surprised me. Every day brought many experiences into the lives of human beings, but none of us had the interest or the insight to understand them.

Christina had grown fond of me, I knew. I worried she might be too fond of me already. I feared I might be influenced by her feelings. But if she wanted me, why did she? What could I offer her while I lived under Palpasa's shadow?

Hours later, Christina still hadn't come back. Where was she? Had she really left for the Netherlands? Or was she waiting for me somewhere, in a restaurant or at her hotel? Maybe she was waiting for me at my house. It was good she'd left me in peace, even if it was for just three hours.

But then I wondered if it was possible, that she'd really left the country. The night before she'd asked me a lot of questions.

'Why did you kiss me?' she'd asked.

Her question wiped the sweet taste from my lips.

I asked, 'Why did you close your eyes?'

'That's not an answer to my question.'

'I got confused.'

'You're a liar.'

'No,' I said, defending myself. 'You touched my nose with your fingertips and I couldn't resist.'

'Do you love me?' she asked.

'You're a very dear friend,' I said, removing my fingers from the nape of her neck. 'And always will be.'

'Then why did you kiss me?'

'Was it a mistake?'

'You kiss me and then say I'm your friend!' she said, obviously upset.

'I'm sorry.'

'I can't forgive such a mixed-up person. So you didn't kiss me out of love?'

'Maybe that's true.'

'You don't know the real meaning of a kiss,' she said. 'You only want a physical relationship with me.'

I said nothing. She was close to tears. I felt bad.

'What do you want?' I finally asked.

'I want you to be honest with me. You're flirting with me while thinking about Palpasa. And I don't like it.'

'Are you jealous of Palpasa?' I asked.

'I'm not jealous of that poor dead girl,' she said, 'but I am jealous of your memories of her and the time you spend thinking about her.'

'What can I do about that?' I said, 'Can you tell me when you'll be free of that jealousy?'

'I can't.' Looking tearful, she pulled back her hair and tied it behind her head.

'Well, could you leave your boyfriend?' I asked.

'He doesn't have a problem with my friendship with you. He isn't worried.'

'Even though he knows we've slept in the same room?'

'He knows I've spent nights in the houses of my male friends in Amsterdam,' she said. 'We're open with each other. That's the difference between Nepalis and westerners. He trusts me.'

'What would your boyfriend think about me if he found out I've kissed you?'

'He wouldn't think about you. He'd only think about me.'

'Will you tell him I kissed you?'

'That's why we trust each other,' she said. 'He knows I don't hide anything from him.'

Surprised, I sat back. Under the dim light of the red bulb, I looked at her face. She was very pretty. She'd untied her hair again and her face was partly hidden by the falls of her hair.

'You just think of me as a typical western woman,' she said.

'Aren't you?'

'And you believe all western women are easy, that we'll sleep with anyone.'

'I never thought of you like that,' I said. 'You love art. I didn't think of you as western or eastern.'

'I spent the night here just to see how you paint,' she said. 'I simply came to observe. But you took advantage of me.'

'Sorry,' I said.

'No. Don't be sorry,' she said. 'If you want, I could be your girlfriend.'

'Wouldn't that be betraying your boyfriend?' I asked in surprise.

'It wouldn't be betrayal,' she said. 'I'd explain to him how I came to love you and we'd break up on friendly terms.'

'So, are you starting to love me?' I asked.

'I had started to love you,' she said.

'Had?'

'But I can forget that now.'

'It seems you've got a problem with love too,' I said. 'It seems you see love as a game you can switch on and off.'

'I don't want to waste my time with a person like you who has double standards.'

'So what do I need to do?' I asked.

'You have to be clear with yourself,' she said. 'I know how much you miss Palpasa. Of course, you can't rid yourself of your memories of her. But don't use me as a substitute, as a way of trying to push her out of your mind.'

'And then what should I do?'

'Well, don't think that just because I'm a westerner, I'd be satisfied with only a physical relationship.'

'I don't think that,' I said.

'How can I trust you?'

'What can I do to prove you can trust me?'

'Tell me honestly,' she said. 'Do you love me?'

I couldn't answer. I looked at her. She looked back at me.

'Do you even know what love means?' she asked.

I still couldn't say a word.

'I don't think you loved Palpasa either.'

'How can you say that?' I cried.

'It seems pretty clear,' she said, 'You were obsessed with her beauty and flattered by the way she looked up to you. She admired your work and you felt affection for her.'

'But isn't affection a way of showing love?' I asked

'If it were real love, you'd never have left her like that in Goa without giving her your address. You met her in Kathmandu just by accident. If you'd loved her, you wouldn't have left for the hills without telling her you were going. And, even though you did go, you'd have found a way of communicating with her.'

'That's just how I am,' I said.

'That's why I'm saying you can't love anyone,' she said. 'You love solitude. You're happy to spend your life looking at the world alone. You don't need company,'

'Does loving solitude mean I can't love another person?'

'It does. The day you start loving someone is the day you don't want to be alone any more.'

'But I've always been this way.'

'And you'll never change.'

'Maybe you're right.'

'But I still like you.'

'Do you?'

'And Palpasa liked you too.'

'Yes, she did.'

'To like you is one thing but to have your love is something else altogether,' she said.

I fell silent again.

'You like colours. You love colours, in fact. You could spend your whole life having a love affair with colours. You're a true artist.'

'Yes?'

'And I love your work.'

'Thank you.'

After that I went back to my work. She kept watching me as I moved my brush. I busied myself on the canvas, away from her gaze. I was trying to find Palpasa's face in my painting.

'This doesn't mean I respect you any less,' she said.

I said, 'I believe you.'

'We'll remain good friends, close friends.'

'We will.'

'And who knows?' she joked.

'What?

'Maybe I'm falling in love with you.'

'Then why don't you kiss me?' I asked.

'Then why don't you close your eyes?' she said, playfully punching my chest.

CHAPTER TWENTY EIGHT

'How do you mix your colours?' the Japanese lady asked softly, raising her eyebrows and fixing me with her gaze.

'It's very easy,' I replied, 'I do it as the mood takes me.' Her husband was studying a painting. 'You have a unique style,' he said.

Fingering the strap to which his glasses were tied, he examined the canvas more closely.

'The colour combinations are very subtle,' he said. 'You mix colours as if mixing milk and water.'

'It looks so natural, doesn't it?' the woman agreed.

'The language of colour is in the eye of the viewer,' I said. Then, realizing they weren't very fluent in English, I rephrased the sentence, putting the idea more simply and slowly. 'Colours depend on the way you see them.'

They nodded their heads in agreement and began to speak between themselves softly in Japanese. They reminded me of a pair of swallows, chirping on the edge of a nest of clay.

When I realized they were happy wandering about my gallery on their own, I left them to their own devices.

I like explaining art to Nepalis more than to foreigners. It's even more satisfying if they're young. Foreigners visiting art galleries already have set tastes and the ability to appreciate art, but very few Nepalis do. Very few Nepalis visit art galleries for a start.

The husband came up to me and pointed to *Palpasa Café*. 'This painting looks like a painting of a dream project.'

'You're right,' I said. 'That's my future. I want to build an art centre based on this design.'

He looked intrigued. 'Great,' he said. You've expressed yourself so well in this whole series. I like this series best because I can see it shows suffering but also hope.'

What could I tell him? I'd finished the Palpasa series long ago, yet it seemed I'd only started it yesterday. It was my best work. The reason every visitor's eye is drawn to it is because I'd poured myself onto those canvases, holding nothing back.

'If you don't mind, I'd like to ask you a question,' the wife said. 'Do your paintings sell?'

'Society here is yet to develop a real appreciation for art,' I said, as she raised her eyebrows in surprise. 'People here don't really recognize art. Those with money buy expensive paintings, but they don't care if they're good or bad. They assume paintings will give their homes prestige simply because they're expensive.'

She asked, 'But isn't it a good sign that people with money choose to buy paintings?'

'There aren't many people with money in our country,' I said. 'And those who do have money are busy advertising the fact. They don't understand the responsibility that money brings. Being rich isn't just a question of having money but what you choose to do with it. Money's a source of power. Wealthy people who're wise don't become slaves to their money. The wise use their money well.'

'I see,' she said, nodding.

'Some rich people, those who've seen the world, just see paintings as objects hanging on the wall to increase the value of their houses,' I said. 'Most don't see art as an essential part of their lives. For them, paintings are just part of a lifestyle, or a fashion.'

'But surely that's just a stage your society's going through?' she said.

I said, 'To be able to make one's life more beautiful, one must first appreciate beauty.'

'You're right,' she said.

'Only beautiful hearts recognize beautiful paintings,' I said. 'For instance, people like you. You've looked at my paintings with so much interest and now you're asking me about my art.'

She blushed and wandered back to her husband. Again, they began to talk between themselves in Japanese. I could hear the swallows chirping again.

She came back, 'But you also want your paintings to be bought?'

'Of course,' I said. 'This is my livelihood.'

'So does that mean that you create paintings that will have a market?'

'That's a good question,' I said, 'but ultimately I think the answer's no.'

'Why not?'

'If I painted with the aim of selling my work, I wouldn't be an artist,' I said. 'I'd be a manufacturer.'

She nodded and joined her husband again.

I went to my desk, switched on my computer, poured some hot water into a glass and put some coffee in it.

The coffee Lahure Kaakaa had given me had the fragrance of the hills, a fragrance that always moved me. Was this a strength or a weakness? Whatever it was, this fragrance affected me deeply, I couldn't free myself from its spell. I felt the hills tugging at me, as if I were a kite on a string. The hills were ancient and I was, after all, a product of the hills. Our bond was deep. Though I lived in Kathmandu, the hills were inside me and the distance between us didn't weaken our bond. The hills had captured me when I was a child and I'd never be free of them.

After checking my e-mails, I made a few phone calls. Then I put the newspapers out in the sun. The delivery boy had brought them wet that day.

I'd been moved by a news story I'd read recently. I was thinking of doing a painting based on it. That story came with a picture. The picture was of Manmaya, a seventy-year-old woman. This picture prevented me from working on any other painting.

The picture showed the old woman walking towards her district's headquarters after the Maoists' 'People's Court' had ordered her to leave her village. Manmaya's daughter-in-law had told the Maoists about some problems she was having with her mother-in-law. Tension between in-laws is a common problem in many households, but in this case the 'People's Court' had taken action against the old woman, ordering her to leave the village within seven days. Even the daughter-in-law had appealed against the sentence as she hadn't expected it to be so harsh. But the verdict couldn't be overturned.

A journalist met Manmaya on her way to the district headquarters. She was carrying only a small bag. The wrinkles on her face were filled with rivulets of tears. Old and stooped, she was making her way towards an uncertain future. When I saw the picture in the newspaper, I recognized my hills. People had been climbing up and down these hills for centuries but Manmaya's journey was a different one. I wanted to start a painting called *Old Woman Coming Down a Mountain* based on that press photo but still hadn't managed to put even one line on canvas.

I had to start working on it today. As the days passed, the inspiration would fade and my energy would dissipate. I kept the newspaper cutting beside me, looking at it now and then. I always became tearful when I looked at the photo of the old woman. She'd already been walking for two days when the picture was taken and had another afternoon's walk left to reach her destination.

'Do you have any relatives in the district headquarters?' the journalist had asked her.

'I hope there's someone there I know,' she replied.

'Such a punishment at such an old age?'

'At least they didn't sentence me to death! I won't lie to you, my son. My daughter-in-law realized she'd been wrong and asked them to change the verdict. But, finally, I left on my own volition. I was too scared to stay. Who isn't scared of them?'

As I re-read the newspaper cutting, someone knocked at the gallery door. 'Just a second,' I called out.

Before answering the door, I took a cup of coffee to the Japanese woman. She wanted to buy my book and asked the price. I showed her the price on the cover. She took out a calculator and converted it to yen. Her husband joined us and talked about some maple trees changing colour with the seasons. 'Do you remember?' he said to his wife. 'Last year, we climbed the hills just as the maple trees were beginning to lose their leaves. So many people were there just to see the red hills.'

The wife explained to me, 'The hills where we live change colour. First they're green, then red, then yellow.'

'And white when they're covered with snow,' I added.

'Yes! That's right. Four seasons in a year and a colour for each season.'

Her husband said, 'I can see a relationship between the hills, the seasons, and the colours you use in your painting. That's the basis of your work. Am I right?'

'Absolutely,' I said. 'I grew up with the colours the flowers painted the hills.'

Again there was a knock at the door. As I left the room to answer, the lady asked me, 'Which painting are you most satisfied with?'

'None,' I said. 'If I'm ever satisfied with any of my work, I won't have the drive to do better. I don't think any artist is ever really satisfied.'

When I opened the door, I saw five strangers.

'Come in, sit down,' I said. I let them in, pointing towards a sofa. I took a chair opposite them, a chair I'd ordered from Taiwan a year ago which was already getting rickety. If the men were carpenters, I'd ask them to fix it.

'Who are you?' I asked, but they didn't react.

I could guess from the men's appearance that they weren't art lovers. They didn't introduce themselves to me. They looked around the gallery, but I could tell they weren't looking at the paintings. A painter can read his audience. The men's attire alone made it clear they had no interest in art. I felt a little awkward.

'Is there anything I can do for you?' I asked finally.

A man wearing a white shirt replied curtly, 'We've come to ask you a few things.'

'What things?' I asked, getting nervous.

'We also came to get to know you,' another said more politely. But he didn't look at me as he spoke and his evasiveness disturbed me.

Another man began looking at the calendar on which I'd marked a few dates. Yet another looked lost, staring blankly at the canvases on the wall. Looking at paintings is one thing, I thought, but understanding them is a different matter.

When I realized they weren't going to leave quickly, I asked, 'Would you like some coffee?'

The first man said quietly, 'We're security personnel.'

I was taken aback. But I tried not to look worried. The Japanese couple was still in the gallery and I didn't want to upset them.

'So?' I asked calmly.

'We've come to ask you a few things.'

'What things?' I asked.

'You have to come with us,' one man said.

'Where?'

Another man stepped closer to me and said forcefully, 'Just come with us.'

I began to tremble but made an effort to appear calm. 'I've got work to do,' I said. 'I can't come now. As you see, there are visitors in the gallery. We made an appointment. I'm too busy to go now.'

Just then my mobile phone rang. It was a friend. I'd made an appointment with him as well and he was waiting for me in a rooftop restaurant. I told him I'd be there soon and asked him to order me something. I didn't tell him about the situation I was in; I didn't even give him a hint. As I hung up, I realized that was a mistake.

The first man said, 'You can finish your work when you get back.'

'How long will it take?' I asked. 'I can't just leave my visitors like this.'

Another man said, 'Just come,' brushing aside my concerns. He looked through the door into the room where the Japanese couple was talking to each other.

'I don't mean to be uncooperative,' I said politely, 'but it isn't clear to me what you want from me.'

'What do you mean?' one man snarled.

'Are you here to arrest me?'

'Not exactly,' the first man said.

'So?'

'Understand it this way,' another man said. 'We've come to take you with us.'

Chilled, I said, 'If you've come to take me, you must have a warrant for my arrest.'

'This discussion is pointless,' one of the men said threateningly. 'We want to ask you a few questions.'

'So ask your questions here,' I insisted. 'You haven't even shown me your identity cards.'

'If we could ask our questions here, we wouldn't be telling you to come with us,' the second man snapped.

I saw, then, a revolver inside his shirt. The man examining the calendar also appeared to have a gun.

'I have to tell my people,' I said, moving towards the phone.

One of the men stopped me. 'Don't cry to be clever,' he said.

Desperately, I said, 'Listen. Amnesty International has placed Nepal at the top of the list of countries with the highest rates of civilian disappearances. All human rights groups are keeping an eye on Nepal.'

The man growled, 'Don't talk like those people who chase US dollars.'

'What will these tourists think?' I protested.

'We don't care.'

'But tourist arrivals are down,' I said desperately. 'What will my visitors think if they see me being taken away like this, right in front of their eyes? They'll never come back to Nepal!'

Finally one of the men took me by the arm. 'Stop talking. Move.'

They wouldn't even let me shut down my computer. There was still some coffee in my cup.

As I was going down the stairs, the Japanese man followed me and asked the price of the Palpasa series. 'Sorry,' I said. 'That's priceless.'

'You haven't decided on a price?' he said, not understanding me.

'I may never decide on a price,' I said.

'Then how can I buy it?'

'Forgive me,' I said, trying to make him understand. 'That series isn't for sale. You can take any of the other paintings but not those.'

He watched, puzzled, as I left with the men. Could he tell I was being forced to go? I didn't want to tell him what was happening. What use would it be if I told him I was being abducted? I didn't want to see the distress on his face.

We reached the street, the five men guarding me closely. I wondered whether any of the people passing by could tell I was being abducted. If only I'd run into someone I knew, I'd have been able to say something.

We crossed the square where a bomb had exploded a few days earlier, the men leading me to a van. I got in meekly. I remembered a cart puller who'd been killed in that explosion. He'd been loading his cart, his little daughter beside him. She'd survived by sheer luck. I'd spent that entire day in my gallery thinking about that man and his little girl, the child's shining eyes haunting me.

The van had moved less than a hundred metres down the road when two of the men pushed my head down towards my knees and blindfolded me. No one could see me in that van. I didn't know where I was being taken or why. I didn't care where they took me. I only hoped it would have a window. All I wanted was to be able to tell day from night.

EPILOGUE

Drishya disappeared long ago. Tired of vainly searching for him, I've completed this novel based on whatever information I've been able to piece together. I haven't been able to stick to the style of most traditional novels since this is the story of a man's life.

After completing my novel, I went to spend the evening at a restaurant in Thamel. Soft music was playing at the bar. I was listening to it when my mobile phone rang. It was a number I didn't know.

'Hello,' said a woman's voice. 'Is this Narayan?'

'Yes.'

'Namaste. I'm Gemini,' she said. 'I came from the States a few days ago. I need to meet you.'

'What for?'

She didn't want to tell me. 'You're the editor of a newspaper,' she said. 'I think you'll be able to help me.'

I told her to come to my office later, but she insisted we needed to meet right away as she wasn't staying long in Kathmandu.

What harm was there in meeting her? After all, journalists meet many people. I told her where I was and asked her to join me there.

After I hung up, I called my office. 'Is there anything urgent?' I asked.

I was told there'd been no big developments, just a few small clashes in a few small places. That was nothing new;

a dozen deaths every day had become routine. The opinion pages were complete. I had time to spare. Of course, I could be called back to the office at any time; the nature of my work was unpredictable. But I felt I could indulge myself a little.

My gin, tonic water, and lemon slices arrived. I asked the waiter to turn up the volume of the music. He went to the bar to do so. Outside, the streets seemed deserted. There weren't many tourists in Thamel these days.

I hadn't brought anything to read, not even a magazine. *The Economist* was bringing out a double issue the next week; *The International Herald Tribune* was too expensive. There hadn't been many international newspapers in the shop downstairs. So I'd decided not to read at all.

But it was difficult sitting there doing nothing. Drishya's disappearance had shaken me to the core. I was glad I'd finished my novel At last I'd finally have some free time. I could start reading books again. I decided I'd go to a bookshop after my drink. I wondered if there were any new books worth reading. In our country, book reviews don't influence readers. We don't have good reviewers, and good books, too, are hard to find. A society without good writers is intellectually bankrupt. I'd always wanted to write a book, but I'd never have written this one if Drishya hadn't given me the inspiration to do it.

One day, I'd asked him, "What kind of book do you think I should write?'

'Write a book you've never read before,' he said.

'In that case,' I said, 'I'll write about you. I've never read a book about an artist like you.'

He laughed at the idea. 'So you want to write my biography?'

'Don't be stupid,' I told him. 'There are already plenty of biographies of artists. *Lust for Life* about Vincent Van Gogh is my favourite.'

'Van Gogh was a great artist.'

'I'm not comparing you to him,' I said. 'I just mean I've never read a book about an ordinary artist. By ordinary, I mean someone like you, whose background's like mine. If I wrote about you, I'd feel like I was telling my own story, sharing my own experiences.'

'All right,' he said. 'What would I have to do?'

'Just give me a few interviews,' I said, setting a condition, 'till I'm satisfied with the material.'

'Don't include too much about my love life!' he laughed.

'So you think of yourself as a romantic?'

'Don't I look like a romantic?'

'I've seen you fall in love.'

'True, I have fallen in love, but it'd be better if you didn't delve too deeply into that.'

'How could I write about you without mentioning your love life?' I'd asked. 'Love's the spice of a novel.'

'You mean you want to write a novel based on me?'

'Your life isn't any less dramatic than a novel.'

'That depends how you see it,' he said.

'But why do you want to keep your love life out of it?' I asked. 'Without that, I won't be able to write a good book.'

'So you really think I'm a good lover?'

'You are. But an unsuccessful lover.'

He laughed. 'If you make my love life public, no woman will ever come near me.'

'Don't worry. I'll cast you in the best possible light.'

'I'm just kidding,' he said. 'I want you to write the truth. I'll help you. If I lied to you or left things out, your writing wouldn't be honest. I'll be completely open with you.'

I finished the first draft of my novel on a cold February night. By then, I'd interviewed Drishya many times and made many changes, but I still felt some things were missing. As I wrote, I become more and more intrigued by Drishya. I asked him to talk about himself time and time again. But on several topics Drishya didn't have the time to talk to me at length and I was worried my novel might feel incomplete.

I didn't interview anyone except Drishya. It was his story, after all, and told from his perspective. How the other characters appeared was entirely my responsibility. I'd constructed them purely from snippets of information Drishya had given me. I understood I mightn't have done them justice. But then, all written works are incomplete. Something's always missing. There's always more to add.

Though my novel was about Drishya, I felt that even his character wasn't fully developed. That didn't surprise me, though, because I'd merely presented the Drishya I knew. I never met Palpasa. If I had, I might've been able to tell her side of the story as well. That would've given my novel another dimension. The period in Drishya's life described in my novel was intimately linked to Palpasa. Even Drishya's dream project was named after her. If Palpasa hadn't met an untimely death, I would've met her some day. I would've liked to have met her. I was intrigued by Drishya's description of this girl who was so independent in her outlook. Drishya had never left the subcontinent, while Palpasa had seen the world. I could imagine the conflicts this might create in their relationship. But such conflicts are always interesting. I would've liked to explore them further.

I was still in touch with Phoolan, but she'd changed. She lost her smile the day Drishya was taken away. She called me just a few days ago, asking if I'd heard any news of him. If Drishya doesn't come back soon, Phoolan might have to go back to her village. And there, she might have to join the Maoists. They're still asking for one recruit from each household.

It was Phoolan who told me Kishore had gone overseas after all. Before he left, he told Phoolan he wanted to have a relationship with her when he got back.

'What did you tell him?' I asked.

'I told him I wasn't interested,' she said. 'I don't want a relationship now.'

It seems that Tshering, the photographer, is Drishya's closest friend in Kathmandu. He's very busy, though, and it's been difficult for me to contact him as he spends months at a time overseas.

To write more honestly about Drishya's experiences, I probably should've trekked through the hills as he did. But I'm a busy man. I don't have time for a long trek like that.

I still didn't know a few basic facts about Drishya. How did he come to be sent to boarding school in Kathmandu? How did his parents pass away? What had made him an artist? When did he start loving solitude? I didn't know about his school or his college days or the things that shaped him then. Many aspects of his life remained a mystery to me. I viewed those aspects like the empty spaces in a painting. Just as paintings do, this novel leaves some empty spaces for the reader to fill in with his or her imagination. I know that, aside from meeting Palpasa, the events of June 1 and the journey with Siddhartha changed Drishya forever. Before that, he was just another young man of Kathmandu. He was content just to paint.

His relationship with Siddhartha certainly couldn't be called ordinary. It's not clear which route Siddhartha had taken Drishya on, or where the two parted. There are very few people I could ask about Drishya. The waiters in the restaurants he frequented don't remember much about him. He had few close friends. If I haven't portrayed him accurately, it's not entirely my fault. His solitary lifestyle has played its part too.

I have managed to clear up one mystery, though. It's about Christina. I found out why she left Kathmandu so suddenly, without even saying goodbye to Drishya. After Drishya's abduction, I went to the gallery to comfort Phoolan. She was busy at the computer. I realized she managed Drishya's mailbox for him. She replied to most of the e-mails he was sent. Drishya was so busy that sometimes he couldn't reply to e-mails for months.

Phoolan looked tense that day.

'It looks like Drishya changed the password to his e-mail account,' she said. 'He was using the old password till the night before he was taken, but now it's not working.'

'Wait.' I asked if I could try a password.

She got off the chair and I sat down.

I asked, 'What words were most precious to him?' And I typed 'Palpasa Café.'

The account opened.

Phoolan was relieved. It didn't feel right for me to read Drishya's e-mails, so I got up and she sat down at the computer. 'Look,' she exclaimed, pointing at the monitor. There are so many e-mails from Christina!'

'Is it all right to read what she's written?' I asked.

'Of course. We have to tell her what's happened.'

'Right. Open them then,' I urged her.

In one of the mails Christina had written:

You must be wondering why I left without saying goodbye.

I thought hard—

Should I stay with you or not?

Should I forget my boyfriend or not?

I was already confused when you came back from the hills, but one day was pivotal—the day I left your gallery in anger. The following day was my birthday, you see. But you didn't wish me happy birthday or give me a present, even though I'd reminded you several times. Either you'd forgotten or you didn't care. I couldn't say which.

But do you know what my boyfriend did?

He called from Amsterdam and got the people at the hotel to bring me a bouquet of flowers. He also faxed a handwritten note, saying he was thinking of me on my special day. The bouquet and fax were there when I opened my door in the morning. I was so touched.

I thought—this dumbo, my boyfriend, is crazy about me.

Then came another surprise—a big birthday cake.

That very day, I rushed to the travel agent and booked my flight back home.

I hope you think I did the right thing.

And, if you say you're busy with your paintings, I'll be even more pleased.

Forgive me if I've disappointed you.

I'd left the gallery after reading this e-mail.

As I was thinking about this, Gemini arrived at the bar. 'Namaste,' she said.

I gestured towards the seat opposite mine.

Of medium height and slim, she wore an ash-coloured sweater zipped up to her neck. She must have been twenty one or twenty two, or maybe twenty three or twenty four.

She hung her handbag over the back of the chair and ran her fingers through her hair. 'I hope I'm not disturbing you,' she said.

'What would you like to drink?' I asked.

'What are you having?'

'Gin and tonic'

'I'll have gin with Sprite.'

The waiter arrived and we placed the order.

First, Gemini asked about me. She was interested in journalism. She asked about politics, the conflict, and where I thought the country was heading. Her questions were quite astute. We talked easily, like old friends. We ordered another round of drinks. Though Gemini seemed engrossed in our conversation, at times I thought I saw tension in her eyes, as if she were searching for something.

Finally, she got to the point of our meeting. 'A friend of mine has disappeared,' she said. 'I know journalists have contacts with the Maoists. I've heard you can help get hostages released.'

'Not exactly,' I said. 'The only thing we can do is exert some pressure through our reporting.'

'I want both,' she said. 'I was hoping you could carry a story and also ask them to release my friend.'

'We don't have two-way contact with the Maoists,' I explained. 'They contact us when they need us. They call from satellite phones so we can't see their numbers.'

The waiter approached and asked if we wanted some snacks. Gemini said she wanted to order dinner and looked at the menu.

After she ordered, she told me she was studying in the US but hoped to come back to Nepal the next year to work on her thesis.

Then she returned to the subject of her friend. 'When I arrived in Nepal, she'd been missing for a long time,' she said.

'Where did she go missing?'

'Somewhere outside Kathmandu, somewhere in the west. I don't know. No one knows for sure.'

'Isn't there anyone at her house?'

'Only her grandmother.'

I was startled. 'What's your friend's name?' I asked.

'Palpasa.'

It felt as though I'd been hit on the head with a hammer. I suddenly felt ill. Palpasa was dead, but her friends and family were still looking for her. They still hoped to find her alive. It was a mark of Drishya's weakness that he hadn't been able to tell Palpasa's grandmother the truth. I'd assumed he'd told her eventually. He should have.

What was I to do?

If I didn't tell Gemini what happened, she might find out in the most painful way. This girl didn't know me. She didn't know about my novel. No one knew about it yet. But everyone would discover the truth when the novel hit the bookstores. Then they'd think I'd been less than honest.

I turned to the waiter and ordered another drink. Gemini was eating pasta, oblivious to my inner turmoil.

I thought, maybe Drishya did make the right decision in not telling Palpasa's grandmother. If he hadn't been on the bus, that terrible event would still have happened. And he wouldn't have known what had happened to Palpasa.

But no, it was wrong of him not to tell her.

'Hajur Aama says Palpasa had fallen in love with an artist,' Gemini said. 'In fact, Palpasa also wrote to me about him and their one-sided affair.'

'What kind of affair?' I asked.

'She wasn't very sentimental,' Gemini said, 'but she was obviously very fond of this man. She wrote that the artist didn't care about her, but she couldn't bring herself to get out of his life.'

I listened in silence.

'I kept asking her why she was staying on in Nepal for so long,' she said. 'She wrote that she was beginning to make a new life here. She said she was starting to understand this society and all its complexities.' She continued, 'Her original plan was to come to Nepal much later. But one day she quarrelled with her parents and decided she wanted a life with no restrictions. She came here in anger. We gave her a big farewell party. She told us she wanted to do something meaningful with her life. We didn't know what she was planning to do, but she looked very determined. She left many friends back in the States. She had both male and female friends, you know. She treated everyone well and wanted to be treated well in return. She stood out in our circle. She could never live alone, yet she left for Nepal by herself.'

'Would you like another drink?' I asked.

'No, thanks. I'm really only drinking to keep you company. Am I boring you?' she asked.

'No,' I said. 'I don't drink much either. I get drunk too easily. But hearing your story, I feel like I need another drink.'

'My story or Palpasa's story?' she asked.

'Both.'

'Where was I? Oh, yes. The artist,' she said. You know, I met him once in Goa. I even went to his gallery in Kathmandu looking for him, but it was locked. No one in the neighbourhood could tell me anything about him. They said the gallery had closed long ago. I couldn't find out his home address. Hajur Aama said the artist came to visit her, and I don't think he and Palpasa left Kathmandu together because he came to see Hajur Aama well after Palpasa had gone. Apparently he didn't seem to know where Palpasa had gone. We know she left Kathmandu with a camera and we think the Maoists might've abducted her. She told Hajur Aama she'd be away for quite some time, but it's been months now. Hajur Aama's really worried. Palpasa was never this irresponsible. I'm sure someone must be holding her against her will.'

Looking at me, she said, 'I need to find out where she is before I go back to the States. I have to take at least some information to her parents. That's why I've come to you.'

By then I'd drunk a peg too much. Without thinking what I was saying, I blurted out, 'She's not coming back.'

She looked into my eyes questioningly. Her disbelieving eyes pierced like thorns. Maybe she thought I'd spoken without thinking. She raised her glass of water but put it down without drinking.

'What are you saying?' she asked.

'I'm telling you what happened.'

'Which is?'

'What did you understand?'

'That she's dead.'

I said, 'Yes.'

She stared at me. 'How do you know?'

'Not because I'm a journalist,' I said.

'So how can you be sure?'

'Do you have some time to spare?' I asked.

'Why?'

'I'll give you a book. It has all the details.'

Her lips went dry. Her eyes moistened. Abruptly, she got up and rushed to the bathroom. When she came back, she asked the waiter for a cigarette.

'Sorry, Madam,' he said. 'We don't sell individual cigarettes.'

'Bring us a packet then,' I told him.

When he brought the packet, she lit a cigarette. I took one too. Gemini exhaled a puff of smoke. I could tell she didn't usually smoke.

It was almost closing time. Silence was descending over Thamel. There were only a few people left on the street. In the distance, we could hear policemen banging their batons as they walked along the road. I realized the bartender had turned off the music.

'Is the book about Palpasa?' she asked.

'What do you think?'

'I'm asking you whether the book's about Palpasa.'

'Do you think I'd lie to you?'

'But how do you know the book's about Palpasa?' she asked.

'Because I wrote it,' I said.

She looked at me in shock. For a long time she didn't blink. Her eyes bore into mine, so much so that I felt scared. I took a drag of my cigarette. When I exhaled, the smoke drifted towards her. The smoke she exhaled drifted towards the ceiling.

The waiter came up to us. 'Excuse me, Sir. We have to close now. The police will be here any minute.'

'Let them come,' I said, irritated. 'I'll talk to them.'

They'll arrest us, Sir. They'll give us trouble. You're our guests tonight, but we might end up their guests forever!'

I wasn't pleased but there was no other choice. 'Let's go,' I said to Gemini.

Getting up, she said, 'Can you give me that book now?'

'It's about to go to press,' I said. 'But I can give you the draft.'

And I handed her the manuscript, printed on A4 paper.

She took it and looked at it incredulously. On the first sheet inside the transparent plastic cover was written in big bold letters—PALPASA CAFÉ.

GLOSSARY

Aama: Mother
Ba: Father; elderly male
Babu: Small boy
Bahini: Younger sister
Bahun: Priest caste
Batti: Wicks for devotional oil lamps
Bhadgaule topi: Black Nepali cap
Chhoila: Buffalo meat prepared in a typical Newari style
Chora: Son
Chori: Daughter
Daal bhaat: Traditional Nepali meal consisting of rice, lentil soup, vegetables and achar
Dai: Elder brother
Dashain; Tihar: The two biggest Nepali festivals
Dhido: Millet porridge
Doko: A woven basket carried by a head strap
Gauncha geeta Nepali . . . Jyotiko pankha uchali: A well-known patriotic song
Hajur Aama: Grandmother
Haku patasi: A black and red sari traditionally worn by the Newar community
Indra Jatra: A festival in Kath-mandu to worship the Living Goddess, Kumari
Kafal: A wild red berry found throughout the Nepali hills
Kaakaa: Uncle
Khukuri: Nepali knife
Koal: A device for pressing oil
Kotha: Room
Lahure Kaakaa: Soldier Uncle
Madal: Nepali drum
Miit (male); miitini (female): Close friend turned ritually into a relative
Narasimha: A musical wind instrument
Pote: A necklace of beads only married women wear
Shreeman Narayana: Popular hymn to Lord Vishnu
Sojo: "Straight"; ingenuous
Sukuti: Dried meat
Thulo Ekadashi: A day of religious significance
Tiriri Murali Bajyo Banaima: Famous Nepali folk song

ACKNOWLEDGEMENTS

It's been said that to write a book is to be indebted to many. As the list of acknowledgements below shows, this adage is only too true. This novel was translated by Bikash Sangruala. Unfortunately, the lack of skilled and enthusiastic translators in Nepal is one reason Nepali literature is not more often published in foreign languages. Bikash's starting the ball rolling was a welcome development, and I am indebted to him for his zeal.

Sangraula's translation was then further honed by Peter J. Karthak and Manjushree Thapa. Throughout every phase of the process Kunda Dixit's suggestions were a guiding force. To all three great figures in the world of Nepalese journalism and literature I'm indebted.

Towards the end of the process an Australian friend of mine, Linda Trigg, spent countless hours making sure my story had been communicated accurately. She was aided by Kiran Krishna Shrestha of nepa~laya, who acted as a bridge, helping her to understand my intentions. Her editing then brought this book into its current form. I will always remember her devotion to polishing this novel to her satisfaction: she spent seemingly endless late nights doing so.

I thank Navin Joshi for coming up with a fresh concept for the cover and Chandra Shekhar Karki and Amrit Gurung for the cover images.

To all those who made suggestions for improving the first edition goes my gratitude. For the editing of this second edition, I thank Perry Thapa.

I would also like to thank Kantipur Publications and all my colleagues there. I also express my respectful thanks and love to my mother, Prem Kumari, and to my younger brother, Janak, for putting up with my bohemian lifestyle.

I also cannot forget my friend, Jyoti Adhikari, who helped me discover the pleasure of trekking.

And last but not least, I would like to thank all those who have discussed, appreciated, and criticized *Palpasa Café* after reading it in Nepali.

Thank you.

Narayan

A NOTE ON THE AUTHOR

Narayan Wagle is an acclaimed journalist and was the editor of Kantipur Daily, Nepal's largest circulating newspaper. *Palpasa Café*, his first novel, was published in 2005 and became a bestseller, selling over 40,000 copies and winning the Madan Puraskar, Nepal's most prestigious literary prize. It was translated into English in 2008. Narayan Wagle lives in Kathmandu.